A BLANCO COUNTY MYSTERY

© 2023 by Ben Rehder.

Cover art and interior design © 2023 by Bijou Graphics & Design.

All rights reserved.

This novel is a work of fiction. Names, characters, places, and incidents are either the product of the author's imagination, or, if real, used fictitiously. No part of this book may be reproduced or transmitted in any form or by any electronic or mechanical means, including photocopying, recording, or by any information storage and retrieval system, without the express written permission of the author or publisher, except where permitted by law.

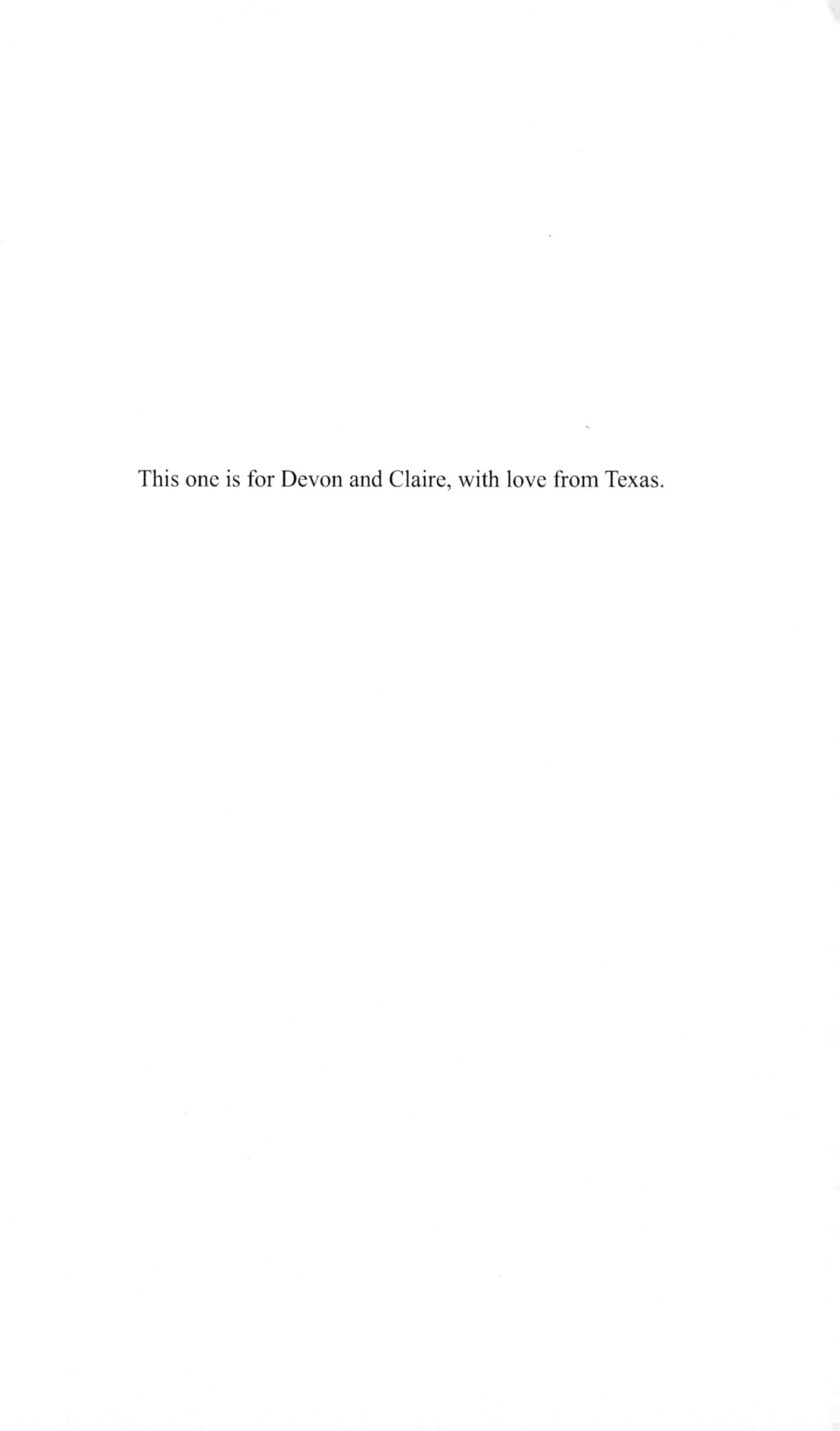

This one is for Devon and Claire, with love from Texas.

ACKNOWLEDGMENTS

Here's the team of people who made this a much better book.
~
Tommy Blackwell
Becky Rehder
Helen Haught Fanick
Mary Summerall
Marsha Moyer
Jo Virgil
Joe Hammer
Linda Biel
Leo Bricker
Naomi West
Richie West
Karen Ortosky
John Strauss
Trey Carpenter
John Barber
Julie Krause Wallace

1

Rodney Bauer was eating lunch at Old 300 BBQ in Blanco when a man with a partially tattooed face walked through the front door with a raccoon perched on his shoulder. Rodney stopped chewing for a moment and watched. The man's face was unmarked on his left side, but the right side was tattooed to look like a skull, including the teeth and the jawbone. Creepy. His hair was short and spiked, mostly white, but with red tips.

It was ten minutes until two and the lunch rush had come and gone, so there was no line at the counter. The tattooed man stopped in front of the cash register and waited for an employee to approach and take his order, and it turned out Melissa was the lucky winner. Rodney liked Melissa, because she was funny and cute and, unlike Rodney's wife, Mabel, Melissa never pointed out that Rodney could stand to go on a diet. Or that he wasn't all that handsome. Or that he didn't earn much money.

"I'm really sorry, but you can't bring that raccoon in here," Melissa said right off the bat to the tattooed man. Firm but sweet. Not reacting at all to the man's appearance.

"He's already in," the man said.

"I see that, and he's cute and everything, but you need to take him back outside," Melissa said. "It's a violation of the health code."

"Moloch is cleaner than anybody in here," the man said.

"That's probably true, but I don't make the rules," Melissa said.

Another man walked in right then, and Rodney recognized him as a local, but he couldn't place the name. Big guy. Ran a backhoe for a living. Wearing jeans so faded they were almost white, along with scuffed work boots and a T-shirt. He was so busy scanning the menu board, he didn't even notice the tattooed man and the raccoon.

"I just need a couple of chopped-beef sandwiches and a pint of pinto beans," the tattooed man said.

"Sir," Melissa said, starting to sound a little irritated, "I cannot serve you. Do you understand? I just can't. I'm sorry. You can take the raccoon out to your car or whatever and then come back inside."

The raccoon began to make an angry chattering noise.

"Who's gonna know if you serve me?" the tattooed man said.

"Sir, this is your last warning before I call the police," Melissa said.

Now the backhoe guy realized that some kind of drama was taking place at the counter, and at the same time, another man came through the door. Smaller guy. Maybe five-seven and no more than one hundred and forty pounds. Rodney could see from here that the man was carrying a handgun in a holster on his right hip, which was perfectly legal in Texas, although you didn't really see it that often. Rodney didn't want to see the tattooed guy get shot simply for being a pushy asshole or a freak, but the situation was getting dicey.

The tattooed man said something back to Melissa, but now the raccoon was making so much noise, Rodney couldn't make it out.

Backhoe Guy obviously heard it, and it must've been something really out of line, because he stepped closer to Raccoon Guy, pointing a finger, and said, "You need to hit the road before I take you outside and shut your mouth."

The raccoon was freaking out and baring its teeth, and Melissa was reaching for the phone, and the smaller guy with the gun said, "You touch my brother and you'll damn sure wish you hadn't."

Backhoe Guy turned around and started to reply, but when he saw the gun on the man's hip, he hesitated. He said, "Take it easy."

"Think you can reach me before I pull this?" the smaller man said, now putting his hand on the butt of the gun.

"No, and I'm not gonna try," Backhoe Guy said.

It had gone completely quiet in the restaurant. Even the raccoon had stopped chattering, as if he were watching the scene unfold.

"But you're a hero," Gun Guy said. "You like to step in when something isn't your business."

"I didn't know," Backhoe Guy said.

"Didn't know what?" the smaller man said.

Backhoe Guy shook his head, plainly having lost his nerve.

"Come on, now," Gun Guy said. "Make a move. You've always wanted to be in a position like this, right? To be a hero? Big, tough guy like you?"

"I like raccoons," Backhoe Guy said, and judging by the expression on his face, he was fully aware how ridiculous he sounded.

Gun Guy started to grin, and then he laughed long and hard. He eventually had to wipe his eyes.

When he was done, Melissa said, "Please just leave." She had a phone in her hand. "We don't want any trouble here. I haven't called the cops yet, but I will. I don't care if you have a gun or not."

The tattooed guy turned to face her again.

"Better to reign in Hell than to serve in Heaven," he said.

"I'm sorry, what?"

"Two chopped beef sandwiches," he said slowly, enunciating every syllable for emphasis. "And a pint of pinto beans."

The raccoon chattered for a few seconds, as if scolding the woman for her insolence.

Another employee quickly slapped together a couple of sandwiches while Melissa dumped some beans into a Styrofoam cup. She put it all in a plastic sack and gave it to Raccoon Guy.

"Well, thank you," he said. "What do I owe?"

"Just get out," Melissa said.

"You don't have to be all uptight about it," the man said. He tossed a couple of bills on the counter, then he and his brother left. The raccoon was looking back over his shoulder as they went out the door.

"Jesus H. Christ," Melissa said. "What the hell was that all about?"

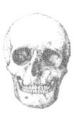

Just before sunset on a clear, dry November evening, Phil Colby hiked to a bluff above Miller Creek and was surprised to look down and see a woman swimming nude in three feet of water. Or maybe she wasn't swimming. Was she bathing? It appeared she'd just put shampoo on her long dark hair and now she was working it into a lather.

Colby didn't mean to stare, but since she was trespassing on his property, he didn't feel obligated to look away, either. He couldn't help himself; the scene was that idyllic. The creek was flowing well after recent rains, and Spanish oak trees beyond the banks would soon turn fiery with vivid shades of red and orange.

And the woman. He judged her to be in her mid-thirties. Slender.

Very fit, from what he could see, which was plenty, considering that the water was only to her midriff.

He stood as motionless as possible and scanned both banks. He saw nobody else. Was she out here alone? It appeared that way. He saw a stack of clothes, a pair of hiking boots, and a camo backpack on the nearer bank. The closest county road was more than half a mile away. Was she homeless? Camping out? Colby had had plenty of interlopers on his ranch before, but none quite like this. The average trespasser was trying to shoot a deer or scavenge firewood, not wash up in the creek.

Two or three times a year, Colby went for a hike on the acreage that had been in his family for generations. Covering it on foot, rather than on horseback or on an ATV, made him feel more connected to the land. The coming night didn't bother him. He could traverse these hills with his eyes closed if he had to.

The woman submerged completely into the waters to rinse her hair, and when she came back up, she finally spotted Colby and froze. She didn't shriek or gasp. Then she lowered herself into the water far enough to cover her breasts.

"The hell're you doing?" she asked.

"That's my line," Colby said.

"You get a good look?" the woman asked. Her tone was aggressive, bordering on angry. But not intimidated in the slightest.

"Pretty good," Colby said. "Now, if I'd gotten here ten minutes ago, before the sun dipped behind the hills, it would've been epic."

"Pervert," she said.

Colby laughed. "Seriously? I randomly find you skinny-dipping and that makes me a pervert?"

"No, but leering from the shadows does," she said.

"I wasn't leering, I was ogling," Colby said. "Big difference."

"Not from where I'm standing."

"Okay, I apologize. But what are you doing here?"

"None of your damn business."

"Actually, it is. This is my ranch. You're trespassing."

"Oh," the woman said.

He said, "Hey, it's not a big deal, as long as you're not hunting or stealing arrowheads or on the run from the law."

The woman didn't reply.

"You're not, right?" Colby said.

"Of course not," she said. The light was fading fast, so it was getting hard to read her expression. "I need to get out now."

"You don't have a towel," he said.

"Don't need a towel. I just need you to turn around for a few minutes while I air dry. Or better yet, you could leave."

"Is that any way to talk to your host?"

She didn't reply. She just waited. Colby turned around.

"Thank you," she said.

"Why are you out here?" he asked over his shoulder.

"None of your business," she said.

"What's your name?"

"That either," she said.

"Are you from around here? You look familiar."

"I'm not," she said.

"Not from here, or not familiar?"

"Either," she said.

"Can I turn around yet?"

"Nope."

"You realize I got cattle?" Colby said. "So that water might not be exactly pristine. Doesn't really matter how well you rinsed. And I hope you didn't drink any of it."

"Your cattle are downstream right now in a fenced pasture," she said. "And I wouldn't drink it anyway."

Strange for her to know where his cattle were, but she was right. Colby had forgotten he'd rotated the herd a few days earlier.

"You got a vehicle?" he asked.

"Not anywhere near here," she said.

"Where are you going now?" he asked.

"Not sure yet."

"You got a flashlight?"

"You ask way too many questions."

"Yes or no? It's a matter of safety. If you don't have one, I'll give you one."

"The moon will be up in about thirty minutes," she said. "That'll be all the light I need."

She was right about that, too. It had been full last night, but it would be nearly full tonight.

"You got a phone?" he asked.

"Why are you so worried about all this stuff?"

"Well, you gotta admit this is all sort of strange," Colby said. "I've never caught anybody taking a bath in the creek before, and it makes me wonder what brought you here."

"The good news is, I'll be gone in a few minutes," she said. "You can turn around now."

"Are you pointing a gun at me?" Colby asked. "I'd hate to turn around and find you pointing a gun at me."

"Don't be an idiot," she said.

"Just my nature," Colby said.

He turned around and she was standing on the bank now, twisting the water out of her hair. She was wearing shorts, the hiking boots, and a lightweight dark-gray sweatshirt.

"You need a place to stay?" he said.

She gave a short laugh, as if there were a joke he didn't get.

"I'm fine."

"You're not in danger?"

Or on drugs? he wondered to himself. *Maybe a little nutty?*

"Nope," she said. "Just wanted to clean up."

"So you hiked half a mile to the nearest creek," Colby said.

"I like nature," she said. "I like hiking. Put the two together and there you go."

"You hungry? I was about to go home and throw something on the grill."

"I have food." She patted the backpack. It was one of the small backpacks like college students carry slung over one shoulder.

What was it about this woman that made him want to know her better?

"Can't be as good as a ribeye steak," he said.

"What I have is fine. I'm not picky."

"You're not going to tell me why you're here? I won't tell anybody."

"There's nothing to tell."

"I'm not buying that for a second," he said.

She shrugged. They stood there looking at each other. A standoff of sorts.

Colby said, "If you need help of any kind, or a place to sleep, or a real meal, my house is right over—"

"I know where your house is," she said.
"Why does that not surprise me?" Colby said.

2

Red O'Brien and his best friend and poaching partner, Billy Don Craddock, were about to have a memorable evening, but at the moment, they were quietly driving north on Highway 281, just about to pull into Blanco.

They'd spent the afternoon trying unsuccessfully to poach deer on a ranch on the south side of the Little Blanco River, but they were irritated because they hadn't seen a single buck, or even a mature doe. Red knew good and well the ranch had plenty of deer on it, because they'd done some cedar-clearing on the ranch that spring and there were deer all over the damn place then.

At the time, Red had casually asked the owner if he was a hunter, and the old geezer said he used to be, but his heart condition had put an end to that a few years earlier. Doctor said it was too much excitement and exertion. So Red dropped some major hints, saying it was getting harder and harder to find a good place to hunt, and leases were too expensive, and where was a fellow to go? But the old man never said anything like, "Hey, come on back to my place anytime." How rude was that?

Didn't really matter, though, because Red was a long-range planner with a devious mind. Pretending to make polite conversation, he asked the old man who else lived there with him, and how many kids he had, and where those kids lived, and what visitors he had on a regular basis—and all of the answers were exactly what Red wanted to hear. The geezer was kind of a loner with only one kid—a son who now lived in Colorado. Nobody came to the ranch regularly.

Then—great news—the old man died. When Red saw the obituary, he said a quick prayer, of course, because that's what a decent person does in that situation. Then he told Billy Don all about this great opportunity to go back to that ranch and get a good buck. They'd be breaking several laws, so they had to be careful, which meant using one of Red's favorite tricks.

Five days earlier, they'd stopped at the ranch gate and placed a dry twig through the lock on the chain that held the gate closed. Earlier today, that twig was still there, so they knew nobody had come and gone. Red cut the lock, drove through the gate, and put one of his own locks on the chain.

Red figured if they did somehow get caught—which wasn't likely—they could just claim they'd talked to the old man last month and he'd given them permission to hunt. Who could prove otherwise? Just because he died, that didn't mean they no longer had permission, did it?

But it turned out all of their careful planning was for nothing. They'd hunted for six solid hours and seen nothing but yearlings and fawns. Good thing they'd brought plenty of beer along.

"You need to quit talking so much in the blind," Red said as they passed Tractor Supply.

"Sure, blame it on me," Billy Don said, his mouth full of Cheetos.

"You wouldn't shut up," Red said.

"I think the problem is the way you smell."

"The way I smell."

"Your cologne, or whatever that crap is. Reminds me of Deep Woods Off. You drove all the bucks away."

"Mandy gave me that cologne," Red said.

Red passed Sonic and Dollar General.

"Maybe she's trying to keep other women away from you," Billy Don said. "But she should know your personality will take care of that. Hey, let's stop at CJ's for some pizza. I'm starving."

Billy Don had already eaten three Slim Jims and was nearly done with the family-size bag of Cheetos, but that was just an appetizer for a man who stood six-four and weighed three hundred pounds.

Red was about to suggest Ronnie's Barbecue in Johnson City instead, but Billy Don would grumble about that, because Johnson City was another fifteen minutes, and that's when the trouble started.

A black van with Louisiana plates came barreling out of the Lowe's Market parking lot, taking a right, and even though Red swerved hard into the left-hand lane, the van clipped his right front fender. Or he thought it did. He wasn't sure. Felt like maybe it did.

"What in the hell?" Red said, laying hard on the horn.

Billy Don stuck his head out the window and yelled, "Learn to fucking drive!"

Billy Don's size gave him the freedom to yell at just about anybody.

"Did he hit me?" Red asked as the van's driver gunned it and started to leave them behind.

"I think so. You know what's weird, though?"

"Huh?"

"It looked like a raccoon was driving."

"What?"

"I saw a raccoon in the window."

"I just need to know if he hit me."

"Then pull over and look."

"If I pull over, he'll get away."

"Then follow him."

"What do you think I'm doing right now?"

He was stepping hard on the gas, but his truck was in desperate need of a tune-up, and it wasn't that fast to begin with.

"I guess it could've been a ferret," Billy Don said. "They sorta look like 'coons, right?"

"I think you drank too many beers this afternoon," Red said.

"Like that's possible."

By the time Red reached the bridge over the river, the van was already on the other side.

"Besides," Billy Don added, "I didn't say a raccoon *was* driving the van, I said it *looked* like it was."

"Or a ferret," Red said.

They passed the Valero gas station, but the van had already passed the Church of Christ. Then they got lucky and the stoplight by the old courthouse turned red. The van was still in the right lane, so Red stayed in the left lane and eased up beside him.

"Ha!" Billy Don said. "Lookee there."

Sure enough, the first thing Red saw was a raccoon, which was riding in the driver's lap with its front paws on the steering wheel. Some kind of weird foreign-sounding music was thumping from the van's stereo system. The van was butt ugly because it had been spray-painted, and not well.

The driver's hair was short and spiky, bleached white as snow, with red tips. He was staring straight ahead, so Red laid on the horn again. He didn't react. Neither did the raccoon.

Billy Don leaned out the window and yelled, "You drive like a damn moron!"

Finally, the driver turned his head, and now Red saw the right side of the man's face was covered with a tattoo of a skull. The left side of his face was normal, but the right side was a skull. Who would do that to himself?

Billy Don said, "What in the—"

Red yelled, "You hit my truck!"

The weirdo said something back, but the music was still blaring, so Red had no idea what it was.

"You hit my truck!" Red yelled again.

The man turned down the stereo and suddenly everything was eerily quiet. The man said, "I prowl like the roaring lion, searching for someone to devour."

"Huh?" Red said.

"What in the speckled hell are you talking about?" Billy Don asked.

"Behold as I trample on serpents and scorpions," the man said.

The raccoon began to chirp and chatter angrily. Maybe he didn't like drama.

"Well, hell, I was hoping to run into a crazy person today, so I guess it's mission accomplished," Billy Don said.

"What're you gonna do about my truck?" Red asked.

The light turned green. The man gave a little salute and said, "See you in hell, gentlemen." Then he drove through the intersection as if everything was perfectly fine.

Red watched him go and said, "Did that just happen?"

"Sure as hell did," Billy Don said. "Follow him."

"Well, of course I'm gonna follow him."

Red hit the gas and his truck grudgingly began to move.

"I want that raccoon," Billy Don said.

"What?"

"I wanna steal it," Billy Don said.

"We ain't stealing no damn raccoon," Red said. "Probably got rabies. That dude's a freak show."

"You never wanted a pet raccoon?" Billy Don asked.

"Nope, because I never wanted my face chewed off in the middle of the night."

"You ever see that video of that old hillbilly dancing with a raccoon?" Billy Don asked.

"Your daddy?" Red asked.

The van was leaving them behind.

"You really need to get your carburetor sorted out," Billy Don said.

The van had already passed the bank, and the Lutheran church, and the liquor store, but he wasn't trying to run away or anything, and Red finally began to close the gap.

"I wonder what his name is," Billy Don said.

"Who cares?" Red said.

"I bet it's something stupid like Bandit," Billy Don said.

Now Red realized Billy Don was still talking about the raccoon, not the driver.

"I'll *buy* the damn raccoon if I have to," Billy Don said. "We can teach him to scare off all the other raccoons. The rabid ones."

"See, Billy Don, that's the thing. You can't scare a rabid raccoon."

Just when Red got within ten yards of the van's bumper, the driver took an abrupt right into the Blanco County Inn, as if he had suddenly remembered where the turn was.

Red braked and made the same turn, following the van as it drove to the north end of the long, narrow building that ran perpendicular to the highway. The van swung into an angled spot in front of the last room, and Red stopped right behind him, blocking him in. There were no other vehicles nearby.

Billy Don was already opening his door and getting out, and as Red reached for his own door handle, he noticed another dude sitting in a chair outside the room, smoking a cigarette. It had to be obvious to anyone watching that some sort of disagreement was about to take place, but the cigarette-smoking dude didn't spring out of his chair or even seem to tense up. Instead, he took one last drag, flicked the butt into the parking lot, and slowly pushed himself up from the chair, like he was in no rush whatsoever and didn't have a care in the world.

That's when Red saw the handgun holstered on his hip.

The parking lot for the Blanco County Inn also connected to Tenth Street, which was directly in front of Red's truck, so if they should need to leave in a hurry, they could just haul ass out of there. In fact, Red decided, upon seeing that gun, that he should just leave the truck running. But as soon as he took his foot off the gas and began to step out of the truck, the engine died.

Great.

Red climbed out and came around the rear of his truck, so he could keep an eye on Cigarette Guy without the van obscuring his view.

"—the black paint right there," Billy Don was saying, and he was pointing at the fender.

"That's not from me," Raccoon Guy said. The raccoon was chattering on his shoulder, plainly getting upset about the entire situation.

"Hell if it ain't," Billy Don said loudly. "It's a goddamn exact match."

Now Red was standing by the rear passenger-side tire, and Cigarette Guy was slowly coming along the passenger side of the van. Red realized Billy Don might not have even seen Cigarette Guy yet. Red's revolver—a Colt Anaconda .45—was in the truck's glove compartment, and now he was wishing he had grabbed it. But there was also the chance that would've made the situation go south in a hurry.

"That's a different shade of black," Raccoon Guy was saying. "Didn't come from my van."

Billy Don stepped closer and the raccoon hunched its back like an angry cat.

"Moloch," Raccoon Guy said, and the raccoon quieted down a little.

"Mole-what?" Billy Don said.

Now Cigarette Guy was standing near the passenger-side fender of the van, where he could see everybody, but he was cloaked in shadows.

"Moloch."

"Do you call him Moe for short?"

"That's the dumbest thing I ever heard."

"Moe is the best Stooge," Billy Don said.

"But you're giving him some competition," Raccoon Guy said.

"A hundred bucks," Billy Don said.

"What?"

"I'll give you a hundred bucks for him."

"Billy Don, let it go," Red said.

"Are you on narcotics?" Raccoon Guy said.

"Two hundred bucks," Billy Don said.

"He's not for sale."

"Then we'll trade fair and square," Billy Don said. "You give us the 'coon and that'll make up for the damage to the truck."

Red could just imagine the headline: *Local men shot outside motel in argument over raccoon.* If Red saw a headline like that, he'd make fun of all the idiots involved.

"I didn't hit the truck," Raccoon Guy said.

If Red was being honest—which he was, sometimes—he could hardly see where the van had brushed against his truck. There was a small black scuff, but the metal wasn't buckled or crumpled or anything like that. If the truck had been sitting by itself in a parking lot when the van had hit it, Red probably wouldn't have even noticed the mark it left behind.

But Billy Don wasn't letting it go—probably because of the stooge remark. He stepped forward and pointed again. "That right there," he said. "You did that. It's the same goddamn paint as your van."

"Just buff it out," Raccoon Guy said.

"That's your job," Billy Don said.

"It would be if I'd hit your truck, but I didn't."

Cigarette Guy finally spoke. "Is this town full of simpletons?"

Billy Don turned his head, surprised to hear another voice. He looked at the man's face, and then down at his hip. There was just enough light to see the gun in the holster.

"Who the hell're you?" Billy Don asked.

"Doesn't matter."

"How is this your bidness?" Billy Don asked.

"Doesn't matter, either. Time for you to hit the road."

"Or what?"

"Are you brain damaged?"

"The only thing damaged is this truck," Billy Don said. "Courtesy of this freak show right here. He drives like an idiot, and he sideswiped us, and he can either pay up, or we call the cops to report an accident. Not just an accident, either. It was hit and run, which is a felony, even in a backwards place like Louisiana."

Red knew Billy Don was bluffing. He would *never* call the cops about anything. He believed in taking care of things himself, and he was usually pretty good at it, because he didn't feel obligated to follow any laws. Plus, his size.

"It's not a felony," Cigarette Guy said.

"Pretty sure it is," Billy Don said.

"You're wrong."

"Well, it oughta be," Billy Don said.

"Let's just go," Red said. "We're gonna get pizza, remember?"

If Red couldn't lure Billy Don away with the prospect of food, then it was going to be a long night.

"You gonna let him get away with this?" Billy Don said. "I say we call the sheriff right now."

Nobody said anything for a long moment. Even the raccoon was quiet. It was a standoff.

Then Raccoon Guy said, "Holy hell, you Texans are a bunch of whiners."

Red heard the raccoon growl again, then realized it had come from Billy Don, who was getting close to losing it. A weirdo like this calling him a whiner? That was too much.

Red said, "If you don't want him calling the cops, the alternative is a whole lot worse."

"I'm going to pay for you to go away," Raccoon Guy said, reaching for his wallet. "That's how annoying you are." He took three one-hundred-dollar bills out and held them up for Billy Don to see.

"Don't do it, Nicky," Cigarette Guy said.

"I'm just tired of hearing them talk," the one named Nicky said, tossing the three bills into the cab of the truck.

"For fuck's sake, that was stupid," Cigarette Guy said.

"There, now. Was that so hard?" Billy Don asked.

Red went around the truck, got behind the wheel, and started the engine.

Cigarette Guy was shaking his head at the whole situation and walked toward the motel room.

The raccoon was chattering again and Nicky was saying something to Billy Don that Red couldn't make out. Billy Don said something back.

"I'm leaving!" Red said. He dropped it into gear, which made Billy Don reluctantly open the passenger door and get in.

Before Billy Don even closed the door, Red hit the gas.

"Next time I'm turning that 'coon into a hat," Billy Don called as they left.

4

There was a gentle rap on Phil Colby's front door at 7:14 the next morning, and when he looked through one of the little glass windows, he saw a familiar face.

He opened the door and said, "Well, this is a surprise. You're fully clothed."

The woman from the creek actually smiled, revealing a killer set of dimples. "That's pretty funny, although that was a fairly obvious line."

"Best I could do on a moment's notice," Colby said. "Come on in." He stepped back and swung the door wider.

"No, thanks. I'm heading out, but I just, uh, wanted to apologize for being a little unfriendly last night. It's just that I didn't expect an audience."

"Well, if you had an audience, at least you—" Colby said, but then he stopped. "Never mind."

"At least I what?"

"I was going to make a tacky joke, but I thought better of it."

"No, let's hear it."

"You sure?"

"Absolutely."

"I was going to say at least you got a standing ovation."

She stared at him for a moment. "That's terrible."

"Yeah, I know. I apologize."

"Kind of funny, though."

The sun was above the hills now, and the golden morning light was sweeping across her face. Colby could see now that she was a bit older than he'd thought last night—probably forty. She had the camo backpack slung over one shoulder. Her long dark hair was pulled into a ponytail and her eyes were the color of bluebonnets. She was lovely.

"I take it you camped by the creek," Colby said, noticing she was wearing the same clothes.

"It was a beautiful night," she said.

He was having trouble placing her accent. Not from Texas or anywhere in the south.

"I have a spare bedroom you could've used."

"I don't *know* you," she said.

"Well, tell me your name and let's fix that."

She hesitated, weighing his request.

"Dixie," she said. "And I don't need any comments about it. People always want to tell me what a terrible name it is. It has so much baggage attached to it. Even Dolly Parton stopped using that name in one of her shows. She said it was ignorant. Plus, some people call me 'Dix' for short, which isn't the greatest nickname."

"What's your last name?"

"Let's stick with just Dixie for now."

"I'm Phil Colby. But if you knew where my house is, I'm guessing you already know my name. Tax rolls are easy to search online. Unless you don't have a phone."

Dixie didn't answer directly. Instead, she said, "Your ranch is beautiful. I was glad to spend a little time here, and thanks for not running me off. Anyway, I need to take off now."

"Got some meetings to attend?" Colby asked. "Busy schedule ahead? More apologies to make?"

"Something like that," she said.

"Why don't you come in and have some breakfast? I was just about to scramble some eggs."

Truth was, Colby had already eaten breakfast.

"I appreciate the offer, but I'd better pass."

"You sure?"

"Yeah, I need to get moving."

"Dixie, I don't know what's going on in your life, but I can promise you I won't make it worse. If you want to talk about it, I'll listen. If you don't want to talk about it, we'll just eat. Then you can take off and attend that important quarterly board meeting or whatever's going on."

He could tell she was considering it. She looked past him, into the house. "Anybody else in there?"

"No wife, no kids," Colby said. "No roommates. Just me. Not even a dog or a cat or a goldfish."

"Must get lonely out here," Dixie said.

"I enjoy solitude."

"That's almost a little sad," Dixie said.

"Says the woman who camped out alone last night," Colby said. "Come on in. Eat some breakfast. Take a shower. Then you can go."

After a pause, she slowly stepped into the house and he closed the door behind her.

"My diabolical plan is working," Colby said.

"You don't strike me as the diabolical type," Dixie said.

Colby said, "I'll start on the eggs and"—he pointed—"the guest bathroom is right down that hall, if you want to shower."

"Are you trying to tell me something?" Dixie asked.

"Yes. Clean towels are in the cabinet above the sink. And a blow dryer."

"You use a blow dryer?" she asked.

"Only when I'm going to the disco," he said.

She turned halfway, then stopped and said, "I appreciate this."

"No problem. Take your time."

He went into the kitchen, where he lined a cookie sheet with foil, then covered it with strips of bacon. Popped it into the oven at four hundred. That would take at least twenty minutes.

Then he cracked half a dozen eggs into a bowl and whisked them for thirty seconds. Pulled a skillet out of the pantry and placed it on the stovetop.

He'd zap some tortillas in the microwave, just in case she wanted to assemble some breakfast tacos. He had grated cheese, jalapenos, and salsa. There would be plenty of leftovers, so she could take a couple of tacos with her. They'd keep for a few hours.

He stopped for a minute and thought about that. Was he just going to let her leave? Well, obviously, he wasn't going to stop her against her will, but should he let her hike away later and vanish into the cedar-covered hills? Where would she go? Would her troubles—whatever they were—follow her? Colby shook his head and tried not to think about it. Not his business.

He washed his hands, then stared out the window above the sink.

Dixie reminded him in some ways of a Blanco County deputy named Lauren Gilchrist, whom Colby had been seeing until recently. They'd had a great time, too. Nothing serious. A month earlier, Lauren had shared the news that she had accepted a job as police chief in

Pampa, up in the Texas Panhandle. She hadn't been looking to make a change, but a former colleague working in that area had recommended her for the job. It was an exciting career move for her, but it would be a seven-hour drive back to Blanco County, and she and Colby had agreed that neither of them was interested in making that kind of round-trip on a regular basis, so…all he had left to do was return her blow dryer before she left town.

Colby heard the shower stop running, so he turned on the heat under the skillet.

A few minutes later, he poured the eggs into the skillet and scrambled them lightly. Put them on a platter with plenty of crisp bacon and placed it on the table. Then he ducked into the hallway, where he saw that the bathroom door was open and the room was dark.

"Dixie?" he said. "If that's your real name."

He stepped further into the hallway and heard slow, heavy breathing. Not snoring, but pretty close. He found her in the guest bedroom, curled on top of the blanket, one towel wrapped around her torso and another around her hair. The room smelled of lavender shampoo.

Colby closed the door quietly as he left.

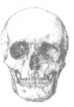

At nine-thirty, Red and Billy Don stopped at El Charro in Johnson City for some breakfast tacos on the way to bid a job near Cypress Mill. When they came out of the restaurant, Billy Don used a handful of wet napkins to wipe the black scuff on the truck's fender.

"Well, lookee there," Billy Don said. "That raccoon feller actually got something right. It did come right off."

Red came around for a look and sure enough, the mark was totally gone.

"Now you made a clean spot, so you'll have to wipe down the rest of my truck."

"Like hell."

"By the way, where's my three hundred dollars?"

"Huh?"

"That cash he tossed into the window last night."

"Must've blown out."

"You think I didn't see you sticking it in your pocket?"

They'd both climbed inside the truck, but when Red turned the key, the engine wouldn't start. It turned over, but it wouldn't catch.

"It ain't starting," Billy Don said.

Red stopped cranking for a second and looked at Billy Don with an expression that said *Did you really just point out the obvious?*

"I'm just saying," Billy Don said.

Red tried again and the engine finally caught, but something definitely wasn't right.

Billy Don pulled out his wallet and passed the three one-hundred-dollar bills to Red. "Guess you're gonna need that to fix your truck after all," he said. "So you're welcome."

Red stuffed the bills into the front pocket of his jeans, and there they stayed until 12:37 that afternoon. By then Red and Billy Don had given a bid to the customer in Cypress Mill, then returned to Johnson City and stopped at a little auto shop Red used regularly on the north side of town. A guy named Jorge ran it, and he knew Ford engines like nobody's business.

They left the truck with him and walked to the feed store two doors over. It was easy to while away some time at the feed store, shooting the breeze, but Jorge called in less than an hour, saying Red's truck was ready.

When Red and Billy Don got back to the shop, Jorge said, "Did you change the air filter recently?"

"About a week ago," Red said.

"When I popped the top off the air cleaner, there was a shop rag in there blocking the top of the carburetor."

Billy Don guffawed.

"That can't be right," Red said.

Jorge shrugged. "Just telling you what I found."

"Probably not a good idea to work on your truck after drinking an eight-pack," Billy Don said.

"Well, it's running a lot better now," Jorge said, "and I got the oil changed, like you asked, so you're good to go."

Jorge rang it up, and Red handed him one of the one-hundred-dollar bills out of his pocket. Jorge went to stick it into the cash register, but then he stopped. He made a funny face and raised the bill over his head, looking at it through the light.

"Uh oh," Billy Don said, but he was grinning, thinking Jorge was joking. "Just printed 'em this morning," he said.

Now Jorge pulled a magnifying glass from a drawer and was taking a closer look at the bill. Then he looked at Red and started shaking his head.

"You're bullshitting me," Red said.

"They tell us how to spot 'em, and this one is definitely fake."

It had felt and looked just fine to Red, so he said, "Now that you mention it, it seemed like something wasn't quite right."

"How could you tell?" Billy Don asked Jorge.

"See the '100' down here in the lower right? That's supposed to be color-shifting ink, but it stays the same color when I move the bill around. And there's no watermark. And there's no microprinting on Ben Franklin's collar."

"Those sonsabitches," Red said.

"Hang on a second," Jorge said. He opened the drawer again and rooted around for a few seconds, then came out with a marker. He popped the cap and made a mark on the bill. "See? It's supposed to be sort of gold or yellow if the bill is real, but this is showing black, because it's reacting to starch in the paper, which means fake for sure. No doubt about it. You know who gave it to you?"

"Yep. In fact, take a look at these other two."

Red pulled them out, and Jorge quickly confirmed they were also fake.

"What I'm supposed to do right now is hang on to these bills and call the cops," Jorge said. "But I don't want the hassle, you know? So you can do it." He handed the bills back to Red. "You'll take care of that, right?"

"Oh, yeah. We'll take care of it," Red said. "Count on it."

5

Dixie slept for five hours.

Colby had planned to run some errands in Austin today, but as the hours ticked past, he blew that off and did a few chores around the house instead.

At eleven, when Dixie had been asleep for three hours, Colby got a text from John Marlin. *Lunch today?*

Colby was tempted to tell Marlin about the sleeping visitor, but then he decided to hold off. Crazy thought, but what if Dixie was on the run from the law? What if she had warrants? But if that were the case, Colby *should* tell Marlin, right? Hell, he didn't know what he should do. It was strange the way Dixie obviously didn't want to talk about her circumstances. Colby replied: *Can't today. Maybe next week.*

At noon, he had a ham sandwich, then he stretched out on the couch in front of the TV. He was woken later by the sound of Dixie emerging from the guest bedroom. He sat up straight on the couch and waited. A moment later, Dixie appeared in the doorway, wrapped in the blanket from the bed. Her long hair was hanging freely now, but it was still damp from the shower hours ago.

"Wow," she said. "Sorry about that. I didn't even plan to sleep."

"Didn't bother me any," Colby said.

"How long was I out?" she asked. "There isn't a clock in that bedroom."

"Well, it's one-thirty now," he said.

"You're kidding. The same day, right?"

"I think you needed it."

"I guess those eggs are kind of cold by now."

"I can make something else. I bet you're starving."

"I am, but right now, you mind if I just sit down? I'm still groggy."

"You don't have to ask," he said.

She lowered herself into the easy chair to his right, using one hand to clasp the blanket closed just below her throat.

He said, "I started to grab your clothes out of the bathroom and throw them in the wash, but—"

"You don't need to do that."

"—I didn't want to sort through your pockets or anything like that."

"There's nothing to find," she said.

"I didn't mean that," he said. "I just, you know, didn't want to invade your privacy. Other than the hidden camera in the bathroom."

"Seriously? You haven't seen enough already? Also, that's creepy. And gross."

"The daily double," Colby said. "You only have that one set of clothes?"

"I've got a second set in my backpack."

"And a whole bunch of other clothes wherever you live," Colby said.

Her eyes had been on the television, absent-mindedly, but now she looked at him and grinned. "I cannot withstand your cunning interrogation. Yes, I live somewhere. I have possessions. That includes other clothes."

"How far away are these clothes?" he asked.

"I would say a medium distance," she said.

"In relation to, say, the county, the state, or the entire country?" he asked.

"Yes," she said.

The blanket had slipped downward a bit, exposing her shoulders. Why did he find that so intriguing, considering, as she had pointed out, that he had seen those shoulders and a lot more just last evening?

"You live in Texas?" he asked.

"For the moment," she said.

"So that means—"

"Phil?"

"Yes?"

"You seem like a solid guy."

"I like to think so."

"Someone I can trust."

"Absolutely."

"So please don't take it personally if I don't answer your questions. I don't want to talk to anybody right now about my situation."

"Understood," he said. "Just know that if you need any help—a place to stay—you're welcome here."

She started to reply, but stopped. Colby thought he might be able to read her expression. Staying in his guest bedroom, even for a night or two, would be a hell of a lot nicer than sleeping on the ground beside a creek.

"That's very nice of you," she said.

He shrugged. "Does that mean you're going to take me up on it?"

She didn't answer right away. Instead, she let out a long breath and seemed to weigh her options for a moment.

"I hardly know you," she said.

"True," Colby said. "Not much I can do about that."

"But you don't know me, either," she said.

"Also true."

"I could be an ax murderer," she said.

"Where would you be carrying the ax?"

"I'm being a pain in the ass," she said. "Here you are making this incredibly generous offer, and I'm not jumping on it."

"Do what you need to do. If you don't want to stay, or you can't for some reason, that's—"

"I'll stay," she said.

Colby found himself happy to hear it.

"But I need to add one condition," Dixie said.

"What is it?"

"You can't tell anybody I'm here. Nobody. I know I'm not in a position to make demands, but that's the one thing I need from you."

"Not a problem."

"I know that seems like I'm—"

"Not a problem. You don't have to explain anything to me."

"You haven't told anybody yet, have you?" she asked.

"I came close to it, but no," Colby said.

"Who did you almost tell?" she asked.

"My best friend."

"Who's that?"

"His name is John Marlin. He's the county game warden."

"And his last name is Marlin?" she asked.

"Yep."

"Like the rifle manufacturer?"

"Or the fish."

"That's perfect."

"If I told him about you, he would help, too. Unless, of course, you're an ax murderer. But I won't tell him."

"I appreciate that."

"I have some leftover lasagna in the fridge," Colby said. "I could zap some of that."

"Oh, my God. My mouth is watering already. Let me get dressed first. I promise I won't fall asleep."

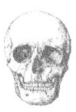

"That really pisses me off," Red said.

"Hey, don't be so hard on yourself," Billy Don said. "You're not a mechanic."

They were sitting in Red's truck in the parking lot of the auto shop. The engine was idling flawlessly and it had a lot more power.

"I'm talking about the fake money," Red said. "He could've gotten me into some serious trouble."

"You think Nicky knew the money was fake?" Billy Don asked.

"You're on a first-name basis now?" Red asked.

"That's his name. What am I supposed to call him?"

"Of course he knew."

"How do you know he knew?"

"When he tossed the bills into my truck, the other scumbag told him not to do it. At the time, I thought he was calling the guy stupid for giving up the cash, but now I think he was calling him stupid for handing out bad bills, like maybe they could get caught for it. You gotta be discreet about that kind of thing."

Billy Don said, "But it wasn't so stupid, was it?"

"How so?"

"He suckered you and got out of a tight spot without spending any real money."

"He suckered me? Hell if he did."

"Yeah, okay. Believe whatever you want."

That made Red even angrier. He'd been ready to let the incident go, but now, not so much. He stewed for a minute, pondering the situation. What could he do to make that punk regret what he'd done? Billy Don was too busy fooling around with his phone now to notice that Red wasn't moving the truck yet.

After a few minutes, Red began to have an idea.

He said, "The question is, what are we gonna do about it?"

"Do about what?" Billy Don asked.

"About those two morons and their Monopoly money," Red said.

Billy Don shrugged and said, "Why bother? That mark buffed right out."

"Yeah, but they were such assholes about it. And don't forget that he insulted you—calling you a stooge and all that. And saying a guy like you wouldn't be smart enough to take care of a raccoon."

Billy Don finally looked up from his phone. "I didn't even hear that part."

"He was really rude, if you wanna be honest."

"In that case, let's go back over there and beat the snot out of them," Billy Don said, repeating his go-to solution for many similar situations in the past. He was never one for subtlety.

"I was thinking the same thing, and that's option number one, for sure," Red said. "Both of those punks could definitely use an attitude adjustment. That's not a bad idea at all. Maybe so. Maayybee so. But I have something else in mind."

"Oh, here we go," Billy Don said.

"No, you're gonna like it," Red said.

"Let's hear it."

"Okay, well, think about it. If they've got three fake bills, they probably have more, right?"

"More fake money?"

"Yeah."

"I don't know. Maybe."

"Why would they have just three fake bills?" Red asked. "That makes no sense."

"I didn't say it did."

"I mean, they probably printed those bills themselves," Red said. "So I figure there's a good chance they have more. Maybe even stacks of it. I mean, if you're gonna print fake money, might as well print a bunch, right?"

"I'll say yes, just so you'll get to the point. What's your plan?"

Red paused for a few seconds to give his words more impact.

"We figure out where they're keeping all that fake money, and then we steal it from them."

Billy Don stared at him, his face blank.

"Did you hear me?" Red said.

"Yeah. But I don't get it. Why would we steal the fake money? You saw how fast Jorge spotted it. How would we use it all up? Where would we spend it?"

"We wouldn't spend it," Red said, almost giggling now, as he grew fonder of his plan.

"Then what would we do with it?"

"Get ready, because that's the best part," Red said.

6

"You're going to need some more clothes," Colby said an hour later. "And toiletries, and whatnot."

"You're right. I'm fresh out of whatnot," Dixie said.

"What I mean is, you probably need some random items and I don't know what they are. We should go online and order whatever you need."

"The problem is, I don't want to use any of my accounts, or my credit cards."

"I'll pay for it."

"I can get by with what I have."

"I don't know what all you have in that backpack, but obviously you're going to need more than that. Just make a list and we'll sit down and order it all. I'm guessing most of it can be here tomorrow. If anything is more urgent than that, I can run into town and pick it up. Or you can go with me, if you're comfortable with that."

"I'll pay you back for everything."

"I'm not worried about it," Colby said.

"But I will."

"That's fine," Colby said.

"You believe me, right?"

"I do."

"I'm a woman you can trust."

"I'm sure you are. We're two extremely trustworthy individuals. Just look at how trustworthy we are."

"The only person I trust more than me is you," she said.

Dixie's mood was lighter now, and Colby was happy to see it.

"There's a Walmart in Marble Falls," he said. "Or one in Fredericksburg. Either is about a thirty-minute drive."

She didn't say anything right away.

"Dixie?"

"I'm thinking about something."

"What is it?"

"There's only so much I can carry in my backpack. I can buy all kinds of great stuff, but I can't carry it. So what's the point?"

They were seated at the small kitchen table beside a bay window overlooking caliche-topped hills to the west.

"You have a vehicle somewhere," Colby said.

"Yeah."

"I'm not trying to be nosy or pushy, but…"

"Where's my vehicle?" she said. "That's what you're wondering?"

"Right."

"Okay, I'll share that with you. It's in San Antonio."

"Did it break down?"

"No, nothing like that."

"Then why is it there?"

She took a breath, then blurted it out.

"I think there's a GPS tracker on it."

"A tracker on your car," Phil Colby repeated.

"Yeah. Now you're wondering what the hell you've gotten into."

"A little, but I'm not worried about it."

"You're not?"

"Not even a little. But I do have some questions."

"I might not answer them."

"I understand. Can I ask anyway?"

"Okay."

"Let's start with an easy one. Where exactly in San Antonio is your car?"

Dixie took a moment to decide if she was going to answer. Then she said, "It's parked in the economy lot at the airport."

"How long has it been there?"

"Let's see…four days, I think. Or five."

"Does it run?"

"Yes."

"Was there anybody with you when you parked it?"

"No."

"Does anybody else know it's there?"

"Just probably the people who put the tracker on it."

"Who are those people?"

"I don't really want to get into that."

"How did you get to my ranch?"

"I walked."

He laughed. She looked at him with a puzzled expression that said *Why are you laughing?*

"Seriously?" he said. "You walked fifty miles on the side of the highway?"

She appeared amused by that question. "No, not on the highway. Why would I walk along the highway?"

"So…you walked…where? Cross country?"

"Parallel to the highway, but yeah, basically a hike. Why is that so weird?"

"You trespassed on literally hundreds of ranches and other private properties? I'm not judging, just asking."

"I used—" She stopped talking abruptly, but it was too late.

"You used Google Maps on your phone to avoid homes and people," Colby said, and he could see he was right. "What does it matter if I know you have a phone?"

"I guess it doesn't really."

"You found water and food?" he asked.

"I carried a quart of water, and I stayed close enough to roads and highways to find a store or restaurant when I needed one."

"How close are you talking about?"

"Within half a mile or so, but usually even less. Couple hundred yards."

"Far enough from the road that you couldn't be seen," Colby said.

"Yeah."

"Crossing fences and creeks and ravines."

"Yeah."

"Where did you sleep?"

"Wherever I wanted to. Usually a nice patch of tall grass, but twice I slept in barns when it was cold."

"You'd just sneak into a barn and sleep there?"

"Yeah, and be gone by daylight. Sometimes I didn't sleep much."

"That doesn't sound like much fun," Colby said. "But it explains why you ate about a pound of lasagna earlier, and why you fell asleep for five hours when you didn't mean to."

She shrugged. "I've always had a big appetite, and I'm active enough that I can eat whatever I want. And I'm a napper."

He thought about all of this crazy information for a moment. "But, uh, my ranch wasn't your destination, right?"

"No. Just passing through. Does that make you feel better?"

"I have no idea," he said. "But back to your car for a second. You left it at the airport because somebody was tracking it?"

"Yes."

"Have you seen the person tracking you?"

"You think I'm making it up, or maybe I'm nuts?"

"Not at all. I'm just wondering whether you've confirmed that somebody is actually tracking you, or if you simply suspect it."

"I've seen the same vehicle a couple of times, in different locations. It's a unique vehicle."

"Which means whoever is following you is pretty stupid, to track you in such an identifiable vehicle," Colby said. "Unless they don't care if you know they're following you. What does the vehicle look like? Will you share that?"

"It's a black cargo van with no windows in the back. On the sides, I mean. The rear doors have windows, but the back part doesn't. And it looks like it was spray-painted."

"You're right, that is identifiable. When did you first see it?"

"I don't know where I first saw it, because I only really noticed it—like thought it was possibly following me—the second time I saw it. I had no reason to worry about it the first time I saw it, so I don't remember where I was. But the second time, I was in Columbus, stopping for gas." She paused, then said, "Let's not talk about this anymore, okay? It's too much."

He could tell she was getting stressed, but Colby had so many more questions:

Have you committed a crime?
Were you a witness to a crime?
Is someone trying to kill you?
Will anyone who helps you be in danger?
Where did you come from?
Are you going somewhere in particular or just rambling aimlessly?
Do you have a history of mental illness? No, really.
How do you hike so far without getting blisters?

He said, "Okay, fine. But I'm going to ask just one more question: Whatever's going on, have you talked to an attorney about it? You don't have to answer, but I want you to think about it. If you talk to an attorney, chances are good that conversation will be confidential. There are only a few exceptions. He or she might come up with some solutions you've never even considered."

Now he really couldn't judge her expression. He didn't know her well enough. Was she considering what he'd suggested? Or was she trying to decide if she should tell him why that wasn't a valid option? Maybe she *had* talked to an attorney and there was no legal solution to her problem. She looked a little lost or confused.

Finally, she said, "I think I could be up for that trip to Walmart, if you don't mind taking me. Instead of shopping online. Is that okay? It'd be nice to get out and not think about anything."

Red loved his idea. Absolutely loved it. But Billy Don didn't seem to get it.

"Sell it back to them?" Billy Don said, repeating what Red had just said.

"Yep. That's the idea."

"Why would they buy the fake money back from us?" Billy Don asked.

But Red had already thought of that question himself, and he had an answer.

"Okay, let's walk through it," Red said. "Let's say we find fifty thousand bucks in fake money in the van."

Billy Don let out a snort of disbelief.

"Hey, you never know!" Red said. "That's only five hundred fake hundred-dollar bills. I did the math. On my phone."

"Keep going."

"To the scumbags, even though the money is fake, it's worth exactly fifty thousand dollars, because they're planning to spend it just like it was real. You follow?"

"It ain't real complicated."

"So if it's worth fifty thousand to them, it's a pretty good bet they'd pay something like ten grand to get it back," Red asked. "They'd still wind up forty thousand dollars ahead."

"You're the math whiz," Billy Don said.

"That's easy money," Red said. "All we have to do is take it."

"Except for the obvious problem," Billy Don said.

"What problem?"

"Why would they pay real money to get fake money back? Why wouldn't they just print more? They can print as much as they want, right? Nothing stopping them."

Red opened his mouth, then shut it again.

They sat for a long moment and watched traffic pass on Highway 281.

But then Red saw the solution.

"I'm a genius," he said. "And because of that, get ready to hear the brilliant answer."

"I'm all ears," Billy Don said.

"Look at the big picture for a minute," Red said. "If you're a scumbag passing fake bills around, as long as you're careful, you could probably get away with it for a long time. Maybe you only spend them at places that don't have security cameras, because you don't want to be on video at a bunch of places where they found fake bills."

"Would you get to the point?"

"It would be a slow process, but you could probably spend at least a couple of hundred-dollar bills every day. Buy something small, get change, and pocket the real money. You could drive from town to town doing that all day, like it was your actual job."

Billy Don started doing a motion with his hand for Red to hurry up.

"You'd have to be careful about getting your fingerprints all over it, because if the Feds started finding the same prints over and over on fake bills, if your prints are in the system, or if you get caught for something else later and—"

"I get it," Billy Don said. "Just tell me the answer that makes you such a genius. Why wouldn't they just print more money and tell us to go blow ourselves?"

"Because once we get ahold of the fake money, we wouldn't just offer to sell it back. We'd tell them if they didn't cooperate, we'd call the cops. That's the deal. That will make all the difference."

Billy Don didn't say anything right away.

Red waited.

Billy Don was thinking it through.

Red waited some more.

Finally Billy Don said, "Why?"

"Why what?"

"Why will that make all the difference? I still don't see it."

"Because even if the two scumbags were real careful not to touch the fake money or use it anywhere with cameras, once the cops know who they are and what they've been doing, they'll figure out how to tie them to it. Think about some of those crime shows we've watched."

"Which ones?"

"Any of them. All of them. See, if I'm right and these guys have a whole bunch of fake cash, the cops take that kind of shit seriously. So they'll put a lot of time and effort into nailing the two scumbags. They'll start by looking at a list of places where counterfeit money has been used in the past few months, and then they'll figure out if Nicky and the other scumbag have been to those places."

Now Billy Don was getting it. "Cell phone records," he said. "Maybe credit card records."

"Hell, yeah," Red said. "And if we're right, it will all match up perfectly. With the way everything's computerized, it wouldn't take the cops more than an hour or two to check all that stuff. Hey, you're quick with your phone. Look up the penalty for counterfeiting."

While Billy Don did that, Red dropped the truck into gear and pulled around to exit onto the highway. Several vehicles were approaching from his left, so he had to wait.

"Whoa," Billy Don said. "This here says up to twenty years in prison and a fine up to a quarter million dollars."

"And *that* right there is why Nicky and his pal are gonna play real nice after we steal their stash. If we ID them, they're screwed."

A maroon Ford F-250 passed on 281, and Red realized it was Phil Colby. He had a woman with him, and she didn't look like that hottie deputy Colby had been dating for a while, but Red didn't get a real good look. If it was the deputy, she'd changed her hair around, and women were known to do that.

Red liked Colby okay, but Colby didn't seem to feel the same way about Red and Billy Don, possibly because of the time they'd threatened him with a gun after a fat-cat lobbyist paid them to steal a massive white-tailed buck Colby had raised from a fawn. Water under the bridge, as far as Red was concerned, but Colby never completely let it go—even though it was only a pellet gun!

Red pulled onto the highway.

"What if you're wrong and there ain't any more fake money?" Billy Don asked.

Red knew that was a strong possibility. It might even be likely.

"No big deal," he said. "We'll just set their van on fire and call it a day."

"Works for me," Billy Don said, finally sounding enthusiastic.

7

"So what's your story?" Dixie said as they went north on Highway 281.

"What do you mean?"

"A guy like you definitely has a story."

"A guy like me?"

"Ruggedly handsome bachelor rancher? Come on. You could be in a Hallmark movie. Why are you still a bachelor? And how did you end up with a ranch? You win the lottery?"

"My family has owned it for more than a hundred years," Colby said.

"So it got passed down to you?"

"Yep. In case you're wondering, that's the easiest way to own a ranch."

"Are you an only child?"

"You sure ask a lot of questions," Colby said, and he gave her a sideways look to show he recognized the irony in his comment.

"You got something to hide?" she asked.

"Absolutely," he said. "The first thing I should tell you is that I have a vehicle parked in the economy lot at the San Antonio airport. I realize that seems like an enormous coincidence, but that's just how we mysterious types roll."

"What if we're parked side by side?" Dixie said. "Wouldn't that be amazing?"

"Mine's a Ferrari," Colby said. "What's yours?"

"Lambo," Dixie said. "Red, of course."

"But to answer your earlier question, yes. Only child."

"Are your parents, uh…"

"They've both passed away."

"Sorry to hear it."

"Thank you. It's been a while. What about you? Brothers and sisters? Parents? A pet iguana?"

She didn't answer right away. They were passing through Round

Mountain, halfway to Marble Falls.

"I can't tell if we're making small talk or you're still trying to squeeze information out of me," she said.

"I'm not sure myself," Colby said. "Obviously, I can't help but be curious about what's going on with you, but I'm trying not to pry."

"I appreciate that."

"So what do we talk about? I can't ask where you're from or where you're going. Family is off limits, and probably your job, too. And where you went to school. Your last name. Can you tell me your favorite color?"

They passed the cloverleaf intersection of 281 and 71.

"I guess purple," she said.

"Okay, progress," Colby said. "Favorite song?"

"Oh, that's easy. *I Don't Want to Miss a Thing*. I know that's corny, but that song was big during my senior year of high school, so I have some good memories about it, and yes, I realize that means you can figure out how old I am."

"By my calculations, you're thirty-four."

"I'm glad you suck at math."

They crossed over Little Flatrock Creek, which had about a foot of water in it—about as deep as it ever got, short of flooding conditions.

"You planning to go inside the Walmart?" Colby asked.

"I figured I would," Dixie said.

"Not worried about anyone seeing you?"

"Not since I left the car at the airport," she said.

A mile passed in silence.

Colby said, "I'm no tech expert, but I know there are ways to follow somebody with their phone. Like I could turn on one setting or another and give you permission to always know my location. Or you could get on my phone and change the setting yourself, possibly without me knowing. I'm not trying to pry about your phone, but..."

"I'm not using my old phone," she said.

"Okay, good."

"I bought a new phone—with cash—and since then basically nobody knows I have it. Except you."

"I feel pretty special," Colby said.

"You should," Dixie said.

Colby slowed as he reached the edge of Marble Falls and crossed the bridge over the Colorado River. It was nearly four o'clock. Dixie reached into her backpack for a pair of sunglasses and a baseball cap.

Colby said, "Maybe, someday, if the planets line up just right, you'll give me your number."

He could feel her looking at him, so he glanced over.

"You're a smart-ass," she said.

"Well, I don't know if I'm smart," Colby said.

"The good news is, I consider that a positive quality."

He said, "Hey, you like pie?"

"Who doesn't like pie?"

He pointed to his right. "See that little diner right there?"

"The Blue Bonnet Café?"

"We should stop there later and have a piece of pie."

"What kind?"

"I always prefer round," Colby said. "They've got about a dozen flavors."

"Banana cream?"

"Yep."

"Sounds good," she said. "It'll be on me."

Colby started to object, but decided against it. Let her buy him a piece of pie.

They continued in silence through the light at 1431.

He was getting a vibe from her—like it was making her anxious to be around so many people all of a sudden.

"It's a pretty town," she said. "Busy."

"The Walmart's gonna be packed," he said. "Just so you know."

She nodded.

Colby eased into the center lane and took a left into the Walmart. He found a spot in the outer reaches of the lot, just because it was easier to park away from the crowd.

He killed the engine, then checked his phone and saw a message on the screen he'd never seen before. He didn't quite understand it.

AirTag found moving with you

**The location of this AirTag
can be seen by the owner**

"What's wrong?" Dixie said.

"I'm not sure," Colby said. "But whatever it is, I don't think it's good."

He showed her the message. He could tell she didn't know what it meant either.

"I've heard of it, but I'm not sure what it is," she said.

"Give me a minute," he said while he did a quick search. A moment later, he had his answer. "It's a tracking device from Apple."

"Son of a bitch," Dixie said.

"Google says it was designed to help people locate keys and purses and things like that. Vehicles."

"Why not people, then?" Dixie asked.

"Good question," Colby said. "Maybe because it gives warnings like the one I just got. It uses Bluetooth, not GPS, so…hang on. Let me figure out what that means."

While Colby was reading, Dixie opened her backpack and began pulling the contents out.

"Here's my understanding," Colby said a minute later. "You buy an AirTag and connect it to your phone by Bluetooth. It only works with iPhones, not other brands. So they are always communicating, but when your phone and the AirTag are not in range of each other, the AirTag will be sending out a signal to any other people nearby with an iPhone or an iPad or an iPod Touch, and that tells the owner of the AirTag where it's located, or at least where it was last seen. Anywhere with cell coverage."

"What do they look like?" Dixie asked, digging through a small zippered pouch.

"About the size of a quarter, but several times thicker," Colby said. "Silver on one side, with the Apple logo. White on the other side."

She obviously wasn't finding anything like that.

Colby kept reading. "If you put one in the middle of nowhere, without any people around, you won't ever be able to find it, since it doesn't use GPS. But if you put one in a package you're shipping across the country, every time somebody with an iPhone gets close enough to that package—Bluetooth range—you'll be able to see where it is."

Dixie stopped rooting around for a minute. "Do the people with iPhones know they're helping locate the AirTag?"

Colby read some more, then said, "No, it's all completely

anonymous. But it's not supposed to be used to stalk people, which is why I got that warning on my phone. When the AirTag is separated from its owner, and then it's around somebody else with an iPhone for an extended period of time, that warning will pop up repeatedly. It's supposed to also send out a little alert sound, but there's a way to disable that. There's also a way for me to disable these alerts, which I'm going to do, so it doesn't keep annoying me."

"I have to admit I'm freaking out a little bit right now," Dixie said. She was looking through the windshield, scanning the parking lot. Searching for anyone suspicious.

"Understandable," Colby said. "You're safe, though. I can guarantee that. But we need to find that AirTag."

"Hang on," she said. "Just one more pocket."

A moment later, her hand came out of the backpack with an AirTag flat on her palm.

Dixie said, "I can't believe this. It's been there all along. There was no GPS tracker on my car. I'm so stupid."

"That's not true. How could you possibly know that? I take it you don't own an iPhone?"

"No."

"Even before all this mess started?"

"Right. I've never owned one."

"And whoever put that AirTag in there probably knew that. Or they didn't know about the warnings that get sent. Anyway, you've been carrying that AirTag with you for who knows how long, and you never would've known unless you hung around somebody with an iPhone."

"That's just downright devious," she said. "That means they know where we are right now, so they could be watching us."

"I guess it's possible, but it doesn't seem likely."

"Why not?"

"It just seems to me that the AirTag is meant to keep tabs on you, so they don't have to follow you."

"What if you're wrong?" Dixie asked. "What if it's specifically so they can keep their eyes on me?"

8

"Do you know who's driving the black van you saw in Columbus?" Colby asked.

"Like their names or anything like that? No."

He said, "I haven't noticed a black cargo van today, but I guess they could be in some other vehicle."

"They could be parked somewhere nearby right now," she said. "You think they saw me hold the backpack up to the light, checking for the AirTag?"

"I think your imagination is getting the best of you, but you know all the details and I don't," Colby said. "Even if they're watching right now, it only looked like you were trying to find something inside your backpack."

She didn't answer.

"Is the person in the van trying to abduct you or harm you?" Colby asked. "Because that would be an important detail. Or do they just want to know where you are?"

Her hesitation showed that she still wasn't ready to tell him everything.

She said, "I want you to know that I trust you. I really do. And I appreciate everything you're doing for me. But I don't want to drag you further into a mess. And, well, there's more to it than that."

"And you're not ready to tell me quite yet," Colby said.

"I might not ever tell you," she said. "You need to get comfortable with that idea. I just don't know. I'm scared, to be honest. Not just for me, but for other people."

Colby wanted to reach for her hand, but he resisted. "That's fine. I don't mean to pressure you. Do what you need to do."

"You sure?"

"Absolutely."

"You can leave me here and go on with your life," she said. "Let everything go back to normal."

"Normal is boring," he said.

"Normally I'd agree," she said. "And I didn't even mean to make that pun. What I mean is, I'd love it if I could have a normal life again."

"Well, you found the tracker, and that might help," Colby said. "Because now you know it's there."

She placed the AirTag on the console between them, where it shined in the sun. "What should I do with it? Hey, I could put it on a train or an eighteen-wheeler!"

She was plainly tickled by that idea.

"Let's take a minute and think about it," Colby said. "Right now, you have an advantage. They don't know you've found it."

"And we know that they know where I've been since the airport—not every minute, obviously, but in general. They know I've been at your house. And they know I'm here at Walmart right now. I should just leave it here, or somewhere else. But I don't want to take it back to your place or they'll know I went back there with you. I want them to think I was there, but now I'm gone and I haven't gone back."

"I think that's probably the best thing," he said. "That way they won't know where you are. But I just thought of another option."

"What?"

"I take the AirTag and carry it around for a few days, and they think I'm you, right? Meanwhile, you take off and go wherever you need to go and do whatever you need to do. I have another truck back at the house—my old truck—and you can take that. It ain't pretty, but it's rock-solid reliable and the registration is current. You'll shake them off your track for good."

He could tell she didn't want to do that, and he thought he knew why. She didn't want to leave him yet. Or was he misreading the situation? Regardless, he found himself wishing he'd met her under other circumstances—like stopping to help her with a flat tire, or, hell, her stopping to help him with a flat tire. Or any of a thousand other ways two people might meet that didn't involve tracking devices or sleeping by the creek or refusing to provide a last name.

He said, "You don't have to make up your mind right now."

"Okay, good. Which means, for the time being, we proceed as if we have no idea the tracker is there. We go inside Walmart and I leave the backpack out here, because that's what I would normally do. Agreed?"

"Yep. Let's go."

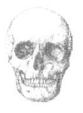

Red drove back home, where they swapped his truck for Billy Don's Ranchero, then drove back to town.

The two scumbags had never seen the Ranchero before, which was a plus, but it was also sort of noticeable, because you hardly ever saw a Ranchero on the road anymore. Some people would notice it right away and might even say, "Check it out. An old Ranchero." But Red and Billy Don only had the two vehicles between them, so the Ranchero it was.

It was nearly six o'clock when they rolled through Johnson City, and it was 6:20 when they approached the north side of Blanco. Billy Don was driving and the windows weren't tinted, so there wasn't much he could do to avoid getting spotted if they got too close to the two scumbags. That's how Red was thinking of them now—"the two scumbags." Or sometimes "Nicky and that other scumbag."

"We should be able to see the van from the road," Red said.

He was calling this a reconnaissance mission, with the objective of seeing if the van was still at the motel, because if it wasn't, and if Red and Billy Don couldn't locate it somewhere else in the small town of Blanco, they might not even get a chance to implement his plan.

"If it *is* there, then what?" Billy Don asked.

"Still ponderin' on that," Red said.

"But we're planning to search the van first? Or the room?"

"I don't know yet. The van would be easier to search, but I'd say the money is probably in the room."

Billy Don had one of those Slim-Jim tools for popping car locks, and an old van would be an easy target. As for the room, Red was hoping the scumbags left it unlocked, feeling safe in a small town like Blanco, but Billy Don could probably force the door open pretty easily, if the van was gone.

"Have we ever blackmailed anybody before?" Billy Don asked.

"Not that I can remember," Red said. "Extortion, yeah, but not blackmail."

"What's the difference?"

"Hang on," Red said. "Slow down a little."

They were about to pass the Blanco County Inn, which was on the left.

"I'm going forty," Billy Don said.

"You see 'em?" Red said, trying to look past Billy Don.

They both looked toward the motel, over a little shrub along the side of the road.

"Don't see the van," Billy Don said.

"Me, either."

Disappointing. Maybe the two scumbags had left town already.

"So now what?" Billy Don asked.

"Just keep going," Red said.

"Where?"

"Don't know yet. Let me think. But watch for the van as you go."

Billy Don stayed in the right-hand lane and went through town nice and slow.

"Make a loop around the courthouse," Red said.

Billy Don took a left on Fourth Street and now the old county courthouse was on their right. Nowadays it was a visitor's center on the bottom floor, and you could rent the top floor for weddings and parties and such. They'd even shot a scene for *True Grit* up there—the new *True Grit*, not the old one with John Wayne. Red liked the new one okay, but he always had a hard time picturing Jeff Bridges as Rooster Cogburn instead of Lebowski.

Billy Don took a right by Old 300 BBQ, then another right, and now they were back at Highway 281.

"Take a left," Red said.

Billy Don turned left, and they cruised slowly through the south part of Blanco. Everything was quiet, which was not a surprise.

"We never did get that pizza," Billy Don said as they passed CJ's. He sounded downright mournful.

"Later," Red said.

"Damn right," Billy Don said. "I'm driving, so we'll go wherever I say we go."

"Keep going south," Red said.

Billy Don kept going south.

They crossed the Blanco River and approached the spot where

they'd originally encountered the black van last night, as it had come barreling out of the Lowe's Market parking lot, which was just ahead, on the left.

Red said, "Billy Don, you know what'd be funny?"

"Huh?"

"If right now the van came out of the Lowe's parking—"

Right then the black van came out of the Lowe's parking lot again.

"—just like that!" Red said.

"What do I do?" Billy Don asked.

The van was coming this way.

"Just keep driving," Red said. "Don't look at them. Don't look. I said don't look."

"I'm not looking!"

It didn't matter, because the setting sun was angling through the van's windshield and Red could clearly see Nicky and the other scumbag. Neither man was paying any attention to the Ranchero.

"Turn around," Red said. "Slowly."

"Where?" Billy Don asked.

"Anywhere," Red said.

He took a right into Seymour's Garage and turned completely around, so now they had to wait at the light before they could get back on Highway 281. This would take a few minutes.

"I still don't know what the difference is," Billy Don said.

"What difference?"

"Between blackmail and extortion."

"Look it up on your phone later," Red said.

"So you don't know either."

"No, I know."

"Then why don't you tell me?"

Red didn't say anything, simply because there was no point in arguing with an ignorant pinhead.

"That's what I thought," Billy Don said.

"Jesus," Red said.

"What?"

"It's like you set out to be annoying," Red said.

"Would you prefer it to be accidental?"

"Blackmail is when you've got something that would make the other person look bad, like photos or recordings or even just because you know something bad about them you can prove, but if they give you money, you'll be cool and not say anything. But extortion is where you're just saying, hey, if you don't give me money, I'll kick your ass or burn down your business. You're not threatening to ruin their reputation or get 'em in trouble with the cops or anything like that. It's like when a bully takes your lunch money."

"Never happened to me," Billy Don said.

"I'm sure it didn't."

"I was the one taking the lunch money," Billy Don said.

"Sounds about right."

"So were you the bully or the one getting your money took?"

"Neither. Never had any money on me," Red said.

"So how did you eat at school?"

"Stole stuff from the snack bar, like a normal kid."

"Sounds about right," Billy Don said.

The light finally changed and Billy Don turned left onto the highway.

They crossed the river and a few minutes later passed the Blanco County Inn again. The black van was once again parked outside the room on the north end of the building.

9

Phil Colby noticed that Dixie went straight to one of the sales racks. Khaki cargo shorts for $14.99. She grabbed a pair and held it up for inspection. Checked the quality. It seemed to meet her needs, so she began to turn away.

"Won't you need more than one pair?" he asked.

"I already have two pairs of shorts," she said. "And, uh…"

"You don't want to spend the money."

"I don't want *you* to spend the money," she said. "Even though I'm going to pay you back. I don't want to put you out or anything."

"Put me out?" Colby said. "Are you suggesting I can't afford a second pair of fifteen-dollar shorts? I'll have you know that I'm deeply and egregiously offended. How dare you say such—"

"Okay," she said, grinning and reaching for another pair. "Whatever you say. Take it easy."

"That's better. My wounded pride is restored."

A few minutes later, as she was looking at T-shirts, Colby noticed a young guy at a nearby rack stealing a glance at Dixie. Then he flipped through several blouses and looked at her again. Colby was fifteen feet away and the other man hadn't paid him the least attention. Colby watched as the young guy looked again, and this time his eyes went from Dixie's face and then traveled the length of her body.

Right then, Dixie looked casually in his direction, and the man immediately returned his attention to the blouses. He pulled one off the rack, double-checked the size, and wandered out of sight.

Dixie walked over to Colby and whispered, "I think that guy was watching me."

Colby said, "I know he was."

"I didn't recognize him, though."

"That's because he was a total stranger."

"How do you know?"

Colby shook his head. "He's just a youngster who hasn't learned how to check out an attractive woman without getting busted."

He could tell the possibility had not occurred to her, but she was amused that he was suggesting it.

"Oh, really?" she said.

"That's the way it looked to me, and I speak from experience."

"From checking out women?"

"And getting busted. It's a rite of passage."

"Surely you have some clever techniques by now."

"At my age? Is that what you're saying?"

"You're, uh, experienced," she said.

"And you're asking me how I check out good-looking women without getting caught?"

"Basically, yeah."

"Okay, well, my latest method—and this one needs work, because I got caught—is that I stumble on them swimming naked in the creek."

"Oh, God."

"I'm serious."

"How many have you seen that way?" she asked.

"Just one so far," Colby said. "But she was…"

He stopped on purpose.

"She was what?" Dixie asked.

"Never mind."

"No, go ahead."

"I really shouldn't be talking about this. I mean, I don't even know your last name."

"She was what?"

There was nobody else in the women's department. No customers. No salespeople.

"She was stunning," Colby said. "And even when she saw me, I couldn't stop looking. I'm not talking about ogling or leering, I'm talking about being struck by beauty in a way that catches you by surprise and takes your breath away for a moment. I was looking at a painting. A poem brought to life."

Dixie was staring at him now with her eyes wide, and he still didn't know her well enough to understand what she was feeling.

Then she looked down at the shorts she was holding and he was pretty sure she was starting to cry, but the bill of her baseball cap was blocking his view.

"You okay?" he asked.

She nodded.

"I'm sorry," he said.

She shook her head, as if to say it wasn't his fault.

So she *was* crying. He had no idea why. He waited.

She wiped her eyes with her free hand. Sniffed a few times. After a moment, she raised her head and looked at him again.

"That came out of nowhere," she said. "I just got real sad for a minute and I'm not sure why. Maybe because my life is a shambles."

"That could do it," Colby said.

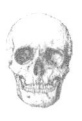

Thirty minutes later, they paid at a register and Colby stopped in the little entry foyer between the two sets of sliding doors.

"You know what?" he said. "Let me go get the truck and pick you up."

He had a bag of merchandise in one hand and his keys in the other.

"Really?" she said.

"Unless you think I'm being silly."

She still hadn't indicated whether she thought she was in danger. He wasn't trying to coerce that information out of her, but it would be helpful in their decision-making. Was there a chance someone might be waiting in the parking lot? If so, might that person or persons take action?

"Yeah, okay," she said.

Good to know.

He began to walk to the truck in the far reaches of the lot, keeping a wary eye in every direction. No black van. Nobody loitering.

Suddenly he had a terrible thought: what if Dixie was gone when he got to the front of the store? He would never know if she had left voluntarily or had been forced to leave. This was a mistake.

He used his key fob to start his truck from twenty yards away. Nobody had parked on either side of him, but right then a beater Lincoln Continental pulled into a space two slots over. Two people in it, now getting out. Young guys. In their twenties. Coming this way.

Colby tried not to think like an old codger, but these guys looked like punks. Both had ragged hair and needed a shave, and they were wearing those saggy pants that were so popular, despite looking ridiculous. One of them was wearing a backward baseball cap. They walked with that little hitch in their step, sort of a strut meant to show how tough they were.

They were ten feet away now, and as Colby closed the gap, one of them looked him in the eye and offered a little upward nod of the head.

"Sup," he said.

Colby nodded back, but he found himself bracing for the worst. Two on one. Even against punks, it would be a challenge. Were they armed?

They walked past him and kept going.

Of course they did.

He climbed into his truck and backed out of the spot. Drove down the row, past the two men, and pulled in front of the store.

Dixie came calmly but quickly through the sliding glass doors and joined him in the truck.

Colby said, "I need you to do something."

"What?"

"Just take a look at these two men and make sure you don't recognize them."

"Where? Those two men walking this way?"

"Yeah."

She studied them for a moment. "Never seen them before."

"Okay, good," Colby said. "I think I'm getting a bit paranoid."

"You know what fixes that?"

"Thorazine?"

"Pie. Like you promised."

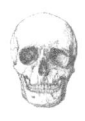

The crowd was light inside the Blue Bonnet Café, which wasn't surprising at 7:45. The place closed in fifteen minutes, and the waitress appeared relieved that Colby and Dixie weren't planning to order anything from the kitchen.

"This," Dixie said, pausing with the fork halfway to her mouth, "is possibly the best piece of pie I've ever had. Good God."

"They know what they're doing, that's for sure," Colby said.

"How long have you been coming here?" she asked.

"Since before I can even remember."

"And how long is that?"

He had chosen a piece of pecan pie with Blue Bell vanilla ice cream on top, but he stopped eating for a moment. "You trying to figure out how old I am?"

"Only seems fair, since you already know how old I am," she said.

They were seated at a small table by the window, and the nearest other customers were three tables away.

"If I told you, it might scare you away," he said.

"From what?" she asked, grinning, and he realized he'd inadvertently made his hopes clear.

"I'm sorry, what?" Colby said.

"What would your age scare me away from?"

"I have no idea what you're talking about," Colby said.

"Uh-huh," she said.

"I've been too busy trying to decide what we should do with that AirTag that was in your backpack," Colby said.

"Got any ideas?"

"Actually, yeah, I do," he said.

"Let's hear it," she said.

"If we put it on somebody's vehicle, like an eighteen-wheeler heading out of town, I'm a little worried that we might be creating some potential trouble for the driver. Is that a reasonable concern?"

She thought about it and said, "Yeah. Probably."

"In fact, almost anywhere we put it, we might create a problem for somebody else," Colby said. "We don't want some innocent person to get an unexpected visitor. Agreed?"

"Agreed."

"So that narrows our options quite a bit," Colby said.

"I'm with you. So what's your idea?"

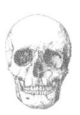

They'd gone back to get pizza, just as Red promised, and now they were seated at one of the tables outside, on the side of the building, near the air compressor where people fill up their tires.

Red had eaten three slices, but right now he was taking a break, trying to figure out what to do next. Billy Don, meanwhile, was still wolfing it down like he was on a deadline.

"The problem is, if we wait for them to go somewhere again, they might be leaving for good, so the money won't be in the room, obviously."

A four-bay car wash sat to the rear of the lot next door, behind the gas pumps, and right now a young woman in a Texas A&M football jersey was vacuuming a red Miata.

"If we decide to search the van first while it's parked outside the room, that could be pretty damn risky," Red said.

Billy Don grunted to indicate he was listening, but Red wasn't convinced. When there was food in front of the big man, he might as well have blinders on and plugs in his ears.

"Or we could wait until they escape to Yugoslavia on the purple bicycle," Red said. "Unless they bring a sandwich loaded with thumbtacks and Vaseline."

Billy Don grunted again.

Red was pissed that Billy Don wasn't focusing, but at the same time, it was probably better that way. Red had always been the idea man, because he was smarter and more devious and just more creative and clever in general— but right now, he had nothing. Nothing at all. Not even the slightest bit of inspiration.

Then—bam!—he had it.

10

It was dark by the time Phil Colby and Dixie entered Johnson City. Colby stayed on 281 through the light at 290, then continued south until he reached Old Austin Highway, where he took a right, and then an immediate left on Alamo, followed by another left on Haley Road, which was not much wider than a single vehicle.

Just four hundred feet later, they were behind the Bill Elsbury Law Enforcement Center—the sheriff's office—which also housed the county jail.

Colby stopped in the road, stepped out of his truck, and, without hesitation, flung the AirTag upward in an arc, and it landed on the roof of the building. He was back in the truck three seconds later and heading down the road.

He and Dixie had had a good laugh earlier when they'd discussed this idea.

What would her pursuers do when they saw that the AirTag was at the sheriff's office? Assume she'd been arrested? Think she'd approached the police for help? Wonder why she'd gone straight from the Blue Bonnet Café to the sheriff's office? They'd be baffled and have no idea how to proceed. It wasn't like they would walk into the sheriff's office and ask about the woman they'd been tracking illegally.

Instead, they'd scour the Internet for any mention of her arrest, and they might even call the jail anonymously to see if she was an inmate. The answer, of course, would be no. But what would that mean? Had she finally had enough and spilled her story? Were the cops keeping the AirTag as evidence? At that point, what options would the men in the van have left? They wouldn't know where she was or what she was doing. They'd be worried the cops would be looking for the black van. Would that convince them to leave the county?

Colby took a left on Fannin, then pulled into the parking lot of the Valero gas station on Highway 281.

"Well, I think that was clever," Dixie said.

"Thank you."

"And hilarious."

"If nothing else, we're amused by it," Colby said. "The question is, what now?"

"What do you mean?"

"Well, now that you're rid of the tracker, you're free, right? You can go anywhere you want. I could take you to get your vehicle at the San Antonio airport, if you'd like."

"Oh," she said. "Honestly, I hadn't thought that far."

"Or I could take you back to my place and you can figure out what you want to do next."

"I, uh…"

"That's what I'm hoping you'll do," Colby said. "In case you were wondering. You're welcome there. As long as you'd like."

"That's very generous," she said. "How about if I make up my mind tomorrow?"

"Whatever you need," Colby said.

"Okay, cool," she said. "You mind if I go into the store for a minute?"

"You need something? I can go get it."

But she was already reaching for the door handle. "No, that's okay. I'll be right back."

She was, too, in less than two minutes. She got back into the truck and showed him what was in the plastic sack—a bottle of cheap champagne.

"The tracker is gone, and I figure that's a good reason to celebrate," she said. "Independence."

"Works for me."

"You like champagne?"

"I don't mind a glass, and after that, I have other options."

"I can't thank you enough for everything you're doing," she said. "I think—"

She hesitated.

"What?" Colby asked.

"I'm just grateful, that's all. Very few people would do what you're doing."

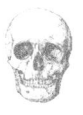

Like Billy Don, Red's girlfriend Mandy was on her phone all the time—watching TikTok videos, or checking Instagram, or shopping, or sometimes just reading—not just memes and stuff, but actual books. Red found her reading habit annoying as hell sometimes, especially when they were in bed at night and he had other things in mind, but as long as she kept one hand free for other stuff, he could deal with it. He figured it was the price he paid for having a smoking-hot girlfriend, and maybe he should just keep his mouth shut. Also, sometimes she read smutty books, and he was all for that, because those fired her up in ways he enjoyed.

He remembered a time a few months ago when Mandy was on her phone yet again and she told him about some guy in Austin griping on Facebook because he got busted for insurance fraud.

"What happened was, he told everybody he got his arm caught in some piece of equipment at work and it tore up some ligaments in his elbow. His doctor said he didn't really need surgery, but he probably would need to rest that elbow for like six months. Apparently they can't just fire somebody outright in a situation like that—or they're not supposed to—so he was basically getting a free vacation. He doesn't come right out and say it, but when you read between the lines, he's telling you he wasn't really injured, or it wasn't that bad, and he was taking advantage of the situation. Sort of playing it up."

"Pretty damn smart," Red said.

"But he got caught," Mandy said. "He was at the grocery store and some good-looking lady in a short skirt needed help loading bags of salt into her cart."

"Softener salt?" Red said.

"Yeah. Forty pound bags."

"Water softeners are for suckers," Red said. "Even if you factor in the cost of replacing appliances, the amount of money you spend on salt over the years is—"

"Focus, Red," Mandy said.

"On what?"

"The story I'm telling," she said. "You interrupted. Anyway, he said he was in the grocery store and this lady needed help with the salt, so he helped her, but somebody else was filming the whole thing. They were using her as bait to trick him into doing something stupid and proving his elbow wasn't really hurt by loading all those bags."

Red thought that kind of set-up was pretty clever.

"You could do something like that," he'd said at the time.

"Lift bags of salt?" Mandy asked.

"No, you could be the bait. Put you in a low-cut blouse and men would drive off a cliff if you told 'em to."

"That's because men are idiots," Mandy said.

"But you agree?"

"Yeah, I guess. Because men are idiots."

"Maybe you have a second career calling," Red said.

And then he'd forgotten all about that conversation. Until now.

When he and Billy Don got back to the trailer later that night, he was glad Mandy was waiting for him, and he was even happier to see she was drinking one of her large tumblers of vodka and orange juice. She was always nicer and more agreeable after one of those tumblers.

Still, when he told her about the encounter with the black van, and how the scumbags had given them fake bills, and what he and Billy Don were planning to do about it, she said, "I swear, y'all come up with the craziest bullshit. What're the odds you're gonna find that money? Probably lower than the odds of getting shot."

He was in his recliner and she was sitting in his lap, which was something else that was more likely to happen if she had a buzz going.

"You mean that *fake* money," Red said. "I figure the odds are pretty good."

"Why?"

"Huh?"

"Why are the odds good?"

"Because where else would they keep it?"

"Oh, I don't know. Wherever they live? Or maybe they don't have any more."

Billy Don was listening from his sunken spot on the couch. "She's prob'ly right," he said.

"So he only had those three bills on him?" Red asked. "That don't seem likely."

"It sure as hell doesn't seem worth the risk to me," Mandy said.

"What if y'all get caught?"

"I don't think we will," Red said.

"Why not?"

"Because you're gonna help make sure that doesn't happen."

"Oh, I am? How am I gonna do that?"

"You 'member telling me about that guy who was lying about his arm being hurt, and that lady got him to lift bags of salt?"

"Oh, good Lord," Mandy said. "What kind of stupid idea did you come up with?"

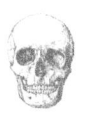

"This, uh, isn't the greatest champagne I've ever had," Dixie said. "Sorry about that."

"I'm surprised," Colby said. "That gas station was profiled in the latest issue of *Wine Connoisseur Weekly*. The hot dogs also received high praise."

"You mentioned—"

"Other options?"

"Yes. Please."

They were seated on the leather sofa in Colby's living room, which featured a large bank of windows facing west. The sun had set long ago, but there was still a faint orange glow on the horizon.

He rose and went to his liquor cabinet.

"Bourbon, scotch, vodka, gin, rum, tequila," he said. "And Irish. And Canadian."

"What are you having?" she asked.

"Bourbon on the rocks."

"Make it two, please," she said.

He went into the kitchen and came back with two lowball glasses filled with ice. Poured a generous amount of Garrison Brothers into each glass, then returned to the couch and handed one to Dixie. They touched glasses and she took a sip.

"Nice," she said. "Very nice."

"The distillery is twenty minutes away," Colby said. "I toured it last year. Kind of cool."

She took another sip, then set the glass down abruptly. "I need to say something before I have any more of that," she said.

"What?"

"I need to ask you something, actually."

"Ask away."

"Just be honest with your answer, okay?"

"I'll do my best."

"Would you like to go to bed?" Then she quickly added, "I mean, if you don't, that's okay. Maybe I got the wrong signals. It's been a long time. So if you—"

Colby set his glass down, too.

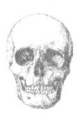

Red was awake at two in the morning when Mandy got up and went to the bathroom, and when she came back to bed and snuggled in close, he said, "You 'member when we went to that fancy dinner last fall?"

"Hmm?" she said.

"At the show barn," Red said.

"You think the wild game dinner is fancy?" Mandy said.

It had always been one of the biggest nights of the year—at least for Red and Billy Don. Great food, booze, door prizes, more booze, a silent auction, and a dance afterward. Last year, Rodney Bauer won a shotgun during the raffle. Lucky son of a bitch. Mabel made him sell it to pay bills.

"Well, I mean we got dressed up," Red said.

"You put on a sport coat," she said. "Whoop-dee-do."

"Okay, so *you* got dressed up," he said.

"I wore a skirt," Mandy said.

"I know, and man, you looked good. I mean good."

"Thank you."

"And that top you were wearing. What do you call that?"

"Just a cropped tank top."

"That green one," Red said.

"Yeah."

"That thing fits just right, I can tell you that much. Tight, like I like it."

"The next size up was too big."

"You were turning heads, big time. I always know you're looking especially good when the other ladies are glaring at you."

"They weren't glaring at me."

"They sure as hell were. All judgy like."

"Well, screw 'em if they were. I dress however I want."

"I know you do. They can't carry it off. That's why they were glaring."

"Why are we talking about this right now?" she asked.

"Oh, no reason," Red said. "Just remembering."

Mandy didn't say anything. She'd probably fall asleep again in less than a minute. She could always do that.

"You still got that top?" Red asked.

11

Syd went outside for a smoke break and sat in the same damn chair outside the motel room. Time was running short. He had to finish it up tonight.

There was a part of Syd—a tiny part—that regretted bringing Nicky along. But what choice had Syd had? He had a rule for situations like this: Always have a backup, because you never knew when you might need one. And who else could Syd bring? Nobody. That was the answer. No-fucking-body. Syd didn't trust anybody except for Nicky, and even that was iffy. Nicky was loyal, but he wasn't that smart, which meant he didn't always make the best decisions, which meant you couldn't always trust him.

And then there was Moloch. That fucking raccoon and Nicky were a package deal. Hell, Moloch was a better traveling companion than Nicky was, to be honest, except that he was always grabbing things with his little hands, which was annoying as hell. Like when he'd throw Syd's cigarettes out the van window. Not individual cigarettes, but full packs, right out the window.

"He hates the smoke," Nicky said at one point.

"Oh, bullshit."

"He does."

"You're telling me this mangy raccoon is smart enough to do something like that? He knows if he gets rid of the cigarettes, there won't be any more smoke?"

"Of course he does. He's smarter than a lot of people."

"Speak for yourself."

"Look at his face, bro. He knows we're talking about him."

Syd had to admit it looked like Moloch was smirking. Taunting him. Daring him to do something about it.

"I should throw *him* out the window," Syd said.

"Don't even joke," Nicky said.

"Oh, I'm not."

And right then Moloch chattered aggressively at him, like he understood the conversation. Kind of creepy.

"They're problem solvers," Nicky said.

"What a load of crap," Syd said.

"Scientists have studied them and it's true," Nicky said. "Like, if they have this one garbage can they always raid, but then you put a strap on it or something, they'll figure out how to take that strap off."

"Then I guess they're goddamn geniuses," Syd said. "I mean, removing a strap. That's brilliant. Send 'em off to college with that kind of IQ. He can get a degree in bungee cords."

As far as Syd was concerned, the best thing about Moloch was that he couldn't talk. Unlike Nicky, Moloch didn't go on and on about stupid bullshit like the Priesthood of Mendes or pentagonal revisionism. What the hell was all that bullshit? Nicky was a member of the Church of Satan, except they didn't really believe in Satan? That's the way Nicky described it, which didn't even make sense. Syd thought Nicky was a member only because he liked having people think he was weird—which was also weird. That's why he had the tattoo and the stupid haircut. Syd figured it was a just a phase, although Nicky was getting too old for "phases."

Sitting outside the motel room, Syd took a long drag and tried not to think about the task at hand. It was what it was. If he didn't do it, somebody else would. Why think about it? And if he didn't do it, you might as well throw his body on the pile. Draco had been pressuring Syd hard, and he'd said something about possibly sending Fernando and Armando to Blanco County, being vague about what he meant. To come after Syd? Was that what he was implying? Or to finish the job Syd had botched?

Syd wasn't scared of much, but Fernando and Armando? Those fuckers gave him chills. When you looked into their eyes, you saw nothing. No, not nothing. That wasn't exactly right. You saw that they viewed you with no regard as a fellow human being. They didn't care if you lived or died. If they saw you—or anyone else—get hit by a bus, they'd go about their business and never think about it again. It would mean nothing to them. Syd wasn't prone to deep thought, but those two psychos made him ponder the nature of empathy. Syd wasn't some snowflake, that's for sure, but he could feel bad for somebody who fell off a building or got some terrible disease.

Syd looked into the dark night. The highway was surprisingly quiet, even for this hour. So was the motel. Most of the rooms were empty, including the one right next to theirs. That was lucky. Syd hated it when you had some idiot stomping around or banging against the walls. Playing music. Turning the TV up too loud. Moaning and groaning as they did things that made the bedsprings squeal and squeak.

Syd finished his cigarette and dropped the butt on the ground. Crushed it with the heel of his bare foot.

Then he pulled his iPhone out and opened the Find My app. Clicked on the Items tab. Just as Syd had seen several hours earlier, the AirTag that had been hidden in the deep pocket of the backpack was still at the sheriff's office in Johnson City, which was pretty damn clever. She'd found the AirTag and tried to throw Syd off track. She or that guy she was with, Phil Colby, had probably tossed it onto the roof of the building. Why bother trying to hide it inside the building? The map didn't know the difference. There was no way she had actually gone inside and talked to anyone about her predicament. Syd wasn't buying that bullshit.

The motel room door opened and Nicky looked out. He was expecting Syd to say something, so Syd kept quiet, mostly because he was sick of Nicky at this point and wanted to piss him off.

Nicky stepped outside, but he left the door open.

"You're letting all the goddamn mosquitoes in," Syd said.

Nicky turned and closed the door. Then he said, "So when are we leaving?"

"I don't know yet," Syd said. "I'm thinking."

"It has to be tonight, right?"

"Yeah."

"Then what's there to think about?" Nicky said.

He really was that dumb. Okay, honestly, *dumb* wasn't the right word. But he didn't think things through. It was like he didn't have the capacity to weigh different options and choose the best one. He always just plowed ahead mindlessly, and then lived with the results, which were often terrible.

Syd, on the other hand, was like a goddamn chess player. Yeah, he knew that sounded kind of smug, but hey, it wasn't bragging if it was true. He could *think*. He could *plan*. He could study all the different possible moves and understand where each one might lead in the long run.

So why had it been so hard to complete this task?

There had been hours at a time when Syd hadn't been able to track the lady at all, especially after she'd parked her car at the airport. That had almost fooled him, but then she'd popped up a few miles north of San Antonio. Then she disappeared again. It went that way multiple times over several days—she would drop off the radar, then reappear several hours later at some convenience store or fast-food restaurant eight or ten miles away from where she'd been before. So he knew she hadn't hitched a ride with anybody, and she wasn't taking a bus or a train.

By the time Syd and Nicky would get to her location, she'd be off the radar again. Syd would drive both ways up and down the highway and never be able to find her. What the fuck? What was she doing, hiking cross-country? Camping out?

Now she was back at Phil Colby's house, all by itself on top of a hill, well away from any neighbors. Syd had always hoped to catch the woman by herself, but maybe this was the ideal situation. Bad luck for Colby, though. He appeared to be a complete stranger to her. Why would he open his home to a random woman like her? What wild story was she telling him to earn his trust?

He checked the time again. Fuck. No more putting it off. He pushed himself up from the chair.

Thank God for the second AirTag hidden inside the woman's backpack, because without it, she could be long gone by now, and Syd would have no idea where to look. He would have failed the assignment miserably and paid the price.

Always have a backup.

12

Dixie and Colby were still in bed and awake at 2:19 when she said, "I'm going to tell you everything now. Okay?"

The offer caught him by surprise.

"Of course it's okay."

They were lying side by side, facing the ceiling. His heart was still beating heavily. The intimacy they had just shared was even more fulfilling than he had imagined it might be.

"Or I can wait until the morning," she said. "I don't want to ruin the moment. Or, more accurately, the past three hours."

"I don't think it's possible to ruin it," Colby said.

"You might be surprised."

"Your call," he said.

"I'll do it now," she said.

"Okay."

"It's going to take a while. It's complicated."

"That's fine. Tell me."

"I don't even know where to begin," she said. "So I'll start with some background. I used to work for the Forest Service. I worked there for sixteen years. I've always loved the outdoors and I loved my job. If you made me work at a desk, I'd go insane."

"I guess that explains why you don't mind hiking fifty miles and bathing in a creek."

She laughed. "That's true. You know the only thing I don't like? Mosquitoes. That's about it. Anyway, I was stationed for a long time at Kisatchie National Forest in Louisiana. Have you heard of it?"

"I don't think so," Colby said.

"It's actually five separate districts, but altogether, it's immense—more than six hundred thousand acres. For comparison, Big Bend is eight hundred thousand acres, so Kisatchie is only a little bit smaller than that. I was a forestry technician at Kisatchie."

"Sounds perfect for you."

"It really was. I loved Kisatchie because it's this really rich and diverse habitat. Four dozen species of mammals, thirty species of amphibians, and more than 150 species of birds. We had gigantic tracts of longleaf pines and seepage bogs and open prairies. Very fertile and lush. It's beautiful. It's also a fantastic place to grow marijuana, partly because there are so many places that are remote and hard to access."

Colby hadn't expected her tale to go in this direction, but he knew it wouldn't lead anywhere good from here on out.

"Have you heard about illegal grow sites on national forests?" she asked.

"I've seen articles about it," he said.

"It's become a big problem, especially in the larger forests, as you would expect. A lot of the sites are in California, but you can find them just about anywhere that marijuana can grow. Some of the sites we found were small-time operations run by some local pothead, meaning just a couple dozen plants. But then there were the big sites—cartel sites with thousands of plants. Several acres."

"Cartel?" Colby said. "Seriously?"

"Yep. We're talking about ruthless, violent people. One large crop alone can be worth millions of dollars, so they'll go to great lengths to protect it. And beyond that, most people don't realize the impact these illegal sites can have on the environment. One marijuana plant alone requires something like nine hundred gallons of water during its growing season. So when you've got thousands of plants in a crop, that's a major drain on the water source in that area."

"But how do they get the water to the crops?"

"The sites are very elaborate. It's not like they're just planting their crops and hoping it rains. It's more like a small farm, and the people working the site will actually live there for months at a time, not just to protect the site, but because there's a lot of work to do. For instance, they'll dig long trenches to divert water from a creek or river and form a holding pond, and from there they'll lay thousands of feet of irrigation pipe and hoses. And they might haul in a thousand pounds of fertilizer—carrying it by hand for miles to get it to the site."

"I had no idea," Colby said.

"The worst part—the part that really pisses me off—is the poison they use. Pesticides, rodenticides—some really toxic crap that puts a lot of animals and plants in danger. Some of it is banned, as it should be. Ever heard of carbofuran? A quarter of a teaspoon will kill a 600-pound animal. They'll just scatter poison all over the place to protect the site, so lots of animals die. Or they'll stick it in cans of tuna or cat food. These people are just fucking evil if you ask me. It creates this terrible circle of death. We saw one case where a bear ate the poison and died, then a vulture ate part of the bear carcass and died, and then another vulture ate part of that first vulture and died. It's just mind-boggling how much destruction it causes. Foxes, bears, ravens, mountain lions, fishers—every animal out there, some of them endangered. Then there's the danger that those chemicals can end up in the water supply for humans."

"How are they able to avoid being caught?" Colby asked. "I mean, I understand they might be miles away from the nearest road, but can't you use drones or helicopters to find the sites?"

"Limited time and manpower and money and so on. And when we do find a site, that requires even more time and manpower and money to clean it up safely. It takes a hazardous materials team, and helicopters, and all kinds of experts, and it ends up costing about forty thousand dollars per site. Oh, and there is no federal funding dedicated to any of this. Where's that money supposed to come from?"

Colby could hear the passion and frustration in her voice. He was tempted to start connecting the dots and make some assumptions about who was following her in a black van, but he resisted.

"Did you ever find any grow sites yourself?" he asked.

"Yeah, a couple, and it's kind of scary, because sometimes the workers are armed. We had some guidelines telling us exactly what to do when we found a site. The first thing you do is turn around and leave. Don't look around, don't take pictures, and don't even mark the spot with GPS, because somebody might be watching you, and if you do any of those things, not only does it waste time getting out of there, but they might decide you're a threat and kill you on the spot. So you just leave immediately. When you're a safe distance away, then you call dispatch and report your location, but you don't mention the grow site on the radio, not even with any kind of code words, although you might have a secret phrase you use to let them know you're in danger, if you think you are. Then you go back to your duty station and that's when you report it to law enforcement. We have our own cops, you know?"

"I didn't know."

"And full investigative teams." She turned her head toward Colby. "Starting to wonder why I'm telling you all this?"

"Writing a script for an action movie?"

"Ha. That's a great idea. But, no. It'll all make sense in a little bit."

"I have no doubt."

"If you can stay awake for it."

"I'll do my best."

"Okay, so, one thing I learned over the years is that a lot of the grow sites go undetected, or we find them after the growers are able to harvest their crops successfully. And when we did find an active site, the cops were rarely able to bust anybody except the low-level laborers, most of whom couldn't even tell you who they're working for. They aren't cartel members, they're paid laborers, sometimes from Mexico or further south, just like the laborers who harvest legal crops. Many of them never understand the risks of what they're doing, or what will happen if they get caught. Sometimes they get forced into helping—basically it's 'Do this or we'll kill you.'"

"And they're the ones who get arrested," Colby said.

"Yep. They usually get charged for manufacturing a controlled substance, plus depredation of forest lands, and possible firearms charges, so we're talking decades in prison. If and when they get out, they're deported, if they're here illegally."

"And their bosses skate?"

"Almost always, yeah. The laborers don't know much, but if they do tell what they know, they could be putting their families at risk."

"That just sucks all the way around," Colby said.

"Despite all of this, I loved my job, and I wouldn't have traded it for anything," Dixie said. "But then I found a big grow site about a year ago. As soon as I recognized what it was, I turned around, and two men were behind me, blocking my path. They were wearing camo from head to toe and one of them was holding a rifle—like an AR-15 kind of rifle. One of them said something to me in Spanish, but I couldn't understand him."

Colby could feel Dixie tensing up beside him.

"What did you do?" he asked.

"I said I didn't speak Spanish, so the other man—the one without the rifle—stepped forward and took my phone away from me. He dropped it on the ground and crushed it with his boot. Then they made me take them to my SUV, where they destroyed my radio. Then they had a conversation and seemed to reach a decision, and they just walked away and vanished into the woods. Later on, I could still remember what one of them had asked the other, even though I didn't understand the words at the time. He had said, 'Should I shoot her?'"

"Jesus," Colby said.

"That's when I had to really think long and hard about whether I wanted to stay in my job, and as luck would have it, something else came along a few months later. I'd gotten to know a lot of employees from timber companies in Louisiana and east Texas, and some of them became good friends. One of them told me about a job opening—they needed someone to act as a caretaker on one of their properties until the next year, when the trees would be mature enough to harvest. It was just over thirty thousand acres, with a home on it and some other infrastructure and equipment that I would need to maintain and protect, but it was pretty minimal. Keep trespassers and poachers out. That sort of thing. They would provide a truck and an ATV."

"More outdoors work," Colby said.

"Yep. And good pay. It was a one-year contract, which would give me time to figure out what I wanted to do after that. Or maybe I'd find a second career in the logging industry, if I liked the way this particular company operated. I already knew they had a reputation for being good stewards of the land."

"Where was the property?"

"East of Woodville in Tyler County."

"Beautiful area," Colby said.

"Sure is."

"So I'm assuming you took the job."

"Absolutely. I gave notice and we moved in to that house one month later. Me and Mark."

"You and who?"

"My husband Mark."

"Your *what*?" Phil Colby said.

13

"My last name is Morrow," Dixie said quietly. "My married name."

Colby propped himself up on one elbow and looked at her in the faint light.

"Maybe I was wrong about your story not ruining the moment," he said.

They were both silent for a moment.

"I wasn't comfortable telling you earlier," she said.

"I can understand why, considering what we just did with each other. I bet Mark would disapprove. Unless he's into that sort of thing."

"Please don't be mad, at least not yet. Let me explain."

"I'm listening," Colby said.

"We didn't do anything wrong," she said. "I'm still married, but it's not really…it's been over for a long time. He knows it, too. We're more like roommates now, but I don't think either of us was quite ready to end it. That's why I've been telling you everything up until now. You need all that background information, so bear with me. Please."

"I'm not going anywhere," he said. He laid on his back again and stared at the ceiling. "I've never done this before."

"Done what?"

"Slept with a married woman. That I know of."

"Are you angry?"

"I wouldn't put it that way."

"Do you feel like I deceived you?"

"I wouldn't say that either—not without knowing the full story."

She reached for his hand and squeezed it. "So you want me to keep going?"

"You mean with your story, or are you gonna climb on top of me again?"

She let out a sharp laugh. "I meant the story, but…"

"Yeah, you should tell it, and then we'll see."

"Okay, then. Mark and I have been married for fourteen years. It's easy to see in hindsight that we weren't a great match, but we pretended our differences weren't an issue at first. For instance, anytime we went to a large city—New York, Chicago, LA—he was totally in his element. He would've lived in any of those places and loved it. But I couldn't get out of there fast enough. I always felt so claustrophobic."

"I'm with you on that," Colby said.

"And I knew from the time I was a kid that I wanted to work outdoors," Dixie said. "I didn't know exactly what I wanted to do, but I knew I didn't want an office job. For a long time I thought about being a wildlife biologist, and then maybe an animal behaviorist, or maybe a game warden, like your best friend. Then I met someone who worked for the Forest Service and I realized how many different types of jobs they offer, and what the purpose of the agency is, so I applied for a job there not long after college."

"Where was this?"

"I grew up in the southeast corner of Colorado—a little town called Campo. In one day, you can drive a loop through Kansas, Oklahoma, Texas, and New Mexico, and be home in time for dinner."

"How did you wind up named Dixie?"

"My parents are from Alabama."

"Which college did you go to?"

"CSUP—Colorado State University Pueblo. That's where I met Mark. He was born and raised in Denver. We had an English class together, and he struggled to get a D—not because he isn't smart, but because he didn't care much about it. That should've been a red flag right there, I guess. He was more interested in smoking pot and going to the lake than studying. But he was good looking and funny and was good at talking me into ditching class. I'm not meaning to go on about Mark, but you'll need to know it for the rest of the story."

"It's fine."

"While I was getting a bachelor's in wildlife and natural resources, Mark was studying business, but he never finished. In fact, he was probably on the verge of being asked to leave. He didn't fail classes so much as simply not go. But he left on his own before they kicked him out. He said he didn't know what he wanted to do next, but college wasn't for him. He said he couldn't see the value in it. I suggested some kind of trade school, but he wasn't interested in that, either."

"Have to say, he sounds like a real winner," Colby said.

"Yeah, I know. I know. You should hear what my mother says. Anyway, he has always bounced from job to job, and I finally realized that was going to be his pattern forever, so I just accepted it. Sometimes he gets it in his head that he wants to pursue some big new career—like he'll want to write a novel or open a restaurant or, my favorite, 'become an inventor'—and a month later, he's forgotten all about it and moved on to something else. As you can probably guess, I've always been the chief breadwinner, and I know that bothers him, although I don't really care about that part myself, as long as we have enough money to get by. Unfortunately, sometimes we don't."

Colby noticed that she was still using the present tense, which didn't give him much confidence that Dixie's marriage was really over.

"What did Mark do?" Colby asked.

"About what?"

"What did he do that somehow ended up with you being on the run and eventually in my bed, telling this story."

"It's that obvious, huh?"

"I don't know where this is going, but I figure he has to play a part or you wouldn't be telling me so much about him. And pot is the common denominator."

"You're right," she said. "I guess I just want you to have a feel for him—what kind of person he is—before you hear the rest. Because he's...he's not a bad person. He might have terrible judgment and bad decision-making skills, but he's not a bad person. Almost everybody likes him."

"I believe you, but at this point, I'm bracing myself for whatever incredibly dumb thing he did," Colby said.

"Smart man," Dixie said. "As I said, Mark's a pot smoker, and he's always going on about how it should be legal everywhere, with no restrictions at all. Even in liberal places like Colorado, you have to be 21, and you can't possess more than two ounces."

"Those laws make sense to me," Colby said.

"But you think it should be legal? For recreational use?"

"Yeah, basically."

"Me, too. Ever gotten high?"

"A couple of times. It's not for me."

"Me, neither. Just give me a glass of wine, or like tonight, a little bourbon. Anyway, whenever I would tell Mark about these grow sites we would find on the job, he would get agitated and go on these rants against the government, which basically included the law-enforcement division of the Forest Service."

"Friction?" Colby asked.

"Yeah, some. I think if he didn't smoke pot, he wouldn't care one way or the other about the laws he griped about."

"So what did he do? Let's hear it."

"Okay, well, as I said, it's hard to find a lot of these illegal grow sites, especially the small ones. Keep in mind that you can grow thousands of plants worth millions of dollars on just two or three acres, so if you hide that site in the middle of thousands of acres, you stand a pretty good chance of getting away with it. The temptation is pretty great."

"Uh-oh," Colby said.

"I made the mistake over the years of telling Mark specific details about the grow sites we found, and how we found them, and—do you ever watch those real-life murder shows on TV?"

"Sure."

"You know how you're thinking, wow, if only he had done this instead, he might've gotten away with it? Apparently, that's what Mark was doing all along—listening to my stories, and combining that with online research, and slowly devising a plan to cultivate a grow site and get away with it. He wasn't alone, either. He was scheming with a friend from Louisiana, and the more they talked, the more convinced they became that they could get away with it."

"Based on what you've told me, he might've been right," Colby said.

"Well, that's true. Sometimes they get lucky. For the cartel, it's a numbers game. If they have dozens of sites and one gets found, well, that's a bummer, but they have all the other ones."

"But if you have just one site..."

"Right. If that gets found, you're done. Everything you've worked for is down the drain. Plus, like I said, the cartel recruits laborers to do all the work and insulate the higher-ups from ever getting caught. But Mark and his friend..."

"It was just the two of them working the site themselves?" Colby said.

"Yep. So the risk was so much worse."

"And they got caught," Colby said.

"Sort of. What happened was—"

They heard a loud, melodic noise outside the bedroom window.

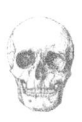

Syd ducked behind a tree trunk and froze.

What the fuck had he just banged into? A wind chime? He'd let his eyes adjust for a long time earlier, and he thought he was seeing well enough to proceed, but apparently not. While he had been looking low, watching for obstructions on the ground, he'd hit the chimes with his forehead. Why would anybody hang wind chimes at forehead level?

Now what?

Run away? Walk away?

He stayed right where he was and waited. The camo hunter's hood over his head was hot and itchy. Sweat was running into his eyes, but he didn't dare move to wipe it away. His .380 was holstered on his hip. He wished he had a rifle instead, but he hadn't expected to make a long-range shot. He was thinking he'd likely be able to find an unlocked door, slip inside, and do what needed to be done.

No lights came on inside or outside the house. That didn't necessarily mean anything. If this Colby guy was smart, he would leave everything dark for a few minutes. He would peek out a window and look for movement. There was enough moonlight that Colby would probably be able to see Syd if he moved. Not well, but enough to know someone—or something—was out here.

Or maybe he hadn't heard it at all. Was he a sound sleeper? What about the woman? Were they sleeping in the same room? Where was the room? Syd figured the master bedroom would be in the back of the house, which was why he had approached from this direction—just in case he might find a lighted room with open curtains and have the chance for an easy shot through a window.

Nicky was waiting in the van about half a mile away. Syd wondered if he should abort the mission and haul ass. Tempting, but Colby or the woman could be watching out a window right now.

For now, Syd waited.

14

Colby could feel Dixie tensing up, so he quickly said, "Wind chimes."

"Is it windy?" she asked. "I don't hear any wind."

They were both speaking in a whisper.

"No, but there's probably another explanation," Colby said as he grabbed his phone off the nightstand. He quickly checked the security cameras along the rear of the house.

"I'm not seeing anything on live view," he said. "No clips from the last few minutes, either, because of the way I have dead zones in the settings. Otherwise, animals and swaying branches would set off a new clip every five minutes. Same with motion-detection lights. I removed those because they were going off and on all night."

"The chimes didn't fall," Dixie said. "They kept ringing too long. Something bumped them or jostled them."

"Maybe a raccoon," Colby said, slipping out of bed and pulling on some shorts from the dresser. "Or an owl or something could've brushed against them."

"You're trying to placate me, and I appreciate it, but you know that wasn't it."

He went to a closet and returned with a .40 caliber semi-automatic. Dixie saw it and said, "You got one for me?"

He said, "This is a question I would ask anybody: have you handled a gun before?"

"Many times," she said.

He handed the gun to her and returned to the closet. This time, he returned with a Remington twelve gauge.

"All the doors are locked with keyless deadbolts," he said. "Nobody is getting inside without us knowing."

"Is there one in the chamber?" she asked.

Colby was pleased to see that she had the barrel pointed at the floor and her finger rested on the trigger guard, not on the trigger itself. Her experience showed.

"Absolutely," he said.

"Full magazine?"

"Yep. Sixteen rounds."

She nodded.

Colby went to the lamp on his nightstand and put his finger on the switch. "Okay, it's gonna get dark in here."

She nodded again.

He turned the lamp off and the room went dark—but after a moment, the faint light from the clock and a nightlight near the bathroom allowed him to navigate. He made his way slowly to the left side of one of the windows and peeked around the edge of the curtain. Dixie positioned herself on the other side of the window, eight feet away. The exterior of the house was limestone, so they were in no danger of being shot through a wall.

A deck ran the length of the rear of the house, with access via a door four feet to Colby's left. To the right of the door was a light switch that controlled three floodlights—one on each rear corner of the house, and another mounted above the door itself.

He said, "If I turn on the floodlights, we might see somebody and know they're out there. Or we might not see anybody, which would be great, but we won't know if anybody was out there earlier."

"Or we'll see a deer standing beside your wind chimes," Dixie said. "Then we'll know we can go back to bed and not worry about it."

"Is that what you want to do?" Colby asked. "Turn the lights on?"

"Beats just sitting here," she said.

"But if somebody's out there, turning on the lights lets them know we think they're out there. Whereas leaving the lights off, they have no idea what we know or don't know. Then they might decide we're still asleep and move around some more, and we might see them."

"That's a lot of *mights*."

"So…turn the lights on?"

"I think so, yeah. But we'd better decide pretty quick. Whatever it was could be leaving right now. Or whoever."

Colby moved over to the light switch and peered through the little window in the door.

"Get ready," he said. "The oak tree with the wind chime in it is straight ahead, about a hundred feet, and there's nothing that would block our view."

"Ready when you are," Dixie said.

Colby flipped the lights on.

Nothing moved. Colby didn't see anything unusual or unexpected.

"I can't see very well," Dixie said. "I have no idea where the chimes are."

"They're too far away to see easily, and they're black, but it's that big oak right in the middle."

"Can you see them?" she asked.

"I can't tell if they are still hanging from the limb or not," Colby said.

Binoculars would be of no use. He'd be looking from a lighted area into a dark area.

"Somebody could easily be hiding behind that trunk," Dixie said. "Or any of the other large trees."

Colby kept watching for a minute longer.

"I'm sorry," Dixie said.

"For what?"

"For dragging you into this."

"You didn't drag me into anything," Colby said, which was true. He had volunteered. Hell, he had practically insisted.

"I'm putting you in danger by being here," she said.

That, too, might be true. Colby didn't care.

"We don't know that anybody was out there," he said. "But if somebody was, I'm not worried. We'll deal with it."

If there had in fact been somebody outside, that meant they hadn't fallen for the ruse of throwing the AirTag on top of the sheriff's office. That, or they had Dixie under surveillance and knew she had returned to Colby's house.

He was getting restless. If somebody was hiding out there, they could stay put for hours. Colby wasn't willing to sit here until dawn.

"Did you ever have any trouble with road hunters at night in the national forest?" Colby said.

"Sometimes. Why? You got a spotlight?"

"Yep. I'll be right back."

Colby hurried out of the bedroom, down a hallway, through the living room and into the kitchen, where he unlocked the door into the garage. His truck—his newer truck—was parked in here, and he kept a spotlight plugged into his dashboard, which kept the battery charged.

He grabbed the spotlight and hurried back to the bedroom.

Any person who had never seen one of these spotlights might not understand how powerful they were. Much more powerful than the average flashlight. This particular spotlight—a million candlepower—could light up a hillside five hundred yards away or more.

This time, Colby stood to the right of the door.

"You should pull back from the window, just in case he shoots," he said.

"What are you going to do?"

"I'm going to swing the door open and stick the light just past the frame."

"And how are you going to see anything?"

"I'll peek a little bit."

"That doesn't make any sense," she said. "If he fires a shot, he'll fire at the light, and he might hit you. But I can be over here, peeking out the window and telling you which way to shine the light—up, down, left, right."

"Works for me."

"Just don't get shot in the hand, okay?"

"I'll do my best."

"We're probably totally wrong anyway," Dixie said. "There isn't anybody out there. And we're going to laugh about it in a minute."

"Yeah, probably," Colby said.

Or they're already gone, he thought.

"Ready now," Dixie said.

"Okay, here goes."

Colby opened the door and stuck the spotlight into the doorway, just far enough that he could shine it toward the trees. Then he pulled the trigger and activated the light.

"Up," Dixie said. "And a little to the right."

Colby followed those instructions.

"Hold it steady right there," Dixie said. "Now I can see the chimes in the tree. I think."

"But you don't see Bigfoot?"

"Just a chupacabra. No Bigfoot. Why don't you sweep to the right?"

Colby slowly moved the spotlight.

"Down a little," Dixie said. "There you go. Keep sweeping."

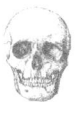

Syd was sweating so badly, he could hardly see. This fucking mask.

They knew he was here. Why else would they be using a spotlight? Had they seen him? After he'd banged into the wind chimes, he'd ducked behind the tree in a matter of seconds. But somehow they knew he was here. Cameras? Or had they seen him before he hit the chimes?

Fortunately, they didn't seem to know exactly where he was now. They'd shined the spotlight directly at his tree at first, but now they were moving it to the right, searching for him.

Or, wait. Maybe they knew where he was, but they were checking to see if anybody else was with him.

Would a guy like Colby shoot Syd in the back without any warning if he ran? Legally, he couldn't do that, even though Syd was trespassing. But if the woman had told Colby everything…

Maybe Colby didn't care what was legal.

Oh, shit. What if the woman was holding the light while Colby was walking this way? Syd wouldn't be able to see him—not with that blinding light shining this way.

Now was the time to make a break for it. Right now. While the spotlight was to his left. They wouldn't see him. Their attention was over there.

Syd turned and scurried away, trying to keep the tree trunk between him and the house. That's when he heard the woman yell.

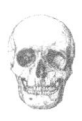

Colby was still sweeping right, and farther right, and still more to the right, when Dixie suddenly shouted, "Left!"

Colby couldn't resist taking a look.

15

He saw a man in full camo running to the north. It looked like he was carrying a handgun.

Colby hadn't expected to make a shot from a great distance. That's why he'd chosen the shotgun—for close combat if somebody tried to enter the home. But it was all he had.

Colby dropped the spotlight, losing sight of the man, and raised the shotgun, picturing in his mind's eye the path the man had been taking.

He fired once. Then again.

Twelve-gauge double aught buckshot.

The chances of hitting the man were small, and if he did hit him, Colby had just exposed himself to all kinds of potential legal problems.

He didn't care. He would deal with that later, if he had to.

Holding the shotgun in his right hand, he picked up the spotlight with his left and searched for the man. Nothing. Not running. Not on the ground. Long gone. That's how quickly it had all happened. Colby swept the light left and right. Nobody.

He closed the door and locked it tight.

"Oh, my God," Dixie said. "Oh, my friggin' God. He was out there."

"Yeah. Did you see a gun in his hand?"

"I think so. It was hard to tell."

"He was holding something," Colby said.

"Absolutely," Dixie said. "Did you hit him?"

"No idea."

Colby was doing his best to breathe slowly and deeply. He could feel his heart slamming in his chest. Well over a hundred beats a minute.

"He could be out there wounded or dead right now," Dixie said.

"I know. Do you wish I hadn't shot?"

"No, I'm glad you did. I'm glad."

Colby walked over to the bed and laid the shotgun on the mattress, the barrel aimed at the headboard. Then he picked the shotgun up, engaged the safety, and put it back down again. Then he went into the closet again and came back with a scoped .270. If he needed to make another long shot, he'd be prepared this time. But he would wager the man wouldn't be coming back. Not tonight.

"No way was I gonna let him just leave," he said returning to his spot beside the window.

"I get it. If you missed him, you probably scared the hell out of him."

"Do you know who it was?" Colby asked.

"Has to be one of the men from the van," she said.

"Do you know who they are?"

"No. If I did know, I'd tell you. It's two men I've never seen before until I saw them at that store in Columbus. They're creepy—that's all I can tell you."

"Creepy how?"

"I only got one quick look, from about fifty feet, and I saw them for maybe two seconds. One of them has a skull tattoo on half his face. Or at least that's what it looked like."

"Yeah, that would be kind of memorable," Colby said. "What exactly happened there?"

"I was at the pump and I saw the van pull into the far side of the parking lot and just sit there. I knew I had seen it before, so after I filled up, I parked in a spot and went inside the store. Then I just watched, and the van sat there for ten minutes. But when I finally left, it stayed where it was, so I was totally relieved. I figured it was all paranoia. But later, when I was almost to San Antonio, there it was in my rearview mirror. I couldn't believe it, but there was no way this was a different van, because it's so unique."

"Was it just hanging behind you or trying to catch you?" Colby asked.

"Just hanging behind, like maybe a hundred yards back," she said. "Anytime I would exit, the van would follow."

"But you got the sense that they didn't think you knew they were there?"

"Right. At that point, I assumed they had a tracker on my vehicle, so I decided I needed to ditch it. I saw a sign for the airport, so I went there and parked in the economy lot. Then I rode the little shuttle to the terminal, like I was going to fly out, but instead I got a cab and asked him to take me to the edge of town. Then I began hiking. I can basically hike all day if I have enough water."

"How did you decide which way to go?"

"I just randomly went north. I figured they'd think I was still headed west, so that was the only direction I didn't want to go."

"Did you tell your parents and in-laws what was happening?"

"You know, I agonized over that decision, but I decided I shouldn't say anything, partly because I didn't want to freak them out, especially since I wasn't sure what to believe, and partly because I knew my dad would report it all, which might make the situation worse."

"I think you made the right call. Do they know where you are now? And what about your boss or supervisor or whoever you report to?"

"Nope. Nobody knows anything. That's the reality about my job as a caretaker—unless somebody physically drives out to check on me, how would they know I'm not there? So they don't know I'm gone. Of course, eventually somebody will notice. Like with the mail stacking up in the mailbox or something."

"So you wandered north along the highway and eventually you ended up in my creek," Colby said.

"Don't you feel lucky?"

"You're being sarcastic, but I really do," Colby said. "Any idea who the two creeps are working for?"

"Yeah," Dixie said. "I have an idea." She paused, then said, "My hands are shaking right now."

"Mine, too," Colby said.

"Really?"

"Yep. You should sit down. I can keep watch."

It was time for a break. She could fill in the rest of the details later.

"You can call 911 if you want to," she said as she turned and sat on the edge of the bed.

He laughed. "Come on. You know me better than that by now."

"I hope you got him, to be honest," she said. "I hope he's out there dead right now."

Colby wasn't sure if he wanted that or not. What would they do? In that case, they really would need to call 911. Right? The only other option would be—

"I'll be right back. I'm going to splash some cold water on my face," Dixie said.

"Yeah, okay," Colby said.

The only other option would be disposing of the body. Bury it deep. He had a tractor with a backhoe. He could do it. Then what? Such a stupid idea. The man in camo was working with somebody, and that person could report what had happened. Not likely, but it could happen. Did Colby want a buried body on his ranch for the rest of his days? A secret that might begin to haunt him? Hell, no.

No, if Colby found the man injured or dead, there was only one option, which was calling it in and describing exactly what had happened. In that case, should he give Dixie a head start? That depended on the rest of her story.

Colby saw no movement outside. He didn't expect to. Who would be stupid enough to approach the house again, knowing Colby was willing to shoot?

"I'm just going to lie down for a minute, okay?" Dixie said as she came back from the bathroom.

"You okay?"

"Yeah, I'm good. Just a little lightheaded from the adrenaline."

She was asleep within five minutes.

"You, uh, gonna get ready?" Red asked at eight-thirty that morning.

"For what?" Mandy replied.

"I was wondering when you're gonna get all dolled up for the mission," he said.

They were seated at the dinette in the kitchen. She was wearing a bathrobe and drinking from a large coffee mug.

"Are you outta your effin' mind?" she asked.

"About what?"

"We just got up."

"Well, twenty minutes ago. So?"

"These guys you're gonna screw around? What time do you think they got up?"

Red wondered if it was a trick question.

"Probably about now," he said. "I mean, it's a Saturday and all."

"If you were just waking up in a motel room on a Saturday morning, what're the odds you're gonna go outside and help some dumb lady with her car?"

"But you're not dumb," Red said.

He could hear—and feel—Billy Don coming down the hallway toward the kitchen. The floor was vibrating.

"I *know* that, but I'm supposed to *play* dumb," Mandy said. "Plus, what am I doing all tarted up on a Saturday morning? I don't ever get dressed like that on a Saturday morning."

"Yeah, but some ladies do."

"What are y'all arguing about?" Billy Don asked as he entered the kitchen.

Red said, "I asked—"

"He wants to do the thing now at the motel in Blanco," Mandy said.

"Too early," Billy Don said.

"Thank you," Mandy said, and she gave Red a look that said *Told you so*.

Billy Don said, "Even if Mandy looks smoking hot, those guys won't want to help anybody this early in the morning. Even if Mandy's got her jugs all hoisted up where—"

"All right," Red said. "I get it. We'll go later. And stop talking about her jugs."

Mandy laughed.

"Whatever," Billy Don said. He went to the coffeemaker and poured himself a mug.

"So what time, then?" Red asked. He didn't like the idea that he wasn't totally in charge of the operation, but what could he do? He needed Mandy, and she was a hardheaded woman. Why wouldn't she just do as she was told, so they could get along better? It would be so much easier for them both. He figured that was a mystery for the ages.

"Couple hours," Mandy said. "Maybe we grab brunch somewhere first."

"Ooh, brunch. Fancy," Billy Don said. "Red's buying."

"Works for me," Mandy said.

16

One year, six months, and eleven days before Syd and Nicky reached the outskirts of Blanco, Texas, their father, Harry Kilton, a press operator by trade, passed away quietly in his sleep after a swim—according to his obituary. In reality, he'd had a heart attack while partying in a hot tub with a couple of enthusiastic Eastern European call girls. He was sixty-eight years old.

Syd and Nicky had loved their dad, despite his shortcomings as a parent. Like forgetting their birthdays. Working late all the time. Drinking and philandering. Getting busted for printing more than four hundred thousand dollars in counterfeit currency.

The arrest happened when Syd was seven years old, so he was old enough to remember most of it. Men with badges came to the house and searched it, along with his dad's little shop in the backyard. Harry was seated on the curb out front, smoking a cigar and drinking a cold beer, when they found the illegal printing plates in the shop and arrested him on the spot. Syd was confused when his dad came home the next day—but it wasn't over yet.

A week later, the two brand-new cars in the driveway were towed away. Syd remembered that a group of neighbors stood outside and watched. His mother quietly told Harry how embarrassing it was.

They almost lost the house, and Syd remembered being confused about that, too. How do you "lose" a house? It was so big and green. Where could it go?

Some kids at school kept saying Syd's dad would be going to jail for a long time, but it never happened. On several occasions, Syd heard his parents talking about some things the lawyer had said, but Syd never understood those discussions. Then, after several months, they no longer talked about the lawyer anymore, so Syd quit thinking about the whole thing. He was relieved. He figured the cops must've made a mistake and arrested the wrong man.

Of course, as Syd got older, he knew that wasn't true. He figured his dad must've finagled his way out of a tight spot somehow, or he'd managed to get probation.

Syd talked to his dad about the arrest exactly one time, when Syd was in his early twenties and he came back to Lake Charles for Christmas Day with his mother. He met Harry for a beer on December 26.

They started with some small talk, which included Harry asking Syd how things were in New Orleans.

"Not bad. Don't know how long I'll stay there."

"Where you working?"

"Assistant manager at a Home Depot," Syd said. Better than telling him the truth, which was that he worked in the lumber department part time, which was why he was also selling weed on the side. Made better money with the weed.

Harry nodded his approval. "Benefits? Health insurance?"

"Yep."

"Nice. That's important. You might not think so right now, but it is."

They both took a swig. They never had much to talk about. They were seated on stools at the bar in Old Town Tavern, Harry's favorite beer joint. Dark place, with lots of neon and a couple of pool tables. He knew all the bartenders' names, mostly young women, and they knew him. Happy hour every weeknight from three to six, with beer for a dollar a can.

"I've always wanted to ask you something," Syd said.

"What's up?"

"When I was a kid, when you got arrested…"

"Yeah?"

"I mean, why did you do it?"

"I was between jobs," Harry said simply. "We needed money."

"Then why not get another job?"

"I tried. Nobody was hiring. Lake Charles is a small town."

"That's not what mom said."

"What did she say?"

"That you had a reputation for showing up late, leaving early, and drinking while you were there. That you spent more time trying to bang female coworkers than doing your job. That you—"

"Yeah, okay. Your mom's not a liar, but I was still a hell of a pressman."

"She said that, too. Which is what got you into trouble."

"I've got this weakness, you know," Harry had said. "It's this flaw—I know it's there—but I can't resist it. I always give in to temptation."

"So what's the flaw?"

"I just told you. I give in to temptation. In this case, it was the temptation to take the easy route. I mean, printing money is a hell of a lot faster than earning it."

"The problem is spending it," Syd said.

"Exactly," Harry said. Then he pointed his cigarette at Syd, like he was proud that his son had recognized the counterfeiter's great dilemma, and Harry again said, "Exactly. *That's* the problem."

"What size bill did you print?"

"Hundreds, which was stupid. Should've gone with twenties. People don't check twenties. But you pull out a C-note and people are like, 'Oh, hey, big spender.' It draws attention. If you're a cashier, they teach you to check those bills. Twenties, not so much."

"How many did you print?"

"At this point, I don't remember exactly. Plenty. Might as well go big, right? I mean, a million bucks in hundreds doesn't take up that much room or use much paper. One bundle with a hundred bills is ten grand. A hundred of those is a million dollars. Took me less than a day to print it and cut it."

On the jukebox, Pink Floyd was preaching about the fleeting nature of time, and the need to use it wisely. The tune was garishly out of place among the other jukebox selections, but Harry had badgered the owner into adding a couple of Pink Floyd songs years back, and he played them every time he came in. His favorite band.

"You wouldn't believe the rush the first time you spend a phony bill," Harry said. "I drove way the hell over to a little corner store in Lafayette. I remember buying like eighty dollars worth of booze, just so the cashier wouldn't have to give me much change back. My heart was pounding, but it was busy in there, and the cashier didn't look twice. Just took the bill and moved on. I felt so damn smart—because I'd beaten the system."

"How many times did you do that? How many bills did you manage to spend?"

"I don't really remember, but it was enough that your mother started wondering how I was paying bills."

"So she didn't know what you were doing?"

Harry turned and looked at Syd. "Of course not. Your mother never would've gone for that. She had too much integrity."

"Where else did you spend it?" Syd asked. "I mean, you couldn't just keep going to the same corner stores."

"Before I got sloppy? Mostly I'd take these road trips and spend it along the way—bars, restaurants, bowling alleys, drugstores, whatever. Those trips were kind of fun, actually. I went places I never woulda gone."

And left your family at home, Syd thought.

"God help me, I paid a couple of hookers with those bills," Harry said. "It doesn't get much lower than that."

Syd didn't comment on that. What was the point? Harry already knew what kind of person he was, and what a poor father he'd been.

"So you basically spent one bill at a time," Syd said.

Two men at one of the pool tables got rowdy as one of them apparently made a difficult bank shot on the eight ball.

"Mostly, but if I ever saw a chance to buy something big I could turn around and sell, I'd do that," Harry said.

"Like what?"

"Anything. Like one time I saw a guy on the side of the road selling a little sailboat, and it came on a trailer. So I bought it for eight hundred bucks. I was thinking if I could flip it for five or six hundred, that's fine, because that money would be clean. So I brought it home, cleaned it up a little, and ended up selling it for a thousand bucks."

"I remember that boat," Syd said. "Me and Nicky would climb all over it and pretend we were out on a lake."

Harry was about to reply, but he stopped and took a drink of beer instead. What had he almost said? Sorry I never took you out in that boat?

Finally he simply said, "It was a Sunfish. I remember that. Sunfish. Solid little boat."

"So how did they catch you?"

"I got cocky and started spending the bills a little too close to home, and what I didn't realize was, even if the cashier wasn't checking the bill right when I spent it, there was a good chance it was getting checked at the bank later, when the store went to deposit it. So then the investigators come back to the cashier and say, 'You remember anybody giving you a hundred-dollar bill last week?' And she says, 'Sure, ol' Harry did. Bought a carton of smokes and only had a hundred-dollar bill.' When that happens a couple of times—they name me—and they know what I do for a living, well, pretty soon they got enough for a warrant. So, yeah, I got stupid. It was my own damn fault."

Syd realized his attitude about his dad's legal troubles had changed over the years. When Syd was a kid, he'd felt a deep shame that his dad had broken the law and gotten arrested. His friends made fun of him for it, and he hated that. But for the past few years, he realized he was only disappointed that Harry had gotten caught. Like his dad, Syd found himself contemplating where Harry went wrong, and what he could have done differently.

"How come you never went to jail?" Syd asked. "I always wondered about that. I mean other than that one night."

"It was two nights," Harry said.

"It was? I thought it was one."

"There was a problem with the search warrant. Something wasn't filled out right, and my lawyer managed to turn that into a plea deal for probation. Technicality, but I'll take it, right? You want another beer? Shirley, another round over here."

Harry was putting them back fast, but he didn't appear drunk at all.

"Did you ever do it again?" Syd asked.

Harry hesitated for half a second, then said, "Hell, no."

Syd wondered about that, but he let it drop. Eventually, they moved on to other topics.

In the years after that conversation, Syd saw less and less of Harry, and in the last three years, they didn't speak at all, and then Harry died. Syd got the news from the manager at the seedy little apartment complex where Harry had been living. Harry had listed Syd as his emergency contact on the lease. Syd could still remember the phone call.

"I need to talk to you about your father's health," the manager said.

"Yeah? What's up?"

Syd was imagining his dad in the emergency department after a heart attack, or a stroke, or liver failure.

"I'm afraid he passed away."

Who the fuck phrases it that way?

Then she went on to say Harry was way past due on his rent, so Syd needed to clear all his belongings out within a week. Syd would've told her to fuck off and handle it herself, but he wanted to see what might be in his dad's stuff. Old letters? Photo albums? Anything worth keeping or pawning?

So he and Nicky went over there one weekend to clean the place out. Most of it was junk that went straight into the dumpster, or out to the curb with a "Free" sign on it. There was no will, which was fine, because Harry had nothing to leave to anybody.

Then Syd found a Braniff Airlines duffle bag crammed in a small utility closet beside the water heater. Braniff? Really? With a bag that old, who knew how long it might've been there. Maybe it wasn't even Harry's. Maybe some other tenant had stuffed it in there forty years earlier.

Syd opened it up, and for maybe half a second, his heart leapt, because he thought he'd struck gold. The bag was brimming with cash. Bundles and bundles of it. Fresh, crisp one-hundred-dollar bills. Syd was amazed and wondered where his dad had gotten that amount of—

Oh. Right.

17

Dixie was still asleep when the sun rose, so Colby left her alone and returned to his spot by the window every few minutes, just in case.

At 8:42, he went into the kitchen for coffee, then ducked into the garage to retrieve a pair of binoculars from his truck.

When he came back to the bedroom, Dixie was sitting up in bed. She said, "Wow. What time is it?"

"Eight forty-five."

"I don't normally sleep like this," she said. "I'm sure that's hard to believe, since this is the second time I've done it."

"I'm jealous, to be honest."

"Everything good?" she asked.

"Yeah. Nothing out there. But it's about time for me to go take a better look."

Colby hadn't wanted to go until she'd woken. If the delay meant the man in camo had had to lie wounded for a few extra hours, well, that was his problem, not Colby's.

"No, I'll go instead," Dixie said. "It's my mess. I should go."

"You don't know the land like I do," Colby said. "He could be anywhere from here to the county road on the back side."

"Then we'll both go," she said.

Colby wasn't crazy about that idea, but it made sense, strategically. Two pairs of eyes were better than one, and the man in camo would be more likely to hesitate when facing two people, especially if they kept a distance between them. Not easy to pick off two people twenty or thirty yards apart.

"I'm tempted to ask you to finish your story first, but there's a little part of me that wants to make sure he isn't out there suffering."

"You're a humanitarian," she said.

"A softie," he said.

"Well, definitely not that," she said.

He had to grin at that one. "You caught me on a good night," he said.

Colby went to his closet again, but this time he returned with camo shirts, pants, and hats for them both.

Five minutes later, they were dressed and ready to go outside.

"I'm thinking we go out the front door, then go around different sides of the house."

Dixie nodded. She looked a little tense. He was sure he did, too.

"Unless you have a better idea," he said.

"Nope. I don't see any way we can look for him without exposing ourselves to some degree."

Their simple plan was to duck from tree to tree. If the man in camo was still out there, he was wounded, which would impact his shooting abilities. He would be scared and nervous and trembling. None of which precluded the possibility he might squeeze off a lucky shot from a great distance with a handgun—but the odds were low.

Ten minutes later, they exited the front door and walked in opposite directions around the circumference of the house. When they reached the corners at the back of the house, Colby went first, quickly moving from one tree to the next, until he'd covered about forty or fifty yards. Then Dixie did the same. And they repeated the process over and over. Each of them was armed with a deer rifle. Colby kept his eyes on the horizon, except for brief moments when he scanned the ground, looking for blood. He saw none, but he knew from hunting deer that some serious wounds don't bleed much, especially if the round doesn't exit.

They got farther and farther from the house, which he had locked behind them.

No sign of the man in camo, and no footprints. The tall native grasses were too thick, and there had been no overnight dew to show any foot traffic.

By the time they reached the county road thirty minutes later, Colby was finally beginning to relax. Dixie still kept her distance, but she was able to hear Colby say he was going to check the shoulder of the road. Maybe he could find a spot where a vehicle had pulled over recently. She nodded and indicated she would stay behind the trunk of a large cedar tree.

Colby double-checked the safety on his rifle and leaned it securely in the Y of two tree branches. Then he dropped to the ground and shimmied under the lowest strand of barbed wire. On the other side, he rose to his feet and began walking slowly along the pavement, moving to the south.

The county hadn't mowed along this shoulder for quite some time, so the grass was as tall as it was on the other side of the fence. That was good news. If somebody had pulled over, he'd be able to—

Right there. He could see it. Two tracks in the grass. Somebody had parked right there, or had at least driven off the road and then back on. The grass was crushed and bent over. Recently, too.

Colby stepped closer. Now he saw a wet brownish-black patch on the ground. Motor oil. The vehicle had a leak. A fairly significant leak, too. Which confirmed that the vehicle had parked there for more than a few minutes.

If he was a cop, he'd gather a sample of that oil for analysis, just in case the man in camo actually managed to kill somebody later on. Then the crime lab could get a second sample from the oil in the vehicle's engine for comparison. But he wasn't a cop. And the man in camo hadn't killed anybody, as far as Colby knew. Instead, he snapped a couple of photos, because why not? Then he used a mapping app to drop a pin at these coordinates, just in case.

He walked further, covering about forty yards, but he saw nothing else of interest. He turned around and proceeded back the other way.

When he reached the parking spot again, he saw another drop of oil, but this one was on the pavement, likely falling as the vehicle pulled away.

Hang on a second.

He bent down and looked closer.

It wasn't oil, it was blood. Then he saw several more drops.

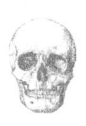

"Dang it, Billy Don, stop," Red said.

"Stop what?"

"Staring at Mandy."

"That's kind of the point, isn't it?"

The three of them were seated at a table at the Chess Club Café in Blanco, which was between the Dollar General and the Sonic. Red was having the Cowboy Breakfast, which included chicken-fried steak, two eggs, home fries, and toast. Something light to start the day.

"Yeah, Red, isn't that the point?" Mandy asked.

Mandy was plainly enjoying the moment—not because Billy Don was staring, but because the staring was making Red squirm, and that pissed him off.

He liked it when Mandy dressed up all sexy, but he didn't like people outright gawking at her. It was disrespectful to him, and, sure, to her, too, he guessed. She wasn't a piece of meat. She was a woman. In a cropped tank top. A tight one. But that was no reason to leer. Anyone wanting a better look was supposed to sneak a peek from time to time, not just stare.

"We need to refine the plan," Red said.

"What exactly *is* the plan?" Billy Don asked.

"She parks outside their room and pretends to have car trouble," Red said. "Her car won't start."

"Okay, and then what?" Billy Don asked. "How does that get them away from the motel?"

"She asks them to take her to get the part she needs to fix it," Red said.

"Which part?" Billy Don said.

"Something that makes it so the car won't start," Red said.

"And that part is…?"

"Just any part that stops it from starting," Red said.

"Eventually you're gonna have to name a part," Billy Don said.

"Maybe we loosen the distributor cap."

"And maybe they tighten it right back up," Billy Don said. "Maybe one of them knows cars good enough to figure it out. They'll follow the lines back from the spark plugs and—"

"Okay," Red said. "Jesus. Not the distributor cap, then."

Red hated it when Billy Don questioned his plans, and he hated it even more when the big man had a point. Billy Don hardly ever had ideas of his own—or at least not good ones—but he loved trying to shoot holes in Red's ideas. Okay, fine, so his plan was missing a key detail. All he had to do was fill that detail in.

"Maybe we remove a fuse," Red said.

"And they look in the fuse box and see one missing," Billy Don said. "Which would seem weird. How does a fuse go missing?"

"Then we put a blown fuse in there," Red said.

"And they pop it out and see that it's blown," Billy Don said. "And maybe they've got some spare fuses on hand. Lots of people do."

"Who says they're gonna be willing to put in that much effort instead of running her over to the NAPA store? Hell, it's less than a mile away."

"Because they'll wanna be her hero," Billy Don said. "I mean, yeah, giving her a ride is nice and all, but fixing her car? Getting her back on the road? That's a whole different deal. Anyway, none of this even makes sense. Let's say you're right and they don't check the fuses. What's she gonna tell 'em? Start at the beginning. She pretends her car dies, and they come out of the motel room, and she says what? Her car won't start and she needs a ride to the auto-parts store. Right? You *know* they're gonna ask what the problem is. I mean, if she knows what part she needs, she has to know what's wrong with the car, right? So when they ask, she's gonna need a good answer."

"Okay, smart guy," Red said. "You figure it out."

"You want me to take your crummy plan and fix it?" Billy Don asked.

"If it wouldn't be too much trouble," Red said. "Seeing as how you're a genius and all."

"Y'all are giving me a headache," Mandy said.

Sure it wasn't the vodka last night? Red thought, but he wasn't dumb enough to say it out loud.

"Just remember air, fuel and spark," Billy Don said.

"That band from the seventies?" Red said.

"Huh?" Billy Don said.

"Never mind. What about those things?"

"Without those things, an engine won't run."

"Gee, you're so smart," Red said. "Without wings, a bird can't fly. So what?"

"All I'm saying is, we need to take one of those things away, so her car don't run. Hey, what if she ran out of gas?"

"How are we gonna time it just right so she runs out at the motel?" Red asked.

"She parks, and then we siphon all the gas out."

"Yeah, perfect," Red said. "Nobody would ever see us out there with a hose in her gas tank."

"Okay, then. That's what we'll do."

"I was joking," Red said.

"Then she can just tell 'em she ran out of gas," Billy Don said. "And say she needs a ride to get some."

"You're also forgetting there's a Shell station about a hundred yards away," Red said.

"I'd say it's more like two hundred," Billy Don said.

"My head," Mandy said. "I swear to God my head is gonna explode if y'all keep this up."

And that's when Red finally figured it out.

"We're looking at this all wrong," he said. "What if the problem has nothing to do with her car?"

18

"Just how deadly is buckshot at that distance?" Dixie asked.

They were slowly making their way back toward the house. Now they were walking side by side, because the man in camo was obviously long gone. They both felt confident there was no immediate danger.

"I imagine he was about eighty or ninety yards away, so it would've lost a lot of velocity, but it could still kill him," Colby said. "Absolutely it could. Or send him to the emergency room. If it hit him in the right place."

"And obviously you hit him."

"Sure looks that way. Can't imagine he was bleeding from some other random injury or wound, but I guess it's a possibility. Maybe he scraped himself on a dried cedar branch."

They were moving slowly, looking for any other signs of blood. If they found more—like, say, a pool of it—then they might be able to better gauge the severity of the wound. But if they didn't find more, that wouldn't necessarily indicate that the wound was superficial.

It wasn't a matter of concern for the man's wellbeing. It was a matter of practicality, and of being prepared should a sheriff's investigator arrive at Colby's front gate. Was the man in camo lying in a hospital bed right now? Dead in the back of a black van? Walking around with a round of shot in his ass? Or hardly grazed? Lots of possibilities.

They covered the distance to the rear of the house in roughly the same time it had taken to reach the county road.

Colby walked to the area behind the wind chimes—approximately where the man in camo had been running when Colby fired the shots—and he paced the distance to the house, counting as he went.

"Eighty-seven yards," he said.

"Damn, that was a good shot," Dixie said. "Would it bleed a lot if it hit him, say, in the back?"

"Not necessarily," Colby said.

"Would it exit?"

"At that distance, almost no chance."

"But it could go deep enough to pierce a lung?"

"I'd say so, but I'm guessing."

They went into the house, and Colby locked the door behind them. Then he put the shotgun in a utility closet near the kitchen. Fast, easy access, but not immediately visible to any potential intruder.

"You gonna be okay?" he asked.

"Yeah," she said. "I'm good. It's just wild, that's all. A month ago, I never would've pictured my life taking this turn. Not in a million years."

She sat down at the table. He leaned against the counter. He was too hyped up to sit right now.

He said, "The offer of my old truck still stands, if you want to leave all this craziness behind."

"So if the cops show up, I'd just leave you here to deal with that alone?" she said.

"I don't think they're gonna show."

"They still could," she said.

"Just doesn't seem likely," Colby said. "If they did, I could always rat you out. I have your first and last name and know where you live. Sort of."

She laughed as she popped the magazine out of the handgun, then racked the slide and ejected the round from the chamber. "All jokes aside, do you want me to leave? You can tell me if you do. I'm a big girl. You won't hurt my feelings."

"No."

"This might be more then you bargained for."

"No. I don't want you to leave," he said.

"What a coincidence. I don't want to leave," she said.

They were staring at each other, and they both started grinning.

"I want you to stay as long as you'd like," he said.

"Unless, of course, we both get arrested."

"Well, yeah," he said. "Ever been arrested before?"

"No. You?"

"I've managed to avoid it so far."

"But you've come close?"

"I was a suspect when a man was murdered a few years back, so the sheriff took me in for questioning. I've known the sheriff since I was a kid—but that's his job, to question people. What I learned was, don't talk to the cops. Hate to say it, but that's my opinion. Not unless you have an ironclad alibi. And my best friend is a cop."

"The game warden?"

"Yep."

"You wouldn't talk to him if he was conducting some kind of investigation?"

"Only with an ironclad alibi."

"So if the sheriff shows up in an hour…?"

"You'd better believe I'm not saying a word. Especially since I'm, uh…what's the word I'm looking for? Guilty. That's right."

"Guilty of shooting him, but that doesn't mean you're guilty of a crime, does it? I mean, this is Texas, right?"

"I'm pretty sure you're required to warn a trespasser before you open fire," Colby said.

"So you'd just refuse to answer any questions?"

"Right. Not until I talk to an attorney. I was innocent that other time, by the way. In case you were wondering."

"Oh, sure. I know you were."

He went to the refrigerator and got a can of Dr Pepper. Showed it to Dixie, who nodded, so he grabbed another one and placed them both on the table. He sat across from her.

"You think he'll come back?" Dixie asked.

"Honestly, no, but I figure we have to prepare as if he will."

He popped the top on his can and took a long drink. She did the same.

"You want to hear the rest of the story at some point, I guess," she said.

"When you're ready," he said.

"It's not like I'm trying to stall," she said. "I'm just tired of it all, to be honest. So I guess I'm procrastinating."

"Which isn't the same as stalling at all," Colby said.

"It isn't!" Dixie insisted, but she laughed. "Similar but not the same."

She looked at the clock on the stove.

"You taking medicine?" Colby asked.

"What?"

"Nothing. A friend used to say that whenever I checked the time. I bet you're getting hungry."

"I am. Let's have lunch, and then I'll tell you the rest," she said.

"I'll fix lunch while you talk," Colby said.

"Deal."

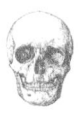

Syd was in bed, lying on his left side. Waiting.

He remembered when he and Nicky had set their house on fire when they were teenagers. They'd been fucking around, killing wasps with a makeshift flame thrower, which was a Bic lighter and a can of hair spray. A wasp landed on a spigot on the front of the house and Syd had torched it. He didn't realize until later that the flame had entered the hole where the pipe exited the siding and ignited the insulation inside the wall.

Ten minutes later, Syd was inside, watching TV, when he saw smoke drifting past one of the windows. Long story short, he and Nicky ripped a piece of four-by-eight siding in half to get to the fire, and once they had it out, there was a moment of wondering whether the fire was up in the attic, too. If it was, chances were good that the entire house was about to go up.

So they waited. And it was terrible. What would they do if flames suddenly appeared in the second-story windows? At that point, well, they'd have to give up. Tell their parents what they'd done. Suffer the consequences, which would be terrible. What an amazing relief when the smoke slowly cleared.

Syd felt that same way right now. Waiting. Not knowing.

Maybe he was fine. Or maybe he was slowly bleeding to death. How would he know? He had one little hole in his back, under his right shoulder blade. What was it, buckshot? Had to be. How deep had it gone? An inch? More? Had it hit any arteries? Seems like it would have hit his right lung, but he wasn't having any trouble breathing. Not yet. Should he get Nicky to dig it out? Probably not. It would either work itself out eventually or the wound would heal around it.

Syd had the TV tuned to an LSU football game, but he wasn't

watching closely. Too much on his mind. What was Draco going to say? Would he give Syd more time? The alternative wasn't pretty.

Nicky finished showering and came out of the bathroom, towel-drying his hair.

"You hungry?" he said.

Syd gave a slight shake of his head.

"Thirsty?"

"No."

"Well, I need to get something to eat," Nicky said.

"Then go."

"You don't want anything?"

"If you ask again, I will beat you to death."

"I'm gonna bring you something anyway, because you'll get hungry when you smell it. Then you'll get cranky because I didn't get you anything."

"Would you just get the fuck out of here?" Syd said.

But Nicky didn't leave. Instead, he went to Moloch's crate and let him out. The raccoon immediately climbed up to Nicky's shoulder.

"Want me to check your back again?" Nicky asked.

"No."

"If you ain't dead yet, you're probably gonna be fine," Nicky said.

"What're you, a medical expert?" Syd said.

"Can you tell if it's bleeding?"

"I think it stopped."

"So why don't you get out of bed?"

"Because then it might start bleeding again, Einstein."

"Or it might not. Get out of bed and find out."

"For what?"

"Huh?"

"I could get out of bed, but why would I? You got a plan? I sure as hell don't. Those fucking wind chimes ruined everything."

"So we're giving up?" Nicky asked.

"Oh, sure," Syd said. "Let's just give up. I'll go back and say, hey guys, sorry, but it didn't work out."

"Why are you always such an asshole?" Nicky asked.

"What did you say?"

"You never say anything nice or constructive."

"That's not what you said."

"Okay, I asked why you're always such an asshole."

"You're starting to piss me off," Syd said.

"Yeah, sure. Blame me when you're the one who blew it last night. Besides, I didn't even have to come along. I'm here to help you—to save your ass—but you still treat me like crap."

Screw the buckshot in his back. Syd was about to get out of bed and give Nicky a beating, but right then they both heard a car door close outside their room.

19

Red and Billy Don watched from the Ranchero, parked in the far end of the long parking lot, as Mandy pulled her little orange Nissan truck into a slot right next to the black van.

The great thing about Mandy was that she didn't really care if the plan worked or not, so she wasn't nervous at all. Then again, she wasn't normally nervous in most situations. She was one of those gals who was always confident, because she thought most people were idiots who didn't know what they were doing, and most of the time she was right. So what was there to be worried about?

She could be dealing with a lawyer, a doctor, a priest, it didn't matter. She was never intimidated. She didn't worry about what other people thought of her, or what she said to them. Okay, maybe with cops, occasionally, if she'd done something wrong, but then just barely, and that was mostly because she didn't want a hassle. But everyone else she dealt with? Who were they to tell her what to do? Most of them backed down if you pushed. Red had seen it. He knew she wouldn't have any trouble handling a couple of ignorant counterfeiters with a raccoon.

Red, on the other hand—well, he *was* nervous. He didn't want to be, but he was.

What if the plan didn't work? What if the two men in the van weren't the type to help a lady out no matter how she was dressed?

Oh, man. Something new just crossed his mind. A possible problem.

Red must've groaned, because Billy Don said, "What?"

"What if they're gay?" Red asked. "It makes sense, two men traveling around together like that."

"They didn't *seem* gay the other night," Billy Don said.

"You can't always tell just by the way they walk or talk," Red said. "And if they *are* gay, they won't care how Mandy is dressed, will they? Well, okay, they might like her outfit, and might even comment on it, but they won't be suckered into helping her because of what she has on display."

"I think you need to worry more if they *aren't* gay," Billy Don said.

"Why?"

"Mandy looks great and you're sending her off in a van with two random dudes? You didn't think about that part?"

Oh, crap. That was true. Maybe he needed to alter the plan. Billy Don could search the room while Red followed the van and made sure everything was okay. That might work, but Red couldn't think about it anymore right now, because Mandy had just gotten out of the truck and the plan was now in motion.

She closed the door and just stood there for a long moment. She turned her head to the left, and then to the right. Slowly. She shook her head, like she had water in her ears.

This was good stuff. Red hoped the men in the room were watching, but he knew they might not be. Maybe they were in there sleeping. Or watching TV. Or looking at their phones.

Now Mandy was rubbing her eyes and sort of massaging her forehead. Man, she was good. Maybe he didn't need to be nervous after all. Maybe this was going to work out exactly as they'd hoped.

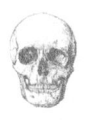

Nicky peeked around a curtain and said, "Some chick. Whoa. A hot chick. Look at the size of those. Driving a little truck."

Syd relaxed. Not a problem. Not a cop. Ever since Nicky had given that redneck those three fake bills, Syd had worried about a cop showing up at their door. Syd would've told him to get lost, but it still would've created yet another unexpected hassle.

Nicky said, "She's…I don't know what the hell she's doing. She looks lost."

"Who cares?" Syd said.

"Or drunk," Nicky said. "Or stoned out of her mind."

Now Syd couldn't help being a little curious. "What's she doing?"

"Like…acting like she doesn't know where she is. Or she can't see. I think that's it—she can't see. She's walking toward the room, but she has her hands out in front of her, like she can't see. She's coming this way."

Something didn't seem right. Why was this woman parking in front of their room?

Syd said, "You already said that. Just don't open the—"

Too late. The moron opened the door.

"You all right?" Nicky said.

Syd could hear a reply from the woman, but he couldn't make it out. Shit.

"Nicky," Syd said.

But Nicky stepped outside and closed the door.

Syd was just so damn tired. He wanted to get out of bed, get into the van, and go home. That would feel so good. Forget about the lady with the backpack. Forget about this new lady outside their room. Forget about the failed excursion last night, and forget about getting shot in the back. Forget about Draco and Fernando and Armando.

For that matter, forget about Nicky and Moloch. Just leave them behind. Holy God, that would be amazing. But they'd just get home somehow, and then what?

Hey, what if…

What if Syd didn't go home? What if he left this all behind, but he didn't go home? Not just now, but ever? How far would he have to go? Would they chase him all the way to, say, California or New Jersey? He figured they probably wouldn't, because what would be the purpose at that point? Draco would get past his little temper tantrum and realize he needed to be focused on profits, and protecting his business from competition. That was all that mattered. Chasing Syd more than a thousand miles would be stupid.

Syd couldn't think about all that right now.

Nicky was saying something to the woman outside. The woman was saying something back. What kind of bullshit was going on out there? Why had Nicky opened the door? Just another complication.

"Son of a bitch," Syd muttered to himself, and he swung his feet to the floor and sat on the edge of the bed. Whew. Lightheaded. Spots in his field of vision. That wasn't good.

But after a minute, he felt more normal. The spots went away. Okay. Steady. He wasn't bleeding, as far as he could tell. He stood, got his balance, and walked slowly to the door. Now he could hear the conversation.

"—and I pulled in here," the woman said. "Just in time, too. Now I don't know what to do."

"Think it'll go away?"

"I've got no idea. This has never happened before."

"You can't see at all?"

"Not much. I can see light. And shapes. But it's mostly a blur."

"What do you think the problem is?"

Leave it to Nicky to ask a dumb question like that.

"I don't know, but it's starting to freak me out."

Syd moved to the window and peeked around the edge of the curtain. Whoa. Nicky was right. She was hot, but kind of in a cheap way. Look at that top. She had her hands raised in front of her, the way you might when walking through a darkened room.

"Is it a stroke?" Nicky asked.

"I don't know. I hope not."

"What's your name?"

"Mandy."

"Well, that's a good sign—that you can remember your name. I'm Nicky."

What a fucking moron. Why was he giving his real name?

"What's four plus six?" Nicky asked.

"Ten."

"What month is it?"

"October."

"Well, you're doing okay," Nicky said. "Other than your vision, I mean."

"This is scary," Mandy said.

"Can you call somebody?" Nicky said. "Do you live around here?"

"I don't know who to call," she said.

"Should I call 911?"

Call 911? Everything out of his mouth was idiocy. That would bring a bunch of commotion, and maybe some cops, to their motel.

"No, don't do that," she said. "You know they charge you for that."

"For calling 911?"

"No, for the ambulance ride. Hell if I'm paying two thousand dollars for an ambulance ride," she said. "I can't afford it."

Wait a second. Something wasn't right. What were the odds this lady would park right in front of their room? She was going blind and she was worried about the cost of an ambulance? Syd sure as hell knew that if his vision suddenly disappeared, he'd get to a hospital by any means necessary. Then he'd stiff the ambulance company later. The hospital, too. Screw those bills. Simple solution.

"You want to sit down?" Nicky asked, and he grabbed one of the plastic chairs by the front door. The blind woman named Mandy fumbled around for the arms of the chair, found one, and sat.

"You got, like medical problems or something?" Nicky asked. "I mean before now?"

"No. Nothing," Mandy said. "I'm the healthiest person you'll ever meet."

"You sure *look* healthy," Nicky said.

"Uh, thanks."

"You want some water or something?" Nicky asked.

Moloch had come down from his shoulder and was sniffing at the woman's shoes.

"What do I hear?" the woman asked.

"My raccoon. Don't worry. He won't hurt you. His name is Moloch."

"I'm not going to pet him."

"Seems like you should go to the hospital," Nicky said.

"I really should. Could you take me?"

"To the hospital?"

So that's what it was. She was trying to get Nicky away from the motel. But why? Who was she?

"If you don't mind," she said. "Obviously I can't drive. Do you have a car?"

"That van right there," Nicky said. "Oh, sorry. You can't see it. Yeah, I'll take you. Give me just a second."

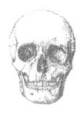

Red was watching, and wondering where the other guy was. Why wasn't he coming out of the room? This was a problem Red hadn't anticipated. He had figured that if a woman like Mandy showed up, the two men would be tripping over each other to help her out. He figured if one guy came out, the other would follow pretty quickly, but so far, that hadn't happened.

"Where's the other guy?" Billy Don said.

"Got no idea," Red said. "Maybe he isn't in there."

"Either way, it's a problem," Billy Don said.

"Well, no shit," Red said.

"And you didn't plan for it," Billy Don said.

"Neither did you," Red said. "You had time to say, 'Hey, what if one of them isn't there?' But you never said a word."

"Because it's your plan," Billy Don said. "You get all uptight when people ask questions."

"Just be quiet and let's see what happens," Red said.

"What does it matter if we're quiet?" Billy Don said. "They can't hear us."

Red didn't say anything. If he kept quiet, maybe Billy Don would, too.

"Think Mandy'll know what to do?" Billy Don asked. "I mean, if the other guy doesn't come out?"

Red sighed loudly.

"It's a fair question," Billy Don said. "Is she gonna follow the plan or not?"

Red didn't know the answer to that. Right now, Mandy and Nicky were having a conversation, and Mandy was probably trying to figure out if the other man was inside the room. She was a fast thinker, and clever as hell. Not as clever as Red, of course, but still, damn clever.

Nicky pulled a chair out and Mandy sat down. Okay, so he was a scumbag counterfeiter with a really stupid tattoo on half his face, but at least he was a gentleman. Then he opened the motel door and went inside. What was happening? Was the conversation over? Why was Mandy still sitting in the chair?

20

"I'm a hiker—you already know that—and it was part of my job, hiking all over the property to make sure nobody was trespassing, or poaching, or logging illegally. I kept a plat on the wall, and I'd make notes of all the different places I'd hiked, so I could keep it all straight."

"And Mark saw that map, too," Colby said. He was at the refrigerator, trying to decide what to serve for lunch.

"Right. Yeah. He did," Dixie said.

"So if you went somewhere, he could be reasonably sure you wouldn't go there again anytime soon. I don't mean to jump ahead…"

"No, that's fine. You're on the right track. The place was big enough that I might not ever go there again before my contract expired. Not without a good reason. And there was one corner so thick and remote, and on the other side of a ravine with a creek in it, that it would be a fairly serious effort to get there."

"Which made it perfect for a grow site," Colby said.

"Exactly," Dixie said. "So, of course, one day I decided to hike to that corner. I packed a lunch and took off early that morning, while Mark was still sleeping. I took the ATV as far as I could, then took off on foot. When I reached the creek, I realized it was going to be harder to cross than I thought, because it was basically as wide and deep as some rivers. But it was also a slow-moving creek, so I hiked upstream and found a shallower spot, meaning I was only up to my stomach. I held my backpack over my head and waded across just fine."

"Did you manage to keep your clothes on?" Colby asked, grinning.

"Somehow, yes, but only because there wasn't some pervert watching from behind a tree."

"That word again," Colby said.

"Are we going to quibble about your predilections, or shall I tell the story?"

"By all means, continue," Colby said. "You like chicken?"

"Sure."

He had smoked a chicken two days earlier—on the afternoon before he'd found Dixie bathing in the creek—and he had some leftovers. He pulled all the ingredients to make sandwiches and gestured for Dixie to keep talking.

"So I crossed the creek and continued my hike, and as I got deeper into the woods, it was one of the few times when I felt a little... vulnerable. Like I was going somewhere very remote and maybe I shouldn't be going by myself. What if I broke my ankle or got bitten by a rattlesnake? Or what if I ran into a poacher or a timber thief? It was weird, because there was no reason for me to be spooked—well, no more than normal—but I was. I almost turned back, but I convinced myself I was nervous only because of that scary experience I told you about with those two men at that grow site. I had another mile or so to go to reach the northeast corner, which was my goal, so I pushed on. Then I started to see footprints in mud. Just one kind of shoe, from one person. It had rained heavily two days earlier, so those prints had to have come after that. Nobody has permission to be on that tract of land, so I took some photos of the prints."

"CSI East Texas," Colby said.

"I couldn't tell what brand of shoe it was or anything like that, but I was hoping it was just some random explorer without much respect for trespassing laws. But then I saw more prints from a different brand of shoe, and a different size, and I recognized the pattern. I'd followed Mark on enough hikes that I knew it was the same brand."

"Still not necessarily a problem," Colby said. "Common brand?"

"Common enough."

"So maybe it was a coincidence. Except of course you kept going and it got worse."

"Yep. I found a grow site, and I could tell from the two sets of tracks that it was just the two of them working it. Not a big site—maybe half an acre—but as you know now, that's plenty big enough to generate a lot of plants and a lot of money. I didn't actually enter the site, because of everything I told you earlier. But I lingered longer than I should have, and I walked along the edge of the site for a minute or two. I saw some mature plants that were probably ready for harvest, and then a large area that appeared to already have been harvested. Then I got out of there."

She stopped there for a minute. Colby realized she was about to tell him about the crossroads she had reached at that time. It was a big decision. Turn in your husband? Confront him and see what he says? Ignore the situation entirely? Or come up with some other solution?

"He put you in a hell of a spot," Colby said.

"Yep. And I was pissed. I wanted to believe it wasn't Mark, but I remembered that he had been gone all day the day before. He was supposedly mountain biking with his friend Lionel, which was a new hobby for both of them. So then I started to realize that was probably just a cover story for both of them to get away for long periods and tend the grow site."

"Did you ask him about it?"

"No, not yet. I wanted to be sure."

"But if you had simply told him you'd found a grow site, if it was his, would he have lied about it?"

"Very possibly, yes. I can tell from your expression that you're wondering why I ever married a guy like that."

"My face says that?"

"I see a little disgust mixed with some disbelief."

"Boy, I'm a judgmental SOB."

"Mark has trouble being honest sometimes—"

"Which is a nice way to put it."

"Yeah, okay. Agreed."

"I don't know how you put up with it."

He put the sandwiches on plates, along with some tortilla chips, and returned to the table.

"I tried to change him for a couple of years, but that doesn't work. I realized he's a liar, and he will always be a liar. It's hard for normal people to understand why someone would be that way, and why I would stay with him for as long as I did, but we're getting sidetracked."

"Sorry. Go ahead."

"The next day, I hid a game camera on the trail I'd followed to the site. The kind of camera that uses a cell signal, so the photos go straight to my phone. If I could get pictures of Mark coming and going from the site, he wouldn't have a chance to deny it. He would know I was obligated to report it, so I was also preparing for the possibility that he might try to talk me out of it."

"And involve you in a crime that could ruin your career and land you in prison," Colby said.

Dixie's expression was grim, but she didn't say anything.

"Okay, so how did the camera work out?" Colby asked.

She had just taken a bite of her sandwich and her eyes widened. "Wow, this is really good."

"Thanks."

"Do you smoke a lot of meat?"

"Oh, yeah."

"You're good at it."

"Thanks."

"Anyway, Mark said he had some errands to run in Woodville the next day, and about three hours after he left, he walked in front of the camera. He walked back out four hours later. I can't tell you how incredibly disappointed I was. Plus, my life was about to become one big mess, and I was angry about that. Selfish, huh?"

"Not at all."

"I didn't get Lionel on the camera, but maybe they took turns tending the plants on some days. When Mark came home, I asked about his errands, and he said it all went fine. He didn't say a word about it. So now it was undeniable—at least for normal people like you and me. But then I realized he might say he found the site for the first time that day and he didn't want to freak me out, so he didn't tell me about it. That's the kind of thing I have to do on a regular basis—anticipate the lies he might tell and prepare for them. So I waited until I got him on camera again, which was three days later, and Lionel was with him that time."

"So then you busted him," Colby said.

"Still not yet," Dixie said.

"Good God, woman."

"I think you might agree with what I did next."

"Which was…?"

"Well, for starters, understand that I was totally done at that point. Done with Mark, I mean. As far as I was concerned, our marriage was over the minute he triggered that camera, and he was probably going to prison, and there was no way I was going to let him bring me down with him. So, the next day, I met with a criminal defense attorney. I wanted some advice on what I should do next, and how I could come out of it with as little damage as possible."

"Well done," Colby said. "What did the lawyer say?"

"This surprised me, but she told me I had no legal obligation to report it, since it wasn't a crime involving serious bodily injury or death. Plus, I had spousal privilege, meaning nobody could force me to testify against Mark. But there was my job to consider, and my reputation. So I decided I was going to report it anyway. Plus, to be honest, I figured it might be relevant during the divorce proceedings, in case Mark tried to hire a slick lawyer and take all our assets. So I had a conversation with him that night—told him what I knew and how I knew it. And I recorded it."

"Smart."

"I was worried he might try to blame some of it on me whenever the cops grabbed him and stuck him in a little interview room. He might say it was all my idea. And if Lionel went along with him…"

"Two against one."

"Yep."

"What is Lionel like?"

"Just your basic pothead," Dixie said. "I don't really know him that well, but he strikes me as a halfway decent guy, and I figured Mark probably talked him into the whole thing. If Mark were to lie and say I was involved with the grow site, I think Lionel probably wouldn't go along with it, but he might just stay quiet, if that's what his lawyer advised, and his silence might be damning enough."

"Then he's not a halfway decent guy," Colby said.

"Maybe you're right," Dixie said. "But you mentioned human nature a minute ago, and I'd say it's human nature to want to keep yourself out of prison."

"So what did you do?"

"I ambushed Mark, so he didn't have time to prepare for the conversation. Told him flat out that I'd found the grow site and I had pictures of him on the trail on two different days. I knew that it was his site, and Lionel's, and what the hell was he thinking? Honestly, I had worked myself into a state of fury, and that came through."

"And what did he say?"

They'd both finished their sandwiches, so Colby rose and put the plates in the sink.

"He surprised me by admitting everything. Didn't deny it for even a second. Then he told me some details, and the situation was worse than I thought. Way worse."

21

As soon as Nicky stepped back inside, Syd held a finger to his lips for silence. Nicky closed the door and came closer.

"I don't want her to know I'm in here," Syd said.

"She needs to go to the hospital," Nicky said.

"That's bullshit," Syd said.

"Huh?"

"It's all a story," Syd said. "She's trying to get us both away from the motel."

"Why? Who is she?"

"I don't know, but we're gonna find out."

"How?"

"You're gonna take her to the hospital and I'm gonna stay here and wait."

"For what?"

The AC shut off and Syd had to lower his voice even more.

"To see who shows up," he said.

Nicky appeared skeptical. "Where are you getting all this? I don't even know what you're talking about."

"There isn't time for me to explain, and if I'm wrong, so what?" Syd said. "Just go. But if she asks about me, you need to tell her I'm not in here, and that I won't be back for a couple of hours."

"I think you're fuckin' nuts," Nicky said, and he turned for the door.

"You just watch," Syd whispered. "When she gets to the hospital, suddenly her eyesight will come back. She'll be just fine."

Nicky and his stupid raccoon came out of the room again, but still, no other guy. Red and Billy Don could only watch as Nicky guided Mandy to the passenger side of his van and eased her inside. Then he went around, got behind the wheel, backed out, and drove away.

"What now?" Billy Don asked.

"I don't know yet. Let me think."

"Where do you think they're going?"

"To the hospital. That was the entire plan. Where else would they be going?"

"So are we gonna check the room or not?"

"Would you stop asking questions for just one minute and let me think?"

"That's a question," Billy Don said. "If you don't like questions, maybe you should stop asking them yourself."

Red was pretty sure Mandy wouldn't have gone with Nicky if she knew the other guy was inside the room. She would've abandoned the plan instead, rather than risk Red and Billy Don getting caught.

But what if she wasn't sure where the other guy was?

How much time did they have? Maybe thirty minutes if Nicky helped Mandy inside the hospital and hung around a bit. It would probably take them five minutes to search the room, so there was no need to rush. Yet.

"Maybe Mandy will text and let us know what's going on," Billy Don said.

"Really?"

"What?"

"She's supposedly blind, remember?" Red said. "If she sends a text, Raccoon Boy will know she can really see."

Right then, both of their phones dinged with a text from Mandy.

Stopped for gas he says his brother Syd is hanging out with a friend until late this afternoon.

They were brothers. Syd and Nicky. This was working out great. Not only was the room empty, but Mandy was alone with just Nicky, and he was kind of scrawny. He wouldn't dare get out of line with Mandy or she would kick his ass.

Red sent Mandy a thumbs-up.

"Let's go," he said, reaching for the door handle. "You ready?"

"If you admit I was right," Billy Don said.

"What?"

"Admit I was right."

"About what?"

"About Mandy sending a text."

"Seriously? Don't be a snowflake."

"You're the snowflake. Can't ever admit when you're wrong. Just be a man and admit it."

Red took a deep breath. Exhaled slowly. "Okay, you were right. Now let's go."

They got out of the Ranchero and walked the length of the motel parking lot. Casual as hell. Just two guys doing nothing suspicious at all.

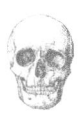

Syd watched from the window, pistol in hand, as two men approached from the other end of the motel. Well, shit. It was those two stupid rednecks from two nights ago. He hadn't expected that. What were they doing here? Had they figured out the bills were fake? And now they were coming to demand real cash? That didn't make any sense. Why would they create an elaborate scheme for that? Maybe the blind woman had nothing to do with these guys. What if she really had been telling the truth?

Now the men were just steps away from Syd's room. What were they going to do? Knock on the door? Syd would just ignore them. Then he realized he hadn't locked the deadbolt after Nicky left.

Surely these imbeciles wouldn't walk right in. That's a great way to get shot. But if Nicky told the woman that nobody was in the room, and if the woman did in fact pass that information along to these two guys...

Syd turned his attention to the door's levered handle now, waiting to see if it moved, and he was confident it wouldn't. No way. Two redneck punks wouldn't raid his motel room. They wouldn't have the balls for that.

Then the lever moved. It friggin' moved, turning downward, and the door slowly swung open.

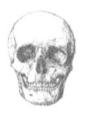

Dixie said, "Mark said that he had already managed to make a sale—a big sale. The day after I found the grow site, while I was hiding the trail camera, he was meeting with the guy who bought it from him. Fifty pounds for twenty thousand dollars. Of course, he had to split that money with Lionel, but that was ten grand, tax free. He had the cash hidden somewhere."

Colby could only shake his head. "The guy's a—I'm sorry, I don't mean to bad mouth your husband, but—"

"Go right ahead."

"What an absolute idiot. Didn't he understand how badly he was screwing you around?"

"It gets worse," Dixie said. "He said his product—that's what he called it, 'product'—was so incredibly good, that they were wanting to hire him to be, like, a consultant on growing methods. They wanted to know his secrets. He was excited, saying this was the break he had always been looking for. This was his big opportunity. He was supposed to have another meeting the next day somewhere near Laredo. He couldn't tell me exactly where or who he was meeting with."

"Oh, good Lord."

"To this day, it still boggles my mind how naïve he was. Lionel, too."

"Once they knew his method, they wouldn't need him anymore."

"Yep."

"So what happened?"

"I told him I wasn't having any of it. I was planning to report the site—but I would give him the next day to talk to a lawyer, so he could be prepared when he got arrested. Then I would report it the day after that."

Colby thought that was a mistake—she should've reported it literally minutes after she'd found the site—but he kept his mouth shut. By waiting two days, she was tempting Mark, and possibly his new "client," to silence her before she went to the police.

"How did he react?"

"He was absolutely furious. I was ruining his new career—new career!—and I might even be putting him in danger. That's when I asked him what he thought would really happen at the meeting the next day. Why wouldn't they just coerce the information out of him—his supposedly amazing growing technique—and then kill him, or at least refuse to pay him? What was he going to do if they held a gun to his head? For half a second, the expression on his face told me he had never even considered that. But then he went back to raging at me, saying he could take care of himself and I should chill out and stop undermining him. He got right in my face and that was the first time I'd ever felt physically threatened by him. I responded by getting equally angry, and since I'm not particularly scared of him, I told him I was filing for divorce."

"Finally," Colby said. "Good for you."

"Funny thing is, that didn't bother him nearly as much as me souring his drug deal. What a creep. How did I waste so many years?"

She paused for a moment. Colby could tell it was taking an emotional toll on her to share her ordeal.

"Wanna take a break?" he asked.

"You know what? I'm getting really antsy. Cabin fever. Why don't we go for another hike? I'd like to see the rest of your ranch. I can tell you the rest as we walk. It's safe now, isn't it?"

Colby thought about it. Was there any danger? At this point, especially in broad daylight, almost certainly not. What were they going to do—stay holed up in the house indefinitely? Not a chance. He wouldn't let the man from last night have that kind of power over them.

"Yeah, sure," he said. "We can walk to the waterfall."

"I like the sound of that," Dixie said.

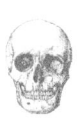

As Red swung the door open, he realized he should've knocked first, just in case. What if somebody was inside? Not Syd, but somebody else? Like, say, some woman they'd picked up at a bar last night? Or some friend who lived nearby?

But it was too late now, because the door was open wide, and as far as Red could see, the room was empty.

Both beds were unmade. The light above the sink just outside the bathroom was on. The AC wasn't running, but surely it would kick on again at any moment.

Red was standing motionless. Billy Don was behind him.

"Hello?" Red said.

There was no sound except the traffic behind them on 281. Red was wishing he was carrying his revolver, but the whole point was to enter an empty room. He shouldn't need a gun. And if he did enter the room with a gun and somehow got caught, he would be charged with a much more serious crime. Now he regretted being soft enough to let the law influence him. This was Texas, by God. If there was ever a place he could carry a gun everywhere he went, this was it.

"Hello?" he said again.

"You going in or what?" Billy Don asked.

Something felt wrong. Why was the door unlocked? Sure, this was Blanco, not exactly a crime hotspot, especially during daylight hours, but if these guys were hoarding a suitcase filled with counterfeit bills, you'd think they'd lock the door. Was it simply because Mandy had rushed the guy named Nicky so much that he'd forgotten to lock the door? Maybe.

"I'm going in if you're not," Billy Don said.

Red turned halfway. "You know what? Go right ahead."

"I will, if you don't hurry up."

"Then do it."

"You're not going?"

"Not if you're so gung ho on going yourself."

"I didn't say that," Billy Don said. "What I said was—"

"Now you're changing your story," Red said.

Billy Don let out a huff and stepped forward, shoving past Red and nearly knocking him down in the process. He walked right through the motel room door like he'd booked it for a year, and then he stopped and looked around. He seemed satisfied enough, until he began to turn around to talk to Red—but he stopped short, instead looking at the front corner of the room to the right of the door.

"What the fuck?" Billy Don said.

Somebody was in that corner.

"Who is it?" Red said.

"You'd better point that thing somewhere else real quick," Billy Don said.

Which meant the person in the corner was armed.

Red wanted to run away. He really did. Or at least run back to the Ranchero and get his Anaconda. Maybe he should do that right now.

"The fuck are you doing in my room?" a voice said.

Red was pretty sure it was the one named Syd. Well, crap. That meant they'd been suckered. Nicky had lied to Mandy. It was all a set-up.

"Better put that thing away or I'm gonna shove it up your ass," Billy Don said.

"Are you bulletproof?" Syd asked.

"Billy Don," Red said.

"Last chance," Billy Don said.

The AC kicked on right then, and Syd said something, but Red couldn't hear what it was. It must've pissed off Billy Don, because he shook his head and lumbered out of sight, into the corner of the room.

Red didn't know what to do. Make a break for his gun? That would take too long.

He heard a shout.

A crash.

A thud.

And a gunshot.

Then the unmistakable sound of a fist repeatedly pummeling somebody's face.

22

Twenty minutes later, Colby and Dixie were roughly five hundred yards from the house, heading toward the creek. It was a balmy autumn day in central Texas, with the temperature near eighty. Dixie was leading the way, following a trail wildlife had used for hundreds of years. Dixie was moving slowly, watching for snakes lounging in the sun, and Colby was following with the .40 caliber Glock holstered on his hip. Not for snakes. He was carrying a light blanket with his left hand and a small ice chest with his right.

Dixie continued with her story. "After I told Mark I was filing for a divorce, I left that night and went to a motel in Woodville, just because it would've been really weird to stay in the house. But weirdness or not, I had to go back the next morning, because that was part of my job. I had to be there physically on the property. That house was my headquarters. That's where my computer is, and all my work-related gear, so I had to go back, regardless of what might happen."

"Are you saying you were scared of what Mark might do?"

"I don't know if I'd put it that way. I definitely wanted to avoid the drama, and I knew there'd be more. Mark would continue trying to change my mind about everything. He's very persistent. He wears you down. It's not like he's ugly about anything, but he just keeps arguing—"

"And lying."

"That, too—until you just can't stand it anymore. But I braced myself and I went back the next afternoon—and he wasn't there. He wasn't home, and his truck was gone. No note or anything like that. Despite everything, I was concerned about him, so I called and texted and never got an answer. I was hoping he was meeting with a lawyer, as I had suggested."

"Instead of going to that meeting in Laredo."

"Right. From what I could tell, some of his clothes were missing, along with a small suitcase and some toiletries. I had no idea what I should do at that point. I'd told him I wouldn't report the crop until the next day, so I was wondering—was he considering that to be a head start? Was he, like, fleeing? Was it fair to go back on my word and report the crop now, or should I wait?"

They'd been cutting through a large cedar break and now exited into an open meadow with a sweeping view of the creek below, about a hundred yards away. Dixie stopped for a moment.

"Just gorgeous," she said.

"You should see it in the springtime, with all the wildflowers," Colby said.

"How do you keep this area from getting trampled by your cattle?" Dixie asked.

"There are some portions of the ranch I leave ungrazed," he said. "Or I graze it in the winter. Depends on how much rain we've had."

"It's really a stunning view," she said.

"The sun sets in that direction, and sometimes—not every night—the light will bounce off the creek in a way that...well, I don't even have the words for it."

After another moment, they began to follow the trail down the hill, through more cedar, oak, and mountain laurel.

"Did Mark have a passport?" Colby asked.

"Yep. I wasn't sure where he kept it, so I didn't know if it was gone. Still don't."

"Any credit cards of his own?"

"None that I know about," Dixie said. "I checked our shared card and didn't see any charges for plane tickets or anything like that. Nothing unusual at all, in fact. And no withdrawals from our bank."

"So what did you do?"

Colby saw Dixie's expression change. It was hard to read. Shame? Regret?

"Honestly, I was worried enough about Mark that I started making some calls, starting with Lionel. He didn't answer, so I asked him to call me back ASAP, but he didn't do that, either. Then I called some more of Mark's friends, but nobody had heard from him."

"This was the same day?"

"Yes, all within an hour or two after I got home from the motel. Then I got a call back from Vince, one of the friends. He told me Lionel had driven to Woodville late the night before and hadn't answered any calls or texts since. Nobody knew where he was."

"So Lionel and Mark were apparently both on the run," Colby said.

"Unless Lionel lied to Vince or asked Vince to lie for him," Dixie said. "What I found is, I started distrusting everybody and everything they told me. You start second-guessing everything. But if Mark and Lionel really were both on the run, I was the only person—among their friends and family—who knew why they might've taken off. Or what might've happened to them. Then I was about to call my lawyer again and see what she recommended, and right then I finally heard from Mark. He was very upset—like bordering on hysteria. He told me Lionel was probably dead and we were both going to be next if we didn't get out of town immediately."

When Syd came to, he was on the bed farthest from the front door and his left eye wasn't working. He wondered at first if it had gone blind. Then he realized it was swollen shut. That whole side of his face felt tender and misshapen.

He had to turn his head sharply to his left to see the rest of the room with his right eye.

The smaller redneck was leaning against the door, which was now closed, and he had Syd's .380 in his right hand. The big redneck was sitting on the edge of the other bed, just a few feet away from Syd.

"No cops?" Syd said, remembering he had fired the gun.

"Not so far," the smaller one said, going over and peeking around the curtains. "If you're lucky, nobody knows exactly where the shot came from. Maybe somebody called it in, or maybe nobody did."

Syd sort of remembered what happened. He looked at the ceiling and saw the bullet hole from his .380. Not that powerful, and not that loud. Maybe nobody had heard it, or they'd thought it was a slamming door or a sound from a TV.

He for sure remembered the big guy punching him in the face at least twice. Each blow felt as if it might split his head in two. He remembered being surprised that the big man would rush him instead of leaving. What a moron. Now what?

Syd tried to sit up, but whoa, it wasn't happening. Not yet.

"You fuckers are dead meat," Syd said.

"Hear that, Red?" the big man said. "We're dead meat."

"I'm shaking in my boots," the man called Red said.

"I need some ice," Syd said.

"Making margaritas?" the big man asked.

"For my face. It's killing me."

"It ain't doing much for me, either," the big man said.

"We gotta have a little talk first," Red said.

"About what?"

"Where's the rest?"

"Huh?"

"Where's the rest?"

"The rest of what?"

"You know what I'm talking about."

"Actually, I have no idea."

"The rest of the fake money."

Well, shit. These guys were quickly becoming a major inconvenience, and it was all Nicky's fault.

"What fake money?" Syd asked. "What are you talking about?"

"Right," Red said. "Pretend you don't know."

"Are both of you retarded?" Syd asked. "Is that the issue here?"

Now the big man stood and loomed over Syd. He was like a small mountain dressed in blue jeans and a pearl-snap shirt.

"I'll pound you clean through the other side of that mattress, if you want," he said.

"You're getting in way over your head," Syd said.

He could feel blood on his back again, from the buckshot. It had been a rough twelve hours.

"That's big talk from a dude who just got knocked out," Red said. "I only wish I'd seen it."

"The money," the big man said.

Syd had very few options.

But there was the principle. He was getting bullied—and ripped off—and he didn't like it. Who were these punks? Did they understand who they were messing with?

"Go fuck yourself," Syd said.

23

Like his dad Harry, Syd Kilton had made plenty of mistakes in life, but this mess was the biggest one yet. And he only had himself to blame.

It started when Alejandro, one of the street dealers working under Syd, was approached by a customer named Mark, who had a proposition. Alejandro told Syd about it later, because this guy Mark had crossed way over the line. How? By growing his own crop. Not a small crop for personal use, or maybe to share with a couple of friends, but a large crop that he wanted to sell to somebody. What the fuck? Who was this guy? Did he really think it worked that way? You don't just suddenly become a large-scale supplier from out of nowhere.

"But here's the thing," Alejandro said to Syd. "He gave me some of his product and it was…I don't even know how to describe it. Easily the best stuff I've ever smoked. Ever. From anywhere."

"What makes it so special?" Syd asked.

Alejandro handed him a plastic baggie crammed full of weed. "You'll see."

Syd took it back to his apartment and had a bowl that night. It was good stuff, for sure. A couple of minutes later, it was even better. Then…

Oh-my-fucking-God.

Incredible. He'd never had anything like it.

While Syd was high, he did some thinking. He was still way down in the organization, and it didn't appear he had much chance of moving up. So maybe this was a good chance to earn a little extra something on his own. Just one time. In and out. Who could blame him?

So Syd arranged a meeting with this guy Mark a few days later at a little beer joint between Beaumont and Lake Charles. Syd found a quiet table tucked in a corner, away from anyone who might eavesdrop.

Mark arrived looking like he'd just come off a golf course—Under Armour polo shirt, khakis, and tasseled loafers. Carrying the most expensive Samsung phone. He gave Syd a firm handshake and looked him straight in the eye, as if he were about to sell Syd a time share.

"How long you been growing?" Syd asked, getting right to it.

"For about twenty years, but it was always just a few plants at a time, for myself. I've refined my technique. Read a lot of research. Trial and error. It's all about genetics, Syd."

"Genetics," Syd said.

"That's the starting point. Ground zero. Without top-shelf genetics, none of the rest matters. But that doesn't mean it isn't important."

Mark babbled for several minutes about proper nutrient ratios, including supplements like nitrogen, potassium, and phosphorus—but don't forget calcium and manganese.

Then there were bloom enhancers, of course, and you had to ensure that the water was properly filtered, and monitor the parts per millions of dissolved solids for consistency. Was it all a bunch of bullshit? What did Syd know? He wasn't a grower himself. On the other hand, he had sampled Mark's product, and there was no arguing with the results.

"I've tried hundreds of combinations and I believe I've finally mastered the ideal growing technique. So now I'm just looking for the right partner."

"The right partner," Syd said.

"Absolutely. Someone who recognizes the quality of my product and will price it accordingly so we can all maximize profits and create an enthusiastic customer base. *Repeat* customers. That's the key."

This fucking guy. Sounding like some kid working on his MBA. What an ignorant asshole. He was trying to pretend he knew how things worked. If he hadn't grown some amazing weed, Syd might take him outside and break his legs.

"Anything extra in there?"

"I'm sorry?"

"You didn't lace it with anything?"

"Oh. Ha. No, not at all. Is that what you thought?"

"Your stuff has an extra little kick."

"I'll take that as a compliment."

"Who else you work with?"

"Just me and a friend."

"What's his name?"

Mark hesitated, then said, "Lionel."

"Lionel what?"

"Sorry?"

"What's his last name?"

"Beebe."

Jesus. This guy talked way too easily.

"Nobody else knows?" Syd asked.

"Nobody."

"You got a wedding ring on your finger," Syd said. "You're telling me your wife doesn't know? Or your husband. Or whatever."

"She doesn't know. I don't want her to know. Better if she doesn't."

"What about Lionel? How do you know he hasn't told anybody?"

"Because he said he wouldn't," Mark said. "If you knew the guy, you'd understand. He hardly talks at all, even when he knows you. He can go all fucking day without saying ten words."

Syd nodded. "Does he know about this meeting?"

"No, he's more like my assistant, not a partner. I'm the one who put it all together. He understands our roles."

"How big is your crop?"

Mark kept his voice low. "I have fifty pounds right now, if that's what you mean. Packaged and ready to go."

Son of a bitch. Street value of that weight could be upwards of fifty or sixty thousand.

"How much more coming?" Syd asked.

"Maybe another sixty or seventy pounds," Mark said.

"Where did you grow it?"

"Oh. Uh. You know. Not far from here."

"In Texas or Louisiana?"

"Texas."

Time to shift gears.

Syd leaned in closer, so that his jacket would fall open and the grip of his .380 would be visible. "Here's the deal, Mark. You obviously don't know shit about this business, but I'll clue you in. There is no room for you in the market and there never will be. You get me? If you try to push your way in, you'll wish you hadn't. I'm talking about lifelong regret. Do you understand what I'm saying to you?"

Mark was plainly surprised by this sudden change in the conversation. "But it's a good product. I put a lot of time and effort into it," he said.

"Fuck your time. Fuck your effort. I'm the nicest guy you'll ever meet, but there are some men I know who'd come looking for you, and your life would never be the same after that."

Syd waited for a response. Mark squirmed in his chair, but he didn't say anything. He was noticeably paler than when he'd come in.

"On the other hand, it's a shame to let a crop like that go to waste," Syd said. "I might be willing to make a one-time deal. Just one time. As a favor. What you've got now and what's coming later. When will that be ready?"

"Maybe a week."

"Okay, so we'll do that, and that's the end of it, you understand? You don't grow any more after that."

"But I've come up with—"

"I don't care, Mark. And you'd better stop caring, too."

Mark nodded. "Yeah, okay. That works for me."

Why did Syd get the feeling this guy was lying? He'd grow more next fall and try to sell it to someone else.

"That's assuming we can agree on a price," Syd added.

"I'm sure we can," Mark said. "I'm not greedy."

What a fucking idiot. Not greedy.

"Don't tell anyone, including Lionel, where you sold it," Syd said. "I mean it. Not a word. Not to Alejandro, either. If you tell anyone, that means you're not a man of your word. Men who can't be trusted have bad endings in this business. You follow what I'm saying? It's real important that you understand that."

"I promise I won't say anything to anybody."

Syd stared at him hard until Mark couldn't handle it anymore and looked away.

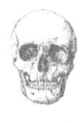

An hour later, back home, Syd told Nicky all about it and gave him a bowl of the weed.

Before he took a hit, Nicky said, "How are you planning to follow through? You don't have that kind of cash."

"Yeah, but I got an idea."

"Let's hear it."

Syd paused for a moment so his statement would have the proper impact. "We pay him with a bunch of dad's old money."

Nicky let out a sharp laugh. "You're fuckin' crazy."

"I'm serious."

"I know you are."

"So what's the problem?"

"I'm not saying there is one."

"It's just sitting there, mostly. Spends just like real money. When are we ever gonna get a chance like this?"

Nicky was thinking it through, so Syd went to the fridge in the kitchen and grabbed two bottles of Jax. Came back and handed one to Nicky, who was lighting up the bowl.

They passed it back and forth a few times, and drank their beers, and after a few minutes, Nicky said, "When he goes to spend that money himself, he's gonna get caught."

"That's his problem."

"But what if he says where he got it?"

"First of all, he'd be too damn scared, and secondly, he'd have to admit to selling a shit-ton of weed. Felony level. So why would he talk?"

"Tell me about this guy," Nicky said.

"What about him?"

"Is he the type to come after you? Holy shit."

"What?"

"This stuff is good."

"I told you."

"Really excellent."

"No, he's not," Syd said. "The type to come after me. Not in a million years. He looks like some guy managing a cell phone store or some shit like that."

Syd leaned back on the couch and felt himself zoning in and out several times—that weird out-of-body feeling that good pot always gave him.

"Oh, I got an idea," Syd said. "Just right now."

"Huh?"

"Hang on. I'm studying it. Don't say anything."

The idea was delicate. If Syd got distracted, he might forget what it was. If he said it out loud, that would help him remember it. "Okay, so, there's no chance he'd talk if he got busted, but why don't I eliminate that risk altogether, just to cover my ass?"

"How?"

"GPS tracker, or one of those Bluetooth trackers. I'll put it in with the money, and then we go take it back. That way, he can't even try to spend it. He thinks he got burglarized or something. Or even if he thinks I screwed him, who cares?"

"Man, that's devious as fuck."

"But you like it? The idea?"

"Yeah, I do."

Syd could tell Nicky was happy that his big brother was asking for his opinion and including him in the scheme. Syd could've done it all on his own, but it would be good to have an extra set of hands.

"So you're in?" Syd asked.

"Hell, yeah."

24

"You getting tired of this story yet?" Dixie asked. She stopped in the trail and turned to face Colby—to gauge his reaction.

"Are you kidding?"

"I keep feeling like I'm dragging you into a nightmare."

"You need to get past that."

"I'm trying."

"If I didn't want to hear it, I'd tell you," Colby said.

"Promise?"

"Yep."

"Same with me being here," Dixie said. "I don't know where I'd be without you right now, but anytime you want me to leave, all you've gotta do—"

"No more of that, okay?" Colby said gently. "Let's hear the rest."

"I'd say I'll try to keep it short, but I'm well past that by now."

"Don't leave anything out," Colby said.

Dixie turned and continued along the trail. They were nearing the creek, and the sound of water rushing over rocks was getting louder, but towering cedar trees on the hillside blocked the view from where they were.

"Okay, so, Mark was freaking out on the phone, but I got him calmed down a little, and he said he had gone over to Lionel's place, which was a trailer in the middle of nowhere, and when he got out of his truck, he heard screams. He looked through a window and saw two men inside torturing Lionel."

"This is the day after you confronted Mark and said you were reporting the site, correct?" Colby said.

"Right."

"So Vince, the other friend, who said Lionel had left town—he was wrong or lying," Colby said. "Or Mark was lying about what he was seeing in Lionel's trailer."

"Yep," Dixie said. "See what I mean about second-guessing

everything?"

"Torturing Lionel how?" Colby asked. "And why? What were they trying to get from him?"

"Mark said he couldn't see exactly what they were doing, but Lionel was screaming for them to stop. They had him duct-taped to a chair. The two men were wearing ski masks."

"Did they not hear Mark drive up to the trailer?"

"I guess not. He didn't say anything about it."

"What does he drive?"

"A Chevy truck. Maybe Lionel's screams covered it up. That's terrible to think about."

"Or, again, maybe Mark made all of it up."

"Possibly."

"Any idea who these two men supposedly were?" Colby asked.

"I don't know for sure. It was a very chaotic phone call. Mark wasn't totally coherent. That's the only way to describe it. Almost like he was having some kind of breakdown, or at least a panic attack."

"Is he prone to panic attacks?"

"Not that I've ever seen."

"Could he fake that kind of emotional distress?"

"I think so, yeah."

"So we don't know what to believe," Colby said.

"You're absolutely right. It's also possible that he truly was freaking out, but he was still lying."

"So he's outside Lionel's trailer…"

"Right, and he said he could hear Lionel telling these two men where Mark and I lived and how to get there. So then Mark said I needed to get out of the house ASAP. I said I was going to call the cops, and he said if I did that, these two men might kill everybody we love. His parents. My parents. My brother in Houston. My grandmother."

"So these are cartel members?"

"I don't know, but bad guys either way, or at least Mark thought so. I mean torturing Lionel makes me think that assessment is on target, and then when Mark was sneaking away from the trailer—"

"Hang on a sec," Colby said. "He left Lionel in there?"

"Yeah. He didn't have a gun or anything, and it was two against one."

Colby started to say it didn't matter. You don't leave a person in those conditions. Any person. Especially a partner, even in a criminal activity. Doesn't matter if you're unarmed and outmanned, you do something. Hell, if nothing else, you hide behind a tree and yell that the cops are on the way. Or throw a rock through a window. Shout that you have a rifle. That might get the men to stop. If they thought the police were coming and there was a witness who could ID them, they might decide it was time to cut their losses and get out of there. But Colby didn't say any of that to Dixie. What was the point? She obviously knew full well about Mark's shortcomings. She was here right now because Mark had no honor or integrity. No courage or character.

Or none of this had actually taken place, because he was a pathological liar.

"We're almost to the creek," Colby said. "This last section is a little steep and the soil is loose in spots, so be careful."

Even an experienced hiker would appreciate the heads-up. They moved slowly, grabbing tree branches for support, and then they reached the flat bank beside the creek. Fifty feet upstream was a small waterfall with a drop of maybe ten feet. Beneath the waterfall was a natural swimming hole surrounded by ferns.

"Oh, my God," Dixie said. "It's beautiful."

"When the water's flowing, yeah," Colby said. "Luckily we had some rain this summer."

"I've lost my bearings. This is all yours? Both sides of the creek?"

"Yep."

"You're a lucky man."

"True. Sometimes I forget that."

"So where I was—where you found me the other night—that was upstream, right?"

"Yeah, maybe three or four hundred yards."

"I had no idea I was that close to paradise," she said.

They stood quietly for a moment.

"Let's get in the water," Dixie said.

"Right now?" Colby said.

In response, Dixie pulled her shirt over her head and unceremoniously dropped it on the ground. Then she removed her bra and dropped it, too.

"Dang," Colby said. "You are a vision."

"Gonna just stand there?" she asked.

"For a minute, anyway," he said. "I'm enjoying myself."

Now she was kneeling to unlace her hiking boots. Those came off, and her socks, and then she stood and unbuttoned her khaki shorts. She began to slide them down over her hips, but she stopped.

"Fair's fair," she said. "Take your shirt off."

He unbuttoned his denim shirt and removed it. Swung it like a lasso over his head and tossed it away.

"Woof," Dixie said.

They both finished undressing and slowly eased into the water, which was nearly to their shoulders. The creek bed was nothing but stones, but they were round and gentle on their bare feet.

"Sad to say, but I can't remember the last time I swam here. Couple years, at least."

"How many women have you brought to this spot?" Dixie asked.

They were facing each other from five feet away. The moment was so pleasant, Colby could almost forget the circumstances.

"Not a lot," he said.

"How many?"

"I think maybe three. But the last one was at least twenty years ago. A couple were girlfriends in high school. It was all a long time ago."

"What we did last night—was that a one-time thing?" Dixie asked.

"You mean a three-time thing?"

"Oh, right. That's more accurate. So was it a one-*night* thing?"

"Not if I can help it," Colby said. "I mean, if that's what you want."

Dixie swam to him and wrapped both arms around his neck. He could feel her breasts pressing against his chest. They kissed deeply, for a long time.

Then she whispered directly into his ear, "How about if we spread the blanket on the grass?"

"What did you say?" the big man asked.

"Go. Fuck. Yourself."

The big man grabbed Syd's wrist and began to twist his arm.

Slowly. Syd tried to resist it, but he didn't have the strength. Not now, with buckshot in his back and possibly a concussion. The pain built, and built some more, and his elbow felt like it was about to snap.

"Okay," Syd said, knowing in his heart that he was going to pay these bastards back in ways they couldn't even imagine. But at least the big man stopped twisting his arm. "It's in the van," Syd said.

"The rest of the fake money is in the van?" Red said.

"Yeah."

"Where in the van?"

Syd couldn't come up with a quick answer.

"Damn liar," Red said. "Speaking of which, why did y'all set us up?"

"What're you talking about?" Syd asked.

"That scumbag Nicky said you were gonna be gone all afternoon."

"That scumbag is my brother," Syd said.

"What is the raccoon, a cousin?" Red said.

The big man laughed and said, "They sorta look alike, now that you mention it."

"That raccoon keeps himself clean as hell, which is more than either of you can say," Syd said.

"Why are you here in Blanco County?" Red asked. "Your plates are from Louisiana. What're you doing here?"

"Just a vacation," Syd said.

"I figured you had to travel to spend the phony bills," Red said.

He pushed himself off the wall and started walking slowly around the small room—not touching anything, but giving everything a good look.

"Okay, yeah, that's pretty much it," Syd said. "It's hard to get rid of that money. Hardly even worth the trouble."

Then Syd heard a chime from a phone. Not his phone, but Red's phone. Then a second chime, this one from the big man's phone. So they'd both been copied on a text. They checked their phones at the same time. Had to be the hot lady telling them that Nicky had dropped her off and was heading back to the motel. Finally. That was great news. These guys would want to leave before Nicky got back. Right?

"Is this all because of that little scratch on your truck?" Syd asked, trying to stall. "My brother shouldn't have paid you with fake bills. That wasn't cool. I can give you some real money and we'll be square, okay?"

Neither of them answered. The big man stayed right where he was, beside the bed. Red continued to look around the room. He wandered near the bathroom, and he stopped beside Syd's small suitcase, which was resting flat on the floor. Red used his boot to lift the zippered top and look inside. Nothing in there but clothes and toiletries.

Then there was the duffle bag right next to it. Zipped closed. Just right there in plain sight. No reason to look inside. Why would Syd keep anything valuable in such a visible spot? On the other hand, it was a Braniff Airlines bag. Vintage. More than forty years old. Was that a red flag? Why hadn't Syd transferred it to some other bag? Stupid, but how could he have known this would happen?

Red knelt beside the duffle bag and unzipped it. He saw the flannel shirt Syd had spread across the top, covering the contents. The answer was, Syd felt oddly sentimental about the bag—and the counterfeit bills.

Syd said, "This is the last warning for both of you motherfuckers. Stay out of my shit. Get out right now and I'll let this slide."

Red reached into the bag and pulled the shirt out, exposing the money underneath. He reached one hand down into the bag and dug around, just to be sure everything was as it seemed.

Then he looked at Syd and grinned.

25

They were lying side by side on the blanket, hands clasped, staring up at the blue sky.

Colby wasn't the type to fall quickly for any woman. Certainly not in a matter of days. It wasn't in his nature.

Until now.

He had developed strong feelings for Dixie. Undeniably.

He also knew Dixie would eventually need to leave, and that reality left an ache in his heart. Or, worse, she could be killed. Or arrested. But he was going to do his best to prevent either of those things from happening. He didn't know how yet, but he was going to help her out of this mess permanently. Then, if she needed or wanted to leave later, at least she'd be safe. Colby couldn't bear to let her leave until he knew the danger was gone.

"So what happened next?" Colby asked.

"Well, as soon as he was ready, they did it a second time," Dixie said.

He turned his head to look at her and she was grinning. She knew what he really meant.

"I probably need another ten minutes," he said. "Is that enough time to finish the story?"

"Ten minutes? You're a machine."

"Maybe fifteen," he said. But now he wished he hadn't asked. "On second thought, let's hold the rest of the story until later."

"Why?"

"You haven't had any normalcy for a while," he said. "I don't want to spoil this little excursion."

"If you think it's normal for me to have sex beside a creek with a man I met just a few days ago, I've got news for you," she said.

"I just figured you might want to wait until we get back to the house," he said.

"I'd just as soon finish telling it and be done. If you don't mind."

"Go for it."

"Okay. Where was I?"

"Mark was sneaking away from the trailer like a coward as two men were torturing Lionel."

"Right. As Mark was leaving, he heard two shots, about three seconds apart. He took that to mean that they'd just executed Lionel."

"Jesus," Colby said. "And how long before he called you?"

"I think just a few minutes later. He was driving. He said those two men would probably come to our house next."

"Did he tell you why any of this was happening?"

"Nope."

"But you ran," Colby said.

"Hell yeah, I ran. If they were in fact cartel members, I knew people like that would absolutely slaughter everybody without a second thought. So I grabbed a few things, stuffed them into a backpack, and took off."

"Why a backpack instead of a suitcase?"

"Easier to carry. We use backpacks for everything."

"Is that your backpack or Mark's?" Colby asked.

"We must have half a dozen backpacks around the house, but that was the first one I saw, and I guess it was Mark's. I don't think I ever used that one."

"Was there anything in it at the time?"

"No, it was empty."

Colby thought about it for a minute. "So it just turned out to have a tracker in it that the men in the van were using to follow you?"

"It doesn't make sense to me, either."

"Had you seen that backpack around the house before?"

"I can't be sure. Mark was always buying new ones, or a couple at a time, if they were on sale. We both used them a lot on hikes, and he usually took one when he went mountain biking or kayaking or whatever."

She looked at him for a moment to see if that satisfied his curiosity about the backpack, and he nodded, so she continued with her tale.

"Okay, well, when I left the house, I wasn't sure if I even believed Mark—but I couldn't take chances. Out there in that house, in the middle of the forest, I would've been an easy target. But it all seemed so surreal—like something out of a movie—and I began to think Mark had made it all up. Maybe it was a weird attempt to stop me from reporting it. So, that night—it was already almost nine o'clock—all I did was go back to the motel in Woodville."

"And you didn't know about the tracker in your bag."

"Right. Maybe I got lucky, but it was a quiet night and nothing happened. I didn't hear from Mark, or anybody else. I was still using my original phone at that point, so I was receiving texts and calls, but nothing out of the ordinary. The next morning, I didn't think I should go home, and I didn't know what else to do, so I just randomly went west on 190, and by the time I reached Livingston, I decided I'd go south to Houston. Talk about a perfect place to hide out. But when I got there, I just couldn't stand it. And I figured nobody could possibly find me at this point, so I should go wherever I wanted and do whatever I wanted. At least for a day or two. You know where I decided to go?"

"I can't even imagine."

"The Alamo. I had never seen it, so I headed for San Antonio on I-10. Then I stopped for gas in Columbus..."

"And noticed the black van for the second time," Colby said.

"Yep. So I went to San Antonio, parked at the airport, and now you're up to date."

"I know everything?"

"Everything that I know."

"Which does not include the reason why the cartel suddenly decided to come after you. I mean, why you? You weren't involved."

They lay in silence for about a minute.

Dixie said, "The only possibility that crossed my mind is that Mark told some lie that somehow incorporated me in their scheme."

"Like what?"

"I can't even imagine. You have any theories?"

"I do, but you're not going to like it."

"Tell me."

"My theory is that Mark didn't lie, he told the truth. You said he was furious because you were undermining him—ruining his big chance. On top of that, you were going to divorce him. Talk about insult on top of injury. He had the meeting planned for the next day, but he couldn't very well go to that while he knew you were about to blow the whistle. So he sold you out. He told his contact—whoever bought the pot from him—that you were planning to report the grow site and turn Mark in. This was going to ruin everything, of course. But Mark had bought some time by warning you that if you went to the cops, your entire family might be in danger. And it worked, even if it wasn't true. Instead of going directly to the police, you ran. So they sent a couple of men after you."

Dixie propped herself on one elbow to look at him.

She said, "The sick thing is, that fits perfectly, except one thing... why did they have to torture Lionel to figure out where we lived? Oh, man. Hang on."

"What?"

"I bet Mark had second thoughts. He stopped cooperating, which is why he called me and warned me what was happening. So those men had to torture Lionel to find out where I was. You see any holes in that?"

Colby thought about it for a long moment. "I think it all lines up. The night after you confronted Mark and told him you were going to report the grow site, he told his contact what you were doing, which immediately placed you in the cartel's crosshairs. But at some point—later that night or that next morning—Mark changed his mind. He probably stopped answering calls and texts. So now the cartel wants you both dead. Or maybe they want Mark alive long enough to get his growing technique from him. But you definitely have to die, or at least be neutralized, unless they happen to find Mark first."

"I was carrying the backpack with the tracker in it when I went to the motel in Woodville, but I must not have gotten close enough to anyone with an iPhone for it to send my location. That or the men in the van didn't want to kill me there. It would've been too public and messy, or maybe they were worried about getting caught or identified."

"We know for sure they were following you the next day," Colby said. "And you know what? Think about it—if Mark cut off contact with them, I bet they thought you and Mark were running away together. At least until they got close enough to see that it was just you in your car."

"I bet you're right. And at that point, they'd focus on me first and plan to deal with Mark later. Because they'd figure Mark wouldn't go to the cops. If he did, he would have to admit everything he had done so far. So he was just running to stay alive."

Dixie lay flat on her back again and they both mulled over their theory, examining it for inconsistencies or inaccuracies. Their long silence said that neither of them could see any flaws.

Colby said, "Any thoughts on what you want to do next?"

"I've been thinking about something. What if I somehow get word to the cartel that I've changed my mind and I won't report it? I just want to be left alone. Maybe I tell Mark and he tells them."

Colby thought about it. "I guess you could try it, but you'd have to trust Mark to be the intermediary—to be truthful with both them and you. At this point, is that a chance you want to take?"

Dixie remained quiet for a moment. "In that case, I'd like to stay here at your ranch and never leave. Never tell anyone where I am. We can swim every day, fool around whenever we feel like it, and pretend none of this crazy stuff ever happened."

"I'm totally on board with all of that," Colby said.

"I can be your ranch hand," she said. "Your housekeeper. But you have to do all the cooking."

The funny thing was, if that were possible, Colby realized he would agree to it in a minute.

26

Always have a backup. Syd had one this time, too. That's why he said *Always*.

This time, the backup was under the mattress. His other handgun. He could feel it beneath him. Not literally, but he could *sense* it under there. Just waiting.

"Don't fucking touch that," Syd said to the one named Red. "Leave it alone. Zip it shut."

"You zip it shut," Red said, and he laughed at his own joke, then looked at the big man to see if he was laughing. This guy was a simpleton.

Syd heard another text tone, but this one was from his phone on the nightstand, and the big man quickly grabbed it and took a look. It must be from Nicky, on his way home from the hospital, saying that Syd was wrong—the woman never said her vision had suddenly returned. He probably still thought her little scam was legit, that she really needed help, and he'd have no way of knowing these two men were in the motel room.

"*You have one more day to find her*," the big man said, reciting the message.

Syd almost laughed. What else could he do? Everything was going to shit. The text wasn't from Nicky, it was from Fernando. Syd had ignored Fernando's most recent text before this one, and now things were getting terse.

"Find who?" Red asked.

"I don't know," the big man said. "Some lady, I guess." He looked at Syd. "Who're ya looking for?"

"I don't even know what that text means," Syd said.

"Who's F? You got the person listed as F, instead of a full name."

"Oh, that's Frank. He's a weirdo. He likes to send dumb messages. Most of the time, I don't even know what he's talking about."

"Why?" Red asked.

"Why does he send them?"

"Yeah."

"No idea. He thinks it's funny. Like I said, he's weird."

"Speaking of weird, what the hell's up with your brother?" Red said. "Why would he do that to his face? Never mind. I don't give a rat's ass."

"We should go, Red," the big man said.

"Hang on. We got time. Something else is going on here." He was looking at Syd with an increasing level of suspicion. "Who are you supposed to find?" Red asked Syd. "And what for?"

"Should I answer this message?" the big man asked.

"Not yet," Red said. He was still looking at Syd, expecting a reply.

"I'm not here to find anybody," Syd said.

He started to sit up, but the big man moved surprisingly fast and pushed him back to the mattress, saying, "Do that again and I'll knock your teeth out."

"Jesus, settle down," Syd said.

"Who's the woman?" Red said.

Son of a bitch. Why did things always have to get so fucked up? Syd wasn't in the mood for this.

"You want me to make up a story?" Syd said. "I can if you want."

Red reached into the bag and pulled out a bundle of wrapped hundreds.

"Is that what all this fake cash is for?" he asked. "To find some lady?"

"Why would I let anybody pay me with fake cash?" Syd asked.

"You tell me. Maybe you didn't realize it was fake until after they paid."

"If that was true, I wouldn't do whatever they were paying me for," Syd said.

"Okay, but that would still mean somebody paid you to find some lady," Red said.

"I'm a private investigator," Syd said. "There. I made something up. No, I work for the Treasury. I busted someone earlier with that bogus money. If you take it, man, you're screwed."

"Then who's the lady?" Red asked.

"Her name is Sally Squattengottit, a notorious counterfeiter. We've been chasing her for years. My boss, Frank, is fed up and losing his patience."

Red shook his head. Not buying it, obviously.

Syd decided to tell the truth.

"My dad printed those bills a long time ago—when I was a kid—and then he got busted for it. But they didn't find all of it. I didn't even know he had any left until I found it after he died."

"Why are you hauling it around?" Red asked.

"Just like you said. We have to travel to spend it. A bill or two at a time."

Red looked at him for a long moment, then broke into a grin. "You're still lying."

"Believe whatever you want. Why would I care?"

"You just haul this big bag of fake cash everywhere?"

"Red, we should take off," Billy Don said.

"In a minute," Red said. He was still looking at Syd, wanting an answer.

"Nobody gave me counterfeit money—or any money—to find anybody," Syd said. "So both of you should get out of here while you can."

If he could just pull the gun from under the mattress, he could stop them from taking the Braniff bag.

Right then, Syd heard the van pulling up outside.

Red moved back to the window and peeked around the curtain. "Shit," he said. "That was faster than I thought."

The big man got up to take a look, and Syd finally had his chance. He slipped his right hand under the mattress and felt the butt of his second .380. He pulled the gun from its hiding spot just as he heard the van door close. Neither of the men were looking toward Syd. Frigging amateurs. How dumb could they be?

Now Red turned around again, obviously intending to grab the Braniff bag, and he said, "Is your brother—"

And he saw Syd sitting up with the gun in his hand, pointing it at Red.

"Y'all fucked up good, huh?" Syd said. "Now what're you gonna do?"

"Billy Don?" Red said to the big man.

Now Syd had both of their names. Might come in handy later when it was time for payback.

Billy Don turned, too, and saw the gun. He actually laughed. "What a buncha bullshit. He's bluffing. He's not gonna shoot anybody for a bag of fake money."

"Try me," Syd said.

He heard the doorknob turn, but the door didn't open. Apparently Red had locked it when Syd was unconscious. "Syd?" Nicky called from outside, and he rapped lightly.

"Already done it once," Billy Don said, and he lumbered toward the Braniff bag.

Now Red had Syd's original .380 pointed at him, just in case.

"Syd, you okay in there?" Nicky said, rapping again.

Syd so badly wanted to shoot both of these fuckers. But what a mess it would create. The cops would come. They'd find the money. Now was not the time. He had to play it cool.

Billy Don grabbed the Braniff bag and turned for the door.

"Don't do it," Syd said. "Final warning."

Billy Don used a kid's voice to say, "You so scawwy."

"I'm gonna find you both," Syd said.

"Good luck with that," Billy Don said, and out the door he went, with Red right behind him. He heard Red say something to Nicky, but Syd couldn't make it out.

"Oh, I won't need luck," Syd mumbled to himself.

27

Fernando and Armando decelerated as they entered the outskirts of Blanco, Texas, because the speed limit dropped to fifty miles per hour, and because they were in no rush. It was never good to rush. Take your time. Do the job right. Remain calm at all times.

The car was a two-year-old Camry. The paint color was predawn gray mica, but most people would simply call it brown, or at least brownish. Boring. Nondescript. Almost invisible. Nobody notices a car like that unless it tailgates you or runs from the cops or has a for-sale sign on it.

Anyone interacting with the two men might mistake them for brothers, but they weren't brothers. They both had the same dull, dark eyes and the wide jaw, but they weren't brothers. However, that didn't stop people from saying, "Are you brothers? You're not? Well, you sure look like brothers. And your names are so similar." It quickly became tiresome.

To the right was a Tractor Supply. Further ahead, a Sonic. A Dollar General. Then a Lowe's Market.

"Is this the entire town?" Armando said from the passenger seat.

Those were the first words Armando had spoken in two hours. Likewise, Fernando had said nothing. There had been nothing to discuss earlier.

"More across the river," Fernando replied.

But not much. Should be easy to find Syd. Only so many places to stay. And he wasn't hiding. He didn't know what was coming. So why would he hide? But he would be keeping a low profile—as best a guy like Syd could, with his limited intelligence and poor judgment.

Draco had instructed Syd to clean up his own mess, but so far, he had failed in spectacular fashion. Finding the woman had been a problem for him. He had bragged about the trackers in her bag, but those hadn't helped him. The last message from Syd said the woman was staying with a man on a ranch and he might have to handle them both. That was last night. Since then, nothing.

Fernando contemplated the possibility that the woman and the rancher had killed Syd. If it were true, Draco would want confirmation that Syd was dead. They would need to confront the woman and the rancher. Make them present the body. Then kill them both. That would leave only Mark. He would surface eventually. They would get what they needed from him first, though.

Fernando crossed the river and dropped the speed of the Camry even lower as they entered the heart of Blanco.

An abandoned gas station on the right.

Valero—open and doing business—on the left.

Dairy Queen on the right.

And so on. All the same shit you'd expect to see in a small Texas town like this, including a church. And another church.

The drive had given Fernando plenty of time to think. He would never share this opinion with anybody—except for Armando—but Draco was too volatile. Too temperamental. He sometimes let his emotions get the better of him. That's why there were occasionally rumors that he was going to be eliminated and replaced. In this case, he had lost his patience and made a rash decision. And he was too proud to admit his mistakes.

Have Syd kill the woman and her husband? Nonsense. Syd did not have the proper skills or experience. And kill them for what purpose? That was the reaction of an angry man, not a rational businessperson. Even if the woman did report what she knew, what could she prove that would harm anyone in the organization? Besides, by now it was obvious she was too fearful to follow through with her threat. And why kill the husband and lose the knowledge he had to offer? Better to find him and return him to the compound, while he was still free. Make him talk, then turn him loose. What could he do? But Draco wanted what he wanted. Any attempt to make him see differently only hardened his resolve to have his way.

Now, a full week later, Draco had added Syd to the list. This, Fernando could understand. Syd had proven that he was a liar, and incompetent, too. He would be replaced quickly and easily. Someone would be promoted from within. There were several candidates for the position. Alejandro, perhaps.

Still, Fernando had to wonder about Draco's methods. Why not simply inform Syd that plans had changed and ask him to return to the compound? There was no need to tell him what the new plans were. But perhaps that would've been too obvious. Syd would have wondered why Draco was aborting the original mission. He would've understood that he had been a failure, and that there couldn't be a good reason to be summoned. Perhaps Draco's judgment had been correct on that one aspect of this debacle.

Instead, Draco had sent Fernando and Armando to find Syd and bring him to the compound. There, Draco might make an example of him. Do terrible things, so word would spread. And dispose of him properly.

Fernando had to stop the Camry at a red light. To their right was the old courthouse.

"No reply yet?" Fernando asked.

Armando had sent Syd a message a few minutes earlier, informing him that he had one more day to find the woman. But the true reason was to make him think he still had time.

Armando checked his phone again. "Nothing. Send another one?"

Fernando thought about it. "Not yet."

"Check the motels?" Armando asked.

There were only three or four places nearby where Syd could be staying. The two men had concluded that the two most likely places were the Blanco County Inn, which was just a few blocks ahead, and the Blanco River Hotel, which was less than a mile north of that. Once they found Syd, they would watch him and wait for him to leave the motel, most likely late tonight. See if he could lead them to the woman. Get them both at once.

Fernando was hungry and needed to take a piss, but it would only take a few minutes to check the motels, so he continued north.

Armando was checking the map on his phone. When they passed a small liquor store, he said, "One more block. Just past this gas station. It is a long building that runs parallel to the highway, so if the van is there, we should be able to see it."

Fernando eased the Camry along slowly and saw the sign for Blanco County Inn, and a place to turn into the parking lot. Fernando passed it by, of course. Because if he pulled in and Syd was actually staying at this motel, he might spot them. That would not do.

"There it is," Armando said. "The van. *Dios mío.*"

When Fernando saw it, he could only shake his head in hopeless disgust.

It was parked in front of the last room on the north end of the building. Syd had told them he had borrowed his brother's black van for the trip, because he might need to carry the woman somewhere—dead or alive. Syd's own vehicle apparently wasn't suitable for such a task. But this van was worse, because it was an eyesore. It appeared to have been painted by hand. Of course, the woman had noticed the van following her, because it—

Fernando slammed the brakes as an orange Nissan truck pulled out of the motel lot directly into the Camry's path. As the vehicles passed within inches of each other, the other driver made an obscene gesture toward Fernando. And right behind the Nissan was an old Ford Ranchero driven by an enormous man. He had the window down and yelled for Fernando to watch where the hell he was going.

What kind of town was this? What kind of people were these?

28

Syd's plan to rip Mark off hadn't worked out as planned.

It started off fine. Smooth, actually. He met Mark in the parking lot at Burger House in Colmesneil and swapped fake money for real weed. Fifty-two pounds, when Syd weighed it. Syd ponied up the cash—twenty grand—and of course Mark never considered the possibility that it might not be real money.

Syd gave Mark the fake money in a camo backpack—the one with two AirTags in it, one in a pocket and one sewn into the lining. He'd already noticed the first time he'd met with Mark that he carried a Samsung phone, so he wouldn't receive any kind of notification about the AirTags. Mark counted the money, seemed thrilled, and left with the backpack.

At that point, Syd had the munchies bad, so he went inside for a double-meat cheeseburger and fries. Damn, it was good. People drove for miles for these burgers.

Syd ate and watched the Find My app for an update on the backpack's location. He got a notification almost immediately that showed Mark at a stoplight on 69, going south, which meant he had probably gotten close to somebody with an iPhone in the four-lane section of the highway, before it narrowed. Cool. Technology was fucking great.

He finished his burger and drove home carefully with the weed.

Checked the app again. No updates on the backpack's location. None later that day, either. Or the next day. Where the hell did this guy live? The middle of nowhere? Syd remembered that Mark's wife used to work for the Forest Service, but he didn't know where they lived. Somewhere closer to Woodville, that's all Syd knew. He went online and tried to find an address, but no luck. Not a big deal. The AirTags would fix that. Eventually. Might take a day or two.

That's when things took a turn for the worse.

Four days after the meeting with Mark, Draco called Syd and said,

"Come see me."

Syd tensed up the minute he saw the number on his phone.

Draco's real name was Felipe, but he absolutely hated that name. Everybody called him Draco—not because of the Harry Potter character, but because he favored a Draco AK47-style pistol. Word was that he had killed several men with it, and one woman, who happened to be his ex-wife. She had committed several sins, including cheating on him, stealing money out of his safe, and calling him Felipe.

Syd told him, "Okay, yeah. Sure. You got it. Everything good?"

"We'll talk when you get here."

Fuck. What was this about?

Draco's compound was just outside Laredo. Still on this side of the border, but in an entirely different world. Some people went down there and never came back—or that's what people said.

"Okay, when?"

"Tomorrow. Seven o'clock. We'll have dinner."

So Syd did it—drove all the way to Draco's compound, which covered about five acres and was enclosed by an eight-foot wall. The house was high on a bluff overlooking the Rio Grande, which was mostly dried up except for a stagnant puddle here and there. Syd had seen a couple of Draco's men inside the house, but they hadn't even looked in Syd's direction. He had taken that as a good sign.

Draco seemed unusually gregarious, and within ten minutes they were seated on the back patio, each with a glass of tequila. Syd was even beginning to wonder if he might be receiving a promotion. That's when Draco said, "You're here because you fucked up. You know that already."

Well, shit. This was terrible. Not unexpected, but terrible.

"Yeah, I know," Syd said, looking down at the ground. "It's all on me."

"Tell me what you did," Draco said.

"Tell you?"

"I want to hear you say it."

Syd did his best to appear terribly ashamed.

"I made a deal on my own," he said.

Draco let out a big laugh, but it wasn't genuine. "Yes, you got tempted, didn't you? Make a little extra money on the side and who's going to know? Who can blame you?"

He even reached over and clapped Syd on the back.

"I'm sorry. It was so stupid."

"It was a lot of product, wasn't it?" Draco said. "How much was it exactly?"

"Fifty pounds," Syd said, which really wasn't that much.

"And two," Draco said. "It was fifty-two."

How did he know all of this? Had Alejandro ratted him out? That was the only explanation Syd could think of. Fucking Alejandro. Stabbing Syd in the back to advance his own career.

"Right. Yeah. Fifty-two," Syd said.

Now two of Draco's men came onto the patio and lingered nearby. Ready for a signal. Syd was starting to panic. He was doomed.

Draco poured him another shot of tequila and Syd downed it.

"The quality was amazing," Syd said, just babbling now to buy some time. "I tried some and it was unreal. I've never had anything like it. I know I screwed up, but maybe this guy is somebody we want to work with. I was going to talk to you about it, but I was, you know, feeling stupid about what I'd done. That's why I haven't sold any. Not one ounce. I brought a little bit, so you could see for yourself."

That was a lie. Syd had brought it for the drive home, figuring he'd want to celebrate if there *was* a drive home. It wasn't much. Just one joint in a baggie that he pulled from his shirt pocket and placed on the table.

Draco stared at Syd for a long moment. Then he reached for his glass and sipped tequila. Swallowed it. Sipped again. Then he put the glass back on the table. Another minute passed. Syd waited.

Draco reached for the baggie and removed the joint. Smelled it like it was a cigar. Syd pulled a lighter from his pants pocket and offered it. Draco ignored it for a moment, then took it and lit the joint. Took a long drag. Held it.

A minute passed. Neither of them spoke.

Another minute passed.

Draco opened his mouth, ready to offer his assessment, but he stopped. His expression now—it was…dreamy. That was the only way to describe it. Contentment, with a hint of a grin.

"You know what I want you to do?" Draco finally said.

Syd said, "Whatever it is, I'll do it."

"I know you will."

"Absolutely."

"Bring him to me," Draco said.

"Bring…bring Mark?"

Did Draco want to meet him? Or kill him?

"Yes," Draco said.

"Here?"

"Yes."

"Okay," Syd said. "Sure. You got it. When?"

"As soon as possible."

"Tomorrow?"

"Yes."

"I'll do it," Syd said.

"We don't need his product," Draco said. Then he tapped his temple with one finger. "We need his secret. The way to grow it."

Syd realized now that he had been terribly short-sighted. The weed itself—the fifty-two pounds—was nothing compared to the value of the growing technique. That's what really mattered. That's why Draco was a lieutenant. He saw the big picture.

The question now: Would Draco pay Mark for the knowledge, or have it extracted from him? Syd knew which was more likely. What was he supposed to do, object? This was his way out. He was getting off easy. His penance was to bring the lamb to the slaughter—a small price to pay.

29

"You really got it?" Mandy said, her eyes wide, staring at the Braniff bag through the passenger side window of her truck. Red had just pulled up outside the hospital. "You actually got the money?"

"Yep. I got it," Red said, trying to be cool, but his heart was pounding. "Here, you drive. I want to look through it."

A minute later, they pulled onto 281 and Billy Don followed in his Ranchero.

"I can't believe you were right," Mandy said.

Red said, "I can barely believe it either. But there was one hang-up."

"What was it?"

"They knew we were coming. The other guy was waiting inside the room."

"Bullshit!"

"I'm serious. He was in there. They were trying to sucker us. He pulled a gun on Billy Don and Billy Don beat the hell out of him and took the gun away."

"No way."

"It was crazy. We coulda been shot."

Red didn't mention that he didn't enter the room until Billy Don had already gotten the gun.

"How did they know?"

"Got no idea."

She was going a little fast for Red's taste—he didn't want to get pulled over—but he didn't say anything.

"I gotta be honest," Mandy said. "That was fun."

"Couldn't have done it without you," Red said.

"Let's see it," Mandy said, nodding toward Red's lap.

"Right now?"

"The money, you moron," Mandy said.

"Oh."

He unzipped the Braniff bag and grabbed a bundle of hundred-dollar bills.

"Holy hell," Mandy said. "How much is there?"

"I got no idea. Haven't counted yet."

She put her hand out and he gave her the bundle. She tried to keep an eye on the highway ahead while studying the money. She put the bundle in her lap and pulled a single bill loose.

"Jesus, this looks so real. It *feels* real."

"Well, if it didn't, they wouldn't print it. They have to be nearly perfect. Those bills they gave me the other night totally faked me out. Watch the road."

"I'm watching," she said. "You think those guys printed these bills? That guy Nicky seemed too stupid to figure anything like that out. Was the other guy any smarter?"

Red was pleased Mandy was so excited about the situation, and that she considered it a success.

"Yeah, a little," Red said. "It's kind of like the difference between Billy Don and me. I have to do most of the thinking."

"It's so weird, though," she said. "Why they're traveling around with all this fake money."

Red was wondering if he should tell her about the text Syd had received—the one about having one more day to find some lady. That explained their traveling, but why complicate things? At this point, Red wasn't even sure what the text meant.

"I guess they need to spend it somehow," Red said. "Look how quick I got caught with those three bills. I'm lucky Jorge didn't get all upset and call the cops or turn me in. I guess it's not as easy to get rid of this stuff as you'd think."

"So what now?" she asked.

That was a good question. The plan had been to get their hands on the fake money without the men knowing who got it. But now they knew. Boy, did they know. Could they figure out who Red and Billy Don were? Could they track them down? Probably wouldn't be too hard. Would they try?

"I'm not sure yet," Red said. "I need a couple of beers to clear my head."

"I still don't understand how you know it's fake," Mandy said.

"It's just that there are things to look for," Red said. "Jorge showed us."

"Like what?"

"Some things are missing and others just aren't quite right, but you need a magnifying glass to see it. Oh, I can use my phone. Hang on."

He pulled his phone, opened the camera, and zoomed in tight on one of the bills as they continued north. It wasn't easy to hold steady as they were moving, and his hands were still shaking from the encounter, but after a minute, he'd gotten a good look at the bill.

"Jesus," he said.

"What?"

"I'm not seeing what I'm supposed to be seeing."

"So what are you saying?" Mandy asked.

Red pulled a different bill and started to study it.

"Red?" Mandy said.

"It's not like I'm some expert, but I think these bills are real."

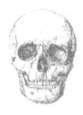

Nicky stepped into the motel room, his face white. Moloch was on his shoulder, chattering softly. The stupid raccoon could sense the tension in the air.

"What the hell just happened?" Nicky asked. "Did they get the money? What happened to your face?"

Syd eased himself down into a chair by the window. He could feel blood running down his back. He was just so tired of all this shit. He said, "Everything just went to hell. That's what happened."

"Why were those guys here again? Were they with that lady?"

"Of course they were with that lady," Syd said. "They set us up. That was the plan. I told you."

"So what went wrong?" Nicky asked. "You were gonna be ready for 'em."

"They're fuckin' crazy, that's what went wrong. The big one, especially."

What kind of person doesn't back down when he has a gun pointed at him? You either have to be crazy or stupid. Now Syd was wishing he'd shot that fucker. It would've felt *so* good. But when it came down to it, he knew that would've ruined everything. He couldn't afford any contact with the cops.

"How did they know about the money?" Nicky asked. "The *real* money? Or do you think they didn't know some of it was real?"

"Just shut up for a minute," Syd said. "And close the damn door."

Nicky did as he was told.

What was Syd going to do without that money? The real money, not his father's remaining counterfeit money. That money was his parachute, so to speak. His emergency raft. Or something. That money was going to allow him to get the hell out of Dodge, which was looking more necessary every minute.

Nicky went to the little refrigerator and removed two bottles of beer. He opened them, handed one to Syd, then sat on the edge of the bed.

It was probably time to run. Syd knew that. If he waited too long, he might not get the chance.

"What happens if you don't get her?" Nicky asked.

"Well, I won't get that promotion I've been hoping for," Syd said. "They might even make me work in the mail room."

After a pause, Nicky said, "But really. Are they gonna kill you instead?"

Syd could tell Nicky was concerned, and it surprised him. His brother loved him. Or maybe Nicky was simply worried he was going to end up as collateral damage. That was probably it. Right now, Draco and Fernando and Armando didn't know Nicky was on this mission with Syd.

"You can always catch a bus back home," Syd said.

"Oh, hell no, bro. I'm not gonna leave you like that," Nicky said. "You wouldn't do that to me."

Syd didn't respond to that. Why tell Nicky the truth?

"I think I need you to bandage this thing on my back again," he said.

Nicky nodded. "And then what?"

At this point, Syd had no answers.

"One step at a time," Syd said. "First we need to get the money back. Then we'll deal with the woman."

"How are we gonna get it back?" Nicky asked.

"How do you think?"

30

"That was a nice break," Dixie said after their trek to the waterfall. Now they were on the back deck of Colby's house, each with a cold bottle of Lone Star. "But back to the real world."

"There are only so many options," Colby said. "You already know that."

"And none of them are good," Dixie said.

"Let's think this through a bit. You told Mark you were going to report him and his grow site, which would've landed him in serious trouble, and it would've soured his deal with the cartel. The cartel doesn't want to get caught up in an investigation, but mostly they want Mark out of prison—at least until they get all the information they can get about his growing technique."

"And then dispose of him," Dixie said.

"Probably."

"Can his pot possibly be so good that they're going to all this trouble?"

"Apparently so," Colby said.

"That's bitter irony for you," Dixie said. "Mark finally finds the one thing he really excels at—his breakthrough opportunity, just like he said—and it's illegal."

"Makes me wonder why he didn't just offer to sell his technique to some legit marijuana operation somewhere."

"These other guys probably promised a lot of money they weren't really going to deliver."

A raven flew overhead, croaking to its mate, who could be heard much farther away.

"I have an idea, but it's not fully formed yet," Colby said.

"Let's hear it."

"You can't just keep running forever, right? At some point, you need to be proactive and take steps to get your life back. Not your old life with Mark, obviously, but your new life."

"With you so far."

"Instead of waiting for the two men in the van to make their next move, we go looking for them instead. Then we make them tell us who they're working for. We want their boss. The person who told them to come after you."

"And what would we do with that information?" Dixie asked.

"We eliminate the problem right at the source."

"Hold on. We kill him?"

"That's what I'm suggesting, yes. Unless you can think of a better way."

"You seriously want to go after some cartel members head on? I'm starting to think you're missing the gene that makes people afraid of scary stuff."

"This is a fight for your survival," Colby said. "Nothing should be out of bounds."

"I agree with everything you're saying. It's just a little overwhelming to face it."

"I'll help you. No matter what happens."

Dixie didn't reply, but Colby could tell she was mulling it over. He took a sip of his beer.

She finally said, "If we find these two men, how do we get them to tell us who their boss is?"

"We torture the hell out of them, just like they tortured Lionel," Colby said.

"And then what? We let them go?"

"I don't know yet. I'm still working on the details."

"Or are you suggesting we kill them, too?"

"Maybe. Whatever keeps you alive, that's what we need to do. You can't run forever, and the problem won't just go away by itself."

"But cold-blooded murder?"

"Is it really murder if they are actively trying to find you and kill you?"

"I just don't know if I have it in me," Dixie said.

"Okay, first things first. We don't have to decide anything right now. Maybe we'll think of a better angle. But in the meantime, we can look for the men and see if it's possible to find them."

"Where do we even start?"

"I figure they're in Blanco or Johnson City, and it won't take long to check the hotels and motels. You up for a drive?"

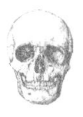

Red couldn't believe it. He *wouldn't* believe it. He wasn't going to get his hopes up and then have them dashed. Surely there was some other way to make counterfeit bills without making all those mistakes Jorge had pointed out. These bills could not be real. So he asked Mandy to stop at Jorge's shop again as they passed through Johnson City.

"Have you counted it?" Mandy asked as she parked out front. Luckily, Jorge's truck was still parked on the side of the building, even though it was ten minutes past closing time.

"Roughly, yeah," Red said. "I counted the bundles, and I'm assuming there aren't any bills missing from the bundles."

"How much is it?"

"I don't think we should be thinking about that because—"

"How much, Red?"

Right then, Billy Don pulled up on Red's side of the truck. Red hadn't texted or called him yet, so Billy Don had no idea why they had stopped. They both lowered their windows.

"What's up?" Billy Don said.

"I'm gonna tell you something, Billy Don, and don't get all excited, okay? Don't yell or shout or get all nutty."

"The hell're you talking about?"

Red kept his voice low. "There's a chance—a *small* chance—that the bills in this bag are real. Now, hang on. I could be wrong. I'm *probably* wrong. So let's just be mellow until we know for sure."

Red could see that Billy Don was doing his best to remain calm. "Why do you think that?" Billy Don asked.

"Because of the things Jorge said earlier about ways to check," Red said. "That marker he has should tell us for sure. So I'm gonna take a few bills inside and ask him to check 'em."

"Isn't he gonna wonder where these new bills came from?" Billy Don asked.

Red started to argue, but Mandy said, "That's a good point. What are you gonna say? Why do you suddenly have more fake bills?"

Damn it. They were causing complications. But he couldn't think of a good answer.

"And if it *is* real, what're we gonna do?" Billy Don added.

"What?"

"Well, it changes things," Billy Don said.

"What does?"

"If the bills are real."

"How the hell does it change things?"

"If you're a counterfeiter and somebody steals a bunch of your fake money, well, maybe it's a hassle, but it isn't real, and you can just print more, right? But if those guys got that money some other way and it's real—think about it. You'd be royally pissed off. You'd sure as hell want that money back. And since they've seen us, and they probably wrote down our license plate numbers, it won't take 'em long to figure out who we are and where we live."

"Oh, great," Mandy said.

"We even used our names," Billy Don said.

"You *introduced* yourselves?" Mandy said, obviously thinking they were idiots.

"No, I just mean while we were talking to each other, we said our names," Billy Don said. "I think. Pretty sure we did."

Red was starting to get angry, but he didn't know what to say. He hadn't considered this aspect. He'd been excited that the money might actually be real, and now he didn't know what would be better—real or fake.

"Let's not get all worked up," Red said. "One step at a time. Let's find out about the bills."

"We should just give the money back to them," Mandy said. "Whether it's real or fake. This was a bad idea from the start."

"Are you serious?" Red said.

"I don't want those psychos coming to *my* house," Mandy said.

"Just hang on," Red said. "We need to think this through."

"What's there to think about?" Mandy asked. "You give it back and tell them to leave you alone. Problem solved."

Red couldn't bear the thought. He said, "We need to find out for sure about the money. If it's fake, we still have leverage on them. They'll be worried we'll turn the bills in and say where we got it all. Then they'll be busted for a federal crime."

"How would we turn the bills in without getting in trouble ourselves?" Billy Don asked.

"That's a good question," Mandy said. "Considering y'all just committed robbery."

"Robbery?" Red said. "I wouldn't call that robbery."

"Then what would you call it?" Mandy asked.

"Robbery," Billy Don said.

"Okay!" Red said. "Let's just stop talking about it for five minutes, okay? There's no point in doing anything until we know about the money one way or the other. So here's what I'll do. I'll go in there and ask Jorge where he got that special marker, and then we'll go get one, even if we have to drive to Austin. Then we'll have our answer. And Jorge won't be suspicious, because I'll just say I want one so I can check bills in the future."

Red waited, and Mandy finally said, "Yeah, whatever. But whether it's fake or real, I'm still not sure I'm going along with any more of this bullshit."

"Same," Billy Don said. "We don't wanna get Mandy in trouble."

"You're sweet," Mandy said.

"Well, neither do I," Red said.

They both just looked at him.

"I'll be right back," he said.

31

They were in Colby's truck, driving east on Miller Creek Loop toward Highway 281. He noticed that she had brought her backpack along, but he hadn't said anything. That backpack had carried all her belongings for a week, so he couldn't blame her. Hard to leave it behind. Or maybe she thought she wouldn't be going back to Colby's, or that she might need to be ready to hit the road again as quickly as possible, depending on what they found in the next hour or so.

The clock on the dashboard read 5:47 when they reached the highway.

"Left to Johnson City, right to Blanco," Colby said. "Got a preference or a hunch?"

"Blanco," she said. "After I parked at the airport, they probably hung around San Antonio until they saw the AirTag pop up at your house, or at points along the way. When they came north, there was no reason to keep going to Johnson City. They would've stopped in Blanco, because it's just as close."

"Good call," Colby said, and he took a right.

He quickly got the truck up to seventy miles per hour.

Dixie pulled a phone from her pocket and checked it—the first time Colby had seen her do that. She did some typing, and after a minute of silence, she said, "If Lionel was killed, there's nothing in the news."

"Interesting," Colby said.

"Mark could've lied, or he might've misinterpreted those two gunshots," Dixie said. "Or I suppose the two men could've dumped the body somewhere—but then you'd think somebody would've reported Lionel missing by now. I know he has a lot of family in East Texas."

They drove another mile in silence as Dixie continued to look at her phone.

"Same with Mark," she said. "Nothing about him in the news."

They were halfway to Blanco.

She added, "You know what else? Judging by my Facebook page, nobody seems to know I'm gone yet or that anything weird is happening. On one hand I'm totally amazed, but on the other, how would they know?"

"That must mean Mark is keeping quiet, too," Colby said.

Dixie held up her phone. "This is my replacement phone," she said. "I still have my old phone, but I haven't turned it on since I left my house, so it couldn't be tracked."

"Who would be tracking it if you didn't commit a crime?" Colby asked.

"I know this sounds paranoid, but I started wondering about this cartel, or whatever they are, and what kind of connections they might have."

"Like somebody working at your cell-phone company," Colby said.

"Right. Is that totally ridiculous?"

"Honestly, I don't know the answer to that question."

"I'm tempted to turn it on and see if there are any texts or voicemails from Mark. Or anybody else."

Colby didn't say anything.

"You think that's a bad idea?" Dixie asked.

"I can't really think of any reason you shouldn't, but if Mark has been in touch, you won't be able to trust anything he says—not unless you can verify it somehow. I guess if you're going to do it, better to do it now than when you're at my house. Because now we're probably connected to a different tower. Or maybe not. Who the hell knows? Surely it can't be the same tower at this point. We're too far from the ranch."

She dug into her backpack and came out with a second phone. She paused for a moment, possibly reconsidering, then pressed the power button. It slowly booted up, and then Dixie said, "I have fourteen texts and three voicemails. Not as many as I was expecting. Then again, I'm not one of those people who uses a phone much."

Colby stayed quiet while she read.

"None of the texts are important," she said. "Good thing I'm usually slow at returning texts or a friend of mine would be wondering if I was okay. I'm going to answer her. It's about having lunch. I'll tell her I'll check with her next week. By then maybe all this craziness will be over."

Colby wasn't optimistic about that, but he kept it to himself.

She typed a response and sent it.

Then she played the voicemails over her speakerphone.

One was from the supervisor at the timber company who'd hired her as caretaker. Nothing important. He was just checking to see how things were going. No need to call back.

The next one was from her mother, asking what Dixie wanted for her birthday next month, and wondering when and where they were going to get together.

"The last one is from an unknown number," Dixie said.

She played it. There was a lot of background noise, like the person was calling from a moving vehicle.

"Dixie, this is Lionel. Jesus effing Christ. I don't even know what to say. Everything went to shit real fast and I hope you're okay. This was all so stupid from the start. Mark talked me into it. I know that doesn't even really matter, but that's what happened. You know how he can be. He gets an idea into his head and he won't let go, and he'll drag you into it with him. A couple of guys were at my trailer earlier today and I thought they were going to kill me. They fired a gun right beside my head and now I think my eardrum is busted. It hurts like a son of a bitch. I think they're going to come for you next, but I don't know why. Maybe Mark knows, but he won't call me back, and I might not get the full story. Anyway, you should get out of town until we know what's going on. Please let me know you're okay. You don't deserve to be a part of this mess, and I'm sorry. I better go. Stay safe."

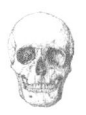

Red came back to Mandy's truck and climbed into the passenger seat, holding a marker. "I told him I want to be prepared the next time anybody gives me a hundred-dollar bill. He said I could have one of his markers."

Mandy said, "Okay, then."

All three of them went quiet, except for Billy Don popping open a beer can in his Ranchero.

Red pulled a bundle of bills from the Braniff bag, then pulled a single bill from the bundle. Uncapped the marker. Ran the marker across the bill, just as he'd seen Jorge do it.

The stripe was gold colored. The bill was real.

"What does that mean?" Mandy said. "Is it real or fake?"

"What color is it?" Billy Don asked.

"Hang on," Red said.

He pulled a bill from a different bundle. Marked it.

Gold. Real.

Red couldn't believe he was disappointed. He was wishing the bills were fake, because Mandy and Billy Don were right. The bills were real, which meant Syd and Nicky wouldn't just let them go. Also, Red and Billy Don had committed a robbery. Or it made it more of a robbery, now that he knew the bills were real. Somehow it didn't seem like much of a crime when he thought they were taking counterfeit money. It was like stealing Monopoly money. What cop would care?

"What color?" Billy Don asked again, because he couldn't see.

"Kind of gold or yellow," Mandy said.

Billy Don laughed, because he was right. "That shit's real," he said. "That's a lot of money and it's real. We robbed the shit out of those sumbitches."

"Y'all should quit saying that," Red said. "You're making me nervous."

He pulled another bill and marked it.

"What the hell?" Mandy said.

"What?" Billy Don said.

"It's black," Mandy said. "The line is black."

"Which means it's fake," Billy Don said.

"So some is real and some is fake?" Mandy asked.

"What in the holy name of Tom Landry is going on here?" Billy Don said.

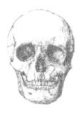

When the message from Lionel ended, Dixie said, "Wow. Okay. At least we know he's alive. Or he was when he left the message."

"When did he leave it?" Colby asked.

Dixie checked the date and time of the voicemail. "The same day the men came to his trailer. A couple of hours after Mark called me. By then I had turned my phone off."

"So he was doing his best to give you a warning."

"Yep. Should I try to call him? Or maybe text him? Maybe he's been in touch with Mark."

"Maybe so, but even if we learn where Mark is, how does that benefit you?"

"I might not know the answer to that question until I hear from both of them," Dixie said.

Reasonable point, but they'd just reached the outskirts of Blanco, so Colby said, "Let's come back to that in a little bit, okay?"

Dixie agreed.

Colby slowed, eased into the left-turn lane, then pulled into the Blanco River Hotel on the east side of the highway. The parking was all directly in front of the three-story building, and it took less than a minute to determine that the van wasn't here.

Colby took a left out of the lot.

They passed the Buggy Barn Museum, then the eye doctor's office.

Colby eased off the gas as they passed the Swiss Lodge, which was small enough that they didn't even need to turn into the lot. They saw no hand-painted black van.

Colby realized there was a chance the two men could have parked the van in some other inconspicuous location—like around the courthouse square or in the Lowe's parking lot—and walked to a motel, but were they that clever? Couldn't rule it out, which meant Colby and Dixie might need to check those places. Still, that wouldn't take long.

They passed the library and the Masonic Lodge.

"I sort of want to find them and also would rather not," Dixie said.

Colby said, "There's still the possibility that the buckshot did the trick. Maybe that guy's dead and the other guy took off for Mexico. Only problem with that is we might never know if—"

"There it is!" Dixie said, pointing toward the Blanco County Inn.

32

After studying all of the bills closely, Red figured out that the fake bills had a tiny piece of one corner cut off. Just a sliver that you wouldn't even notice unless you knew to look for it. The real bills were untouched. That's how the scumbags in the van kept them straight.

"What difference does knowing that make?" Mandy asked. "So some of it is real and some of it is fake. So what?"

"That's kind of weird, isn't it?" Red said.

They were still parked in front of Jorge's place, trying to decide what to do.

"So maybe they were spending the fake bills and keeping the real bills they got in exchange," Billy Don said.

"How do they spend fake hundred-dollar bills and get real hundred-dollar bills back?"

That shut Billy Don up for a minute. But not Mandy.

"I say we take the bag back," she said. "Before they come looking for it. We got no idea what kind of people they are and what they might do."

"Especially after seeing that text," Billy Don said.

Oh, great, Red thought.

"What text?" Mandy asked.

"A text that said they had just one more day to find her," Billy Don said.

"Find who?" Mandy asked.

"No idea."

"So the guy carries a gun, uses counterfeit money, and he's been given an ultimatum about finding some woman?" Mandy said.

"Yep," Billy Don said.

"All of that is more than enough to know we don't want to mess with these guys," Mandy said. "It's not worth the hassle."

"Hey, why don't we just get out of town for a while?" Red said. "Go to the coast for a week. Have a few drinks, go dancing, eat some good food, and when we get back, they'll be gone."

"Sure they will," Billy Don said.

"It's a hell of a lot of money," Red said. "I mean the real money."

"How much?" Billy Don asked.

"Who cares?" Mandy said.

"About thirty-seven thousand in real cash and forty-eight thousand was fake," Red said.

"Whoa," Billy Don said. "They damn sure won't let that much money go."

"Like the amount even matters," Mandy said. "You *stole* it from them. I know you think it's okay because they probably didn't earn it like normal people, but it's stealing either way."

Mandy was lecturing him? Red remembered how she'd behaved when her boyfriend at the time, Dub, had fallen out of a treehouse Red was building behind his trailer. It was going to be shaped like the Alamo, and he had recruited a lot of locals to help with the construction, which had gone smoothly until Dub had taken a header from about fifteen feet. It was Dub's own damn fault, drinking the way he had been, but that didn't stop him from raising the idea of a lawsuit. Then he went missing and Red thought his problems were over. But Mandy said she was going to sue him herself unless he gave her twenty grand, which he did. Then she fled the state, because she was a suspect in Dub's disappearance. Then there was the fact that Mandy had been cheating on Dub with some weird little Mexican kid who had an unhealthy obsession with feet.

Red was wondering if he should bring all that up. Probably not if he ever wanted to see Mandy undressed anytime in the near future.

So he said, "Maybe we make a deal with them."

"What?" Mandy said.

"What kind of deal?" Billy Don asked.

"We keep some of the money and give the rest back."

"Why the hell would they do that?" Billy Don asked.

"No, the question is, why wouldn't they?"

"Would you?" Billy Don asked. "Think about all the money you got locked in the safe back home. If somebody took it and then said you should split it, what would—"

"I got that money fair and square," Red said. "That's the difference."

"Maybe they did, too. At least the legit money. We don't know where they got it, or how."

"Oh, come on."

"Where we going?"

"Why are we even talking about this?" Mandy asked.

Jorge came out of his shop just then and looked surprised to see them still parked out front.

Red quickly stuffed all the bills back into the bag and zipped it up.

Jorge locked the door, then walked over to Red's side.

"Everything okay?" he asked. "You don't have a rag in your air cleaner, do you?"

Red faked a laugh. "Not this time. We're just wondering where to go eat supper."

"Braniff?" Jorge said, looking at the bag in Red's lap. "That old airline?"

"It was my daddy's bag," Red said. "He used to travel some."

"What line of work?" Jorge asked.

"Rodeo clown," Red said. When Jorge grinned, Red said, "No, I'm serious."

"Oh. Cool. He must've had some good stories to tell. Anyway, I'm gonna take off." He rapped on the roof of the truck twice and waved goodbye.

As Jorge got into his truck, Mandy said, "It's two against one. Me and Billy Don want to give the money back."

Red wasn't dumb enough to ask her why she thought she got a vote. Red looked at Billy Don who shrugged, meaning he was siding with Mandy.

Mandy's phone, in the cup holder between them, lit up with an alert. She was always getting alerts, because she loved goofing around on Facebook and Instagram and another one called TikTok.

While she checked it, Red said, "I still think we should keep the real money, or least part of it."

"I just wanna go home, drink some beer, and watch football," Billy Don said.

Red was about to offer a snarky reply when Mandy raised her phone to let him see the screen.

AirTag found moving with you

The location of this AirTag can be seen by the owner

"The hell's an AirTag?" Red said.

"It's some kind of tracker," Mandy said.

"What's going on?" Billy Don asked.

"There's a warning on my phone about an AirTag," Mandy said.

Red's iPhone chimed right then. He checked it and saw the same warning.

Then Billy Don's iPhone chimed, too.

Red looked down at the Braniff bag.

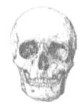

Syd was finally in a good mood. For the moment.

The AirTags in the Braniff bag had performed flawlessly, telling him exactly where the two rednecks had gone with his money, including the real bills he'd been saving up for several years. Screw the counterfeit money, but he wanted the real money back.

First the rednecks had gone to the hospital, probably to pick up the bimbo.

Then they'd gone to some little auto shop in Johnson City, where they sat for quite some time.

Now they were on the move again, going south on 281. Eventually they would go home, and that's when Syd would go after the bag. Maybe later tonight. He had to decide before then what he would do afterward. Continue pursuing the woman, or give up and take off.

Meanwhile, the remaining AirTag in the woman's backpack had also been on the move. It had left Phil Colby's ranch and gone south on the highway, toward Blanco. A few minutes later, the AirTag was located in the parking lot of the Blanco River Hotel, just a mile or so away. Then the AirTag was on the highway again, continuing south.

Syd climbed out of bed, still a little woozy, and went to the window by the door. He moved the curtain slightly with his right hand. At the moment, there was little traffic on the highway. Syd checked the app again and saw that the AirTag was about a hundred yards north of his motel. But it couldn't be the location in real time. How much of a delay was there?

Just then, a maroon Ford truck went past, and the driver was clearly looking toward the motel. A woman in the passenger seat was leaning forward enough to also look in this direction.

"What?" Nicky said.

The truck kept going.

"The guy who shot me just drove by," Syd said.

Nicky sat up quickly and came to the window. Moloch was sleeping in his crate.

"Maybe he's taking her back to the airport in San Antonio," Nicky said.

Syd checked his phone and saw that the AirTags in the Braniff bag were a mile outside Blanco.

"The rednecks are coming this way, too," Syd said.

"That's weird," Nicky said.

"They went all the way to Johnson City, and now they're coming back."

Blood was slowly running down Syd's back, but he ignored it. His face was throbbing from the big man's punch, and his eye was swollen shut, and his elbow hurt, but he ignored all that, too.

"We should follow them," Nicky said.

Syd started to agree, but then he realized the problem with that. "If they see us, they'll figure out we're tracking them."

"You're giving them too much credit. They aren't that smart."

"So what are we supposed to do? Jump in the van, chase them down, and get the bag back, without anybody calling the cops?"

"If any of them has an iPhone, they probably already got a warning about the AirTag," Nicky said.

Which was true, but that was why Syd put two AirTags in each bag. Syd's theory went like this: The person gets a warning about an AirTag, so they look in the bag and find it, like the woman and Phil Colby had done. So they destroy the AirTag, or toss it out a car window, or throw it on top of a building. Then, later, if they get another warning from the second AirTag that's hidden better, they think it's just a technical glitch left over from the first AirTag, so they ignore it.

There was also the fact that some people had no idea what an AirTag was, and when they saw the warning, they would simply dismiss it and go on with their lives. And some people would never get a warning at all, if they had Location Services or Bluetooth turned off.

The AirTags in the Braniff bag were now less than one hundred yards away.

"We're just gonna let them drive by?" Nicky asked.

"They'll go home eventually," Syd said.

"I think that's a mistake," Nicky said.

They both looked out the window and saw the Ford Ranchero making a left into the motel parking lot.

"What the hell?" Syd said.

"I can't believe it," Dixie said as they continued south on Highway 281. "The van was really there. You totally narrowed it down and figured it out."

"You're the one who picked Blanco, and for good reason," Colby said.

He took a left on Fourth Street and drove past the north side of the old courthouse. Then he took a right on Pecan, and another right on Third Street, where he pulled into a parking spot. The old courthouse was dead ahead. Cranberry's Antiques was behind them.

"What're we doing?" Dixie said.

"Figuring out what to do next," Colby said.

"Can we at least drive past again and I'll try to get their license plate? What if they leave while we're sitting here?"

"Normally I'd say that's a great idea, but I know the people who run that motel, and I promise you they have the license plate number and they ran a copy of their driver's license—whichever one of them checked in."

"Even if they paid cash?"

"Especially if they paid cash. Point is, we don't have to worry about getting their identity. We'll be able to get that later."

Dixie took a deep breath and let it out slowly. "I didn't expect to find them so fast."

"Truth is, neither did I."

"It makes me feel kind of...powerful. I like taking the situation into my own hands. Doing something, instead of waiting for them to do something."

"Kind of a rush?"

"Like we turned the tables," Dixie said. "And they don't know we found them."

"That's a big advantage."

"But what are we going to do with it? We can't just knock on their door. I've got this bad feeling they're going to leave before we decide what to do."

"Okay, then let's find a good spot to watch their room," Colby said as he started his truck.

33

Billy Don parked the Ranchero in front of the motel room, next to the black, hand-painted van, and Red said, "Tap the horn."

"What for?"

"I want 'em to know we're here, so I don't spook 'em."

Billy Don tapped the horn.

The Braniff bag was on the bench seat between them. Syd's little .380 was in the glove compartment. Mandy was back at the trailer by now in her truck. She'd said she wanted no more part in this nonsense.

The motel-room door opened and the one named Syd stepped outside. His bruised face looked even worse than before.

Red held both hands up to show that he wasn't armed. Then he opened his door and got out of the Ranchero.

"Come to your senses?" Syd asked.

"Not a chance," Red said.

"Then why are you here?"

"To make a deal," Red said.

"I don't make deals with losers," Syd said.

"Then I guess that rules your mom out," Red said.

"What the fuck are you even talking about?" Syd asked.

"I'm gonna take three hundred bucks to account for the fake money y'all gave me last night."

Red couldn't resist getting *something* out of all this effort. He couldn't just give everything back.

"That's the deal?" Syd said.

"Yep."

"Fine. Whatever. Take it."

"And just so you know, I figured out half the cash is real and half is fake," Red said.

"You're a damn genius is what you are," Syd said. "I shoulda known I was totally outmatched."

Now the guy was being a smart-ass. Red hated smart-asses.

"It wasn't that hard," Red said. "Those phony bills are pretty bad."

"Red," said Billy Don quietly from inside the Ranchero. "Drop it and move on."

Red stared at Syd for a moment, and Syd spread his arms wide, like *Are we gonna do this or what?*

Red reached into the Ranchero, got the Braniff bag, and carried it over to Syd.

"What about my gun?" Syd said.

"I'll put it on the ground when we leave," Red said.

"When exactly will that be?" Syd asked. "Sometime soon?"

Red really hated this guy. He couldn't resist saying, "We found the tracker in your bag, so I guess you aren't that smart, huh?"

Syd took the bag and said, "You found the tracker?"

"Yep."

"What about the other tracker?" Syd asked.

"Huh?"

"See, there's two trackers in there. There's one for suckers like you, and another one hidden in the lining. Guess you didn't find that one. So maybe you're the one who isn't so smart."

It was a rare moment, but Red had no snappy reply. He was glad that Billy Don probably couldn't hear this exchange.

"You can leave now," Syd said.

"I peed all over the money," Red said, which was just stupid, but it was all he could think of, and he walked back to the Ranchero with his face burning.

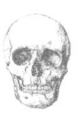

"What the hell?" Colby said, looking through binoculars and seeing Billy Don Craddock's old Ford Ranchero parked next to the black van. "No way. They can't be."

He and Dixie were parked at a convenience store across the highway and catty-corner from the motel. The sun was low in the sky behind Colby's truck, so it was currently bathing the motel room doors in light.

"What?" Dixie said. "Who is it?"

"A couple of local buffoons," Colby said. "But there's no way they're mixed up with these guys."

Sure enough, Red O'Brien was standing on the passenger side of the Ranchero, talking to a man standing in the motel room doorway.

"You saw this guy in Columbus?" Colby asked. "The guy in the doorway."

He handed the binoculars to Dixie and she raised them to her eyes.

"Absolutely. One hundred percent. Tell me about these local buffoons."

"They're garden-variety rednecks," Colby said. "They poach and drive drunk and trespass and occasionally steal things. But something like this…"

"Not their style?"

"I wouldn't think so. But maybe I'm wrong. Or maybe there's something else going on. They always seem to be in the middle of everything in one way or another. If they are involved with your two guys, I can't imagine how or why."

After a short conversation, O'Brien leaned into the Ranchero and emerged with some kind of overnight bag, which he carried over to the man by the door. They had a few more words, and then O'Brien handed the bag to the man, returned to the Ranchero. Craddock reversed it, took a left on Tenth, then a right onto the highway.

Now Colby had a decision to make. Stay here and watch the motel, hoping for a chance to follow the two men to someplace isolated and confront them. Or follow Red O'Brien and Billy Don Craddock and ask them what the hell was going on. What was in the bag? How did they know the men in the motel room? Could they give him useful information? Even if they could, would they do it willingly?

34

Red didn't place Syd's .380 gently on the ground; he dropped it to the pavement, unloaded, as Billy Don reversed out of the parking spot.

"What was that he said at the end?" Billy Don asked as he pulled back onto the highway.

"Huh?"

"I thought I heard him call you a sucker," Billy Don said.

"No, he said he had been a sucker," Red said.

"He was a sucker about what?"

"Hell, I can't even remember what we were talking about."

They had just reached the outskirts of town when Billy Don said, "Is that Phil Colby behind us?"

Red turned and saw a maroon F-250 approaching fast. Sure enough, it was Phil Colby. And there was a woman in the passenger seat—possibly the same woman who'd been riding with Colby the other day, when Red had seen him going north in Johnson City.

Now Colby flashed his headlights, and Billy Don said, "Is he wanting me to get out of the way or pull over?"

"No idea."

"I'm gonna pull over."

Billy Don turned right on San Saba Court, then took another right into the little parking lot behind the Countywide Title office, which was closed at this hour.

Colby parked in a spot, so Billy Don did, too. All three men got out and met behind Colby's truck, but the woman stayed where she was.

Red said, "What's up?" but Colby didn't shake hands or say hello.

Instead, he said, "I need to ask you a question, and I need a straight answer. No bullshit. It's really important. Can y'all do that for me?"

"I guess we can try," Red said.

Billy Don grunted.

Sure, the three men had some bad blood between them, but they were always civil enough when they encountered one another. Red always got the feeling Colby was one of the few men alive who intimidated Billy Don physically, even though Billy Don had at least a hundred-pound advantage. Colby had a way of carrying himself that showed he was prepared to handle himself in any situation. Like now. Just the way he was standing there made Red feel like Colby was going to get what he needed one way or another.

"How do y'all know the men in that motel room?" Colby asked.

Red sure as hell hadn't expected *that* question. Why did Colby want to know—

Then Red had a sudden suspicion about the woman in Colby's truck.

"Long story," Red said. "How much you want?"

"All of it," Colby said.

"We might've, uh, committed a small crime here or there," Red said.

"I won't say a word," Colby said.

So Red told Colby the whole thing, starting with the black van scraping Red's truck, then Jorge identifying the fake money, and Red's idea to lure the men away from the motel room, and so on, and ending with Red giving the Braniff bag back to Syd. Occasionally, Billy Don filled in a detail or two along the way. The entire tale took about fifteen minutes. Colby listened patiently the entire time, his expression unchanging until Red mentioned Syd's last comment—the one about the second tracker in the Braniff bag. That was important, Red could tell, but he didn't know why.

Colby said, "Did he appear injured?"

"After I punched him in the face, he did," Billy Don said proudly. "One eye's swollen shut."

"Before that," Colby said.

"I noticed blood on the bed, and on the back of his shirt," Red said. "Did you do something to him?"

"Shot him with my twelve gauge," Colby said.

Typical Colby. Instead of involving his best friend, John Marlin, the game warden, or the sheriff, Bobby Garza, he'd handled it himself.

"Birdshot or buckshot?" Billy Don asked.

"Buckshot," Colby said.

"Outstanding."

"When this guy heard you read the text about having one more day to find her, how did he react?"

It made Red feel important that he was helping Colby out.

"He said it was a text from a weird friend and it didn't mean anything. Like it was a joke or something."

Colby didn't answer right away. There was obviously more to the story that Red and Billy Don didn't know. Maybe Colby would tell them what it was about someday.

Colby finally said, "Okay, I really do appreciate it."

He turned to leave, but Red said, "That's the woman he's looking for, right? In your truck?"

Colby faced him again. "That's a long story—one I can't share right now."

"Okay. Yeah. I get it. But do you need any help? We'll both help, if you need it."

"Hell, yeah, we will," Billy Don said.

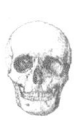

Two hours later, Colby was still trying to decide if he had made a terrible mistake. Or was it the smartest possible move in a desperate situation?

Two extra sets of eyes.

Two extra pairs of hands.

It was the two brains that worried him.

On the other hand, they had already given him useful information, like the fact that there was a second tracker inside Dixie's backpack. He had felt around, squeezing and pinching, and sure enough, there it was, sewn into the lining low on one side. The men in the motel room—Syd and Nicky, according to Red O'Brien and Billy Don Craddock—had made a small incision in the interior of the backpack, slipped the AirTag into the newly created pocket, and glued it shut. It wasn't perfect, but you couldn't see it unless you inspected the interior lining carefully, and why would you do that?

He and Dixie had discussed what they'd learned. Then they'd weighed their options: run or fight? It would be easy enough to take off and avoid the men for the night, but then what? Just because these two particular men might leave didn't mean it would be over. On the other hand, if Colby and Dixie decided to fight, they had information now that they might never have again. They knew the men were almost certain to make another attempt tonight. They had to; they were being pressured from above. They had a time limit.

Dixie wanted to fight. Hadn't wavered for a second. Do it now.

So they'd devised a plan. Not the greatest plan ever, but it would have to do, and even if he came up with a better idea, it would probably be too late to make changes.

Now the backpack was inside Colby's metal barn, more than five hundred yards from the house. Bait. Nobody was in the barn right now, but Colby had left a light on and a small radio playing. The big sliding door was unlocked and open about two feet.

The sun had set a few hours earlier, rendering it pitch dark outside, but the waning moon would be above the tree line soon, nearly three-quarters full, and there would be plenty of natural light then. The two men would want that light, so they wouldn't come before then. Way too dark for them to fumble around in strange territory.

Colby had taken O'Brien and Craddock up on their offer and given them one simple job. Now they were parked at the same convenience store Colby and Dixie had visited earlier to watch the motel. If the men left in the van—or even on foot—O'Brien and Craddock were supposed to alert Colby. But don't get spotted first. Or do anything else. Don't confront the men. Don't follow them. Don't try to stop them or divert them or confuse them. Just text Colby and then wait some more, in case he might ask them to do something else. Like what? Who knows? But just stay put unless Colby told them to move.

Now Colby and Dixie were in the living room, waiting.

"Maybe they won't come," Dixie said.

"You might be right. Maybe they won't."

"But you think they will."

"Yep. Supposedly they have just one more day."

"If they do leave the motel, how much time will we have to get ready?"

"Minimum of fifteen minutes, but possibly a lot more. They'll need to park the van somewhere, and I'm betting they won't use the same spot as last night. Then they'll need to sneak all the way to the barn, most likely without a flashlight. That could take an hour. But I also left the gate open. They might decide to drive right on through."

"What time is it now?" Dixie asked.

Colby realized she was asking questions simply because she was anxious. So was he. Who wouldn't be?

"Ten twenty-five," Colby said.

Five minutes passed.

"If we kill them...then what?"

"Meaning, do we report it?"

"I already figured the answer to that is no. What I mean is, what will we do with the bodies?"

"I have a tractor with a backhoe," Colby said.

Even in the rock-hard Texas soil, he knew some spots near the creek where the digging would be much easier. He could put them at least four or five feet deep.

"I can't believe we're even talking about this," Dixie said. "What about the van?"

"I could crush it," Colby said. "Bury it, too."

"I would feel guilty about it for the rest of my life," Dixie said. "I don't care what they did."

"I can understand that," Colby said. "I guess I probably would, too."

He found himself thinking of his best friend John Marlin, and how incredibly angry he would be if he knew what was happening right now. But what was the reasonable, realistic alternative? There was none that Colby could see.

"Could be a long night," Colby said. "If you want to sleep, go right ahead. It's been a long day."

"I don't think I can. Not right now."

"Then how about a rousing game of Scrabble?" Colby asked.

35

A stakeout required a good supply of food and drinks, so Red and Billy Don had brought an ice chest filled with Keystone Light, along with a variety of snacks, including Slim Jims, honey-roasted peanuts, and pork rinds. If they wanted more later, they were out of luck, because the store was closed.

Now they were in Red's truck, which Syd and Nicky had already seen, but at this distance and at this hour, they wouldn't be able to make it out. Red hadn't had much choice, because Syd and Nicky had also seen Billy Don's Ranchero and Mandy's Nissan.

It was nearly midnight when Red went behind the convenience store to take a leak, and after he was done, when he came around the side of the building, he froze. A dark Toyota Camry was parked two spots over from Red's truck, on the driver's side. It had reversed into a spot, just as Red had done, so Red was looking at the rear bumper. He could see two people in the front seats, or was it just the driver? Hard to tell. No, the passenger's head just moved, so two people.

Meanwhile, Red couldn't see Billy Don through the rear window of the truck. Had he gotten out? Or was he hunkered down, out of sight?

Red stood in place for a long moment, trying to decide what to do. Chances were slim that anyone inside the Camry had seen him. He slowly backed up and went behind the store again.

He pulled his phone out and saw that Billy Don had sent him a text: *Stay where u are a car is here a camry and I don't know who or why maybe you heard it turn in*

Before Red could respond, another one showed up: *I'm laying flat on the seat where they can't see me*

Red's reply was quick and short: *Stay down until they leave*

Why was that Camry parked there? Drug deal? Some kind of pervert hookup? Car trouble? And why did it look familiar? It was a gray or brown Camry and there were a lot of them on the road...but still, he had seen one just like it recently.

Oh, right. When he and Billy Don had pulled out of the motel parking lot this afternoon, a brown Camry had been coming north on 281 and had to hit the brakes.

Kind of a weird coincidence. But there was no way it was the same car. Couldn't be.

Another text arrived from Billy Don: *It's the same camry from earlier*

Red replied: *Yeah, I know*

Billy Don said: *But who the hell are they*

Red said: *Got no idea all we can do is wait and see what they do*

Fortunately, Red could still see the motel room from where he was. If Syd and Nicky left in the van, he'd know it.

A minute later, Billy Don said: *I got to piss real bad*

Red grinned at Billy Don's misfortune, until he realized how this situation might end up. Billy Don would use it as an excuse to pee all over the floorboard, and he would laugh about it later.

So Red sent a reply: *Use a beer can*

A minute later, Billy Don said: *Piss into that little opening while laying sideways yeah right*

Red said: *Then hold it but stop texting so I can watch the Camry*

He put his phone back into his pocket, then edged slowly along the side of the store. The rear of the Camry gradually came into view. Now he could see the back of the driver's seat, and then the passenger seat. Both people were sitting quietly. Very little movement.

Time passed. Slowly.

It occurred to Red that either of the two people in the car might also need to take a leak at any given moment, so he might need to scurry around the side of the building and find a hiding spot.

More time passed. The moon was low in the sky over the little resale shop across the highway. Pretty soon, with the added light, it would be easier for the men in the Camry to see Red in their mirrors, if he wasn't careful.

Red's feet were beginning to ache from standing in one spot without moving.

Then a light appeared in a doorway of a room at the motel, near the end of the building. Syd and Nicky's room? Had to be. Red couldn't tell from here without binoculars. Then the light went away. Had one or both men come outside? Were they still outside or back inside?

The night was quiet and still. No wind. That's why Red was able to hear an engine starting at the motel. It idled for a moment. Then headlights popped on and washed the motel with light. The van. No question. Red could see it now.

It backed up slowly, took a left onto Tenth Street, then took a right onto Highway 281, going north. Phil Colby's ranch was in that direction.

Red slipped behind the building again and texted Phil Colby, copying Billy Don, too: *Van just left, coming your way*

Then Red heard another engine starting. Much closer. Right around the corner of the building. The Camry.

They hadn't actually played Scrabble. That had been a joke. Instead, they'd scrolled through the channels until they'd landed on the movie *Arthur*, midway through. Colby had always enjoyed that movie. Hilarious, if a little dated. So many great lines that Colby was able to lose himself in the story for a bit. Perry's wife was, obviously, the worst.

Then a group text arrived from Red O'Brien: *Van just left, coming your way*

It was nearly one o'clock in the morning.

"What?" Dixie asked.

"They're coming. They just left the motel."

Colby was about to reply, thanking O'Brien, when a second text arrived: *A Camry was sitting at the same store as us watching and it just left too also going north two men in it couldn't get a good look at them probably following the van*

Colby didn't know what to think. Who were these people? Was it a coincidence? This could ruin the plan entirely.

Then a third text from O'Brien: *Want us to follow it*

Colby quickly sent a reply. *Hang on.*

"Know anyone who drives a Camry?" Colby asked Dixie.

"I mean, sure, back home, I guess. But not here, obviously."

"Does Mark or Lionel drive one?"

"No. What's going on?"

"Someone in a Camry just followed the van. Supposedly. These guys could be wrong, though."

"You think they are?"

"I have no idea. Got any guesses who might be following your followers?"

"None whatsoever, but if they were giving this guy Syd just one more day to find me, maybe they sent somebody else to complete the job. Or maybe Syd and Nicky and the men in the Camry are all working together. I'm just guessing. I have no idea."

Time was ticking. Colby needed to decide what to do. If he waited much longer, O'Brien and Craddock might lose the Camry.

Yes follow them. Then he added: *Keep your distance and don't let them know you're following. If it gets too obvious, bail out.*

O'Brien sent a thumbs-up.

Colby said: *How many men in van?*

O'Brien said: *I think one only heard one car door*

Colby said: *Keep me posted and don't do anything that will get you shot.*

O'Brien didn't reply.

Dixie said, "You look a little rattled."

"Yeah, because we're relying on buffoons, and I don't feel good about it. If they're right and the Camry follows the van out here, that changes things, no matter who's in it."

"So what're we gonna do?" Dixie asked. "Follow the plan or scrap it?"

If they were going to get into position, they needed to get moving soon. If they were going to run, they should leave right now.

"I think you need to make that decision," Colby said. "I'm with you either way."

Keep in mind that you might not get another shot like this, because we know the van is coming, he wanted to add, but he kept it to himself.

"I'm so tired of running," she said. "Let's do this."

"That means we might have to wing it—if the Camry shows up, too," Colby said.

"Then let's wing the hell out of it."

Traffic was light.

Syd could see the headlights of one vehicle behind him on the highway, maybe three hundred yards back, and another one beyond that. A couple of vehicles passed him on the other side of the highway, heading south. Late-night travelers? People going home from bars?

To Syd's right, the moon was well above the trees. Plenty of light. He probably wouldn't need a flashlight. He would be able to find the big metal barn easily enough. That's where the woman was hiding out for the night, according to the second AirTag in her backpack. Made sense. Maybe Colby was with her, or maybe he wasn't. Did that mean they were expecting Syd, or were they simply being cautious after last night? Either way, they wouldn't expect Syd to know exactly where she was holed up, so this should be his best chance. His last chance, too, but he tried not to think about that.

Nicky had offered to come with him again, but Syd said no. Not after last night. Nicky was a pain in the ass and a weirdo, but damn it, he was Syd's brother, and Syd didn't want to get him killed. When Syd had left the motel, he had wondered if he would ever see Nicky again.

He began to slow because his turn was coming up. Miller Creek Loop. He got into the left lane and used his blinker. Don't give a deputy or a trooper a reason to pull him over. This time of night, they'd be out cruising for drunks. Looking for reasons to make traffic stops.

Syd braked gently and took a left on the narrow county road. Drove real slow.

He watched in the rearview mirror as the vehicle that had been behind him continued north on the highway, toward Johnson City.

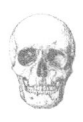

Fernando could see the headlights of one vehicle behind him on the highway, maybe three hundred yards back. When the black van ahead of him turned left on Miller Creek Loop, Fernando knew he couldn't follow without being obvious, so he continued north on the highway. Fortunately, he found a turnaround in the median just two hundred yards ahead. He quickly made a U-turn, hurried back to Miller Creek Loop, and took a right. Now if Syd saw headlights in his mirrors, he would simply think it was some other vehicle, not the one that had been behind him on the highway from Blanco. For the moment, Fernando had no choice but to drive much faster than the speed limit to catch up with the van.

The plan was to get Syd at gunpoint. Bind his hands. Abandon the van and put him in the passenger seat of the Camry. Armando would ride in back. Then they would begin the drive to Laredo. There, they would present Syd to Draco and be done with this debacle.

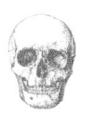

Red wasn't sure what to think.

When the van turned left onto Miller Creek Loop, the Camry kept going north on 281. But then it made a U-turn—so it was definitely following Syd and trying not to be obvious about it.

Red had no choice but to also continue straight on 281, so the men in the Camry wouldn't know he and Billy Don were following them. Fortunately, there was a second turnaround up ahead, and by the time Red made a U-turn, the Camry had already turned right onto Miller Creek Loop.

"Tell Colby what's happening," Red said.

"Already on it," Billy Don said with his phone in his hands. He recited the message as he typed it. "Van...and Camry...both on...Miller Creek."

Red heard that little sound an iPhone makes when a text is sent.

"Tell him we're following," Red said.

"We're...following," Billy Don said, followed by the little text sound again. Then he said, "What happens now?"

"I got no idea," Red said, as he turned off his headlights and took a right on the county road. "I really don't."

36

Colby was kneeling behind a large, tall cedar tree sixty yards to the west of the metal barn. He would've preferred to be closer, but that was the best available cover. There were no other trees closer.

He was armed with a shotgun, a .270 deer rifle, and his Glock. From here, he was on a line almost parallel to the front of the barn, but at just enough angle that he could see the sliding door and the light coming from the interior.

His phone was in easy reach, but he had the display set to dark mode—white text on a black background. Less light that way, so a lower chance he would give himself away.

He had also adjusted the settings to keep everything silent, with one exception. Any call from Dixie would ring. They both knew there might be times when Colby couldn't check his phone, so they'd agreed that if she absolutely needed to reach him immediately, she would call.

Texts, on the other hand, came in with just a vibration. The most recent text from Billy Don Craddock said the black van and the Camry were on Miller Creek Loop, and he and O'Brien were following.

Surely Syd would soon figure out he was being followed, as would the men in the Camry. O'Brien and Craddock might be skilled poachers, but that didn't mean they were good with surveillance.

Colby sent a quick text: *Can you follow with your headlights off?*

O'Brien had grown up in this county, driving these back roads, day and night, well before he even had a license. Headlights? Hell, he could probably drive the road blindfolded.

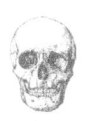

"Haha," Billy Don said. "He's asking if you can follow with your headlights off."

"Tell him—"

"Yeah, I got it. Already...doing...that," Billy Don said as he typed.

Now Red reached under his seat for his secret weapon—a switch that disabled his brake lights. Brilliant. It was an idea he had stolen directly from game wardens who had busted him. Red found it useful when he and Billy Don were cruising the roads late at night, looking for deer. Red had no idea what the penalty was for installing a switch like that, but he figured as long as he always remembered to flip the switch back on, he wouldn't get caught. Why would any cop ever look for a switch like that under the seat?

Red goosed the gas, and a minute later, after rounding a curve, he saw the taillights of the Camry maybe two hundred feet ahead. Red eased off the gas so they wouldn't get too close. If the van was ahead of the Camry, Red couldn't see it.

"Where's Syd going, you think?" Billy Don asked. "Gotta be Colby's, right?"

"I would think so."

"I mean, if he's not going there, where's he going?"

"I don't know."

"He wouldn't go all the way back to Johnson City, would he?" Billy Don asked.

"Would you stop asking questions?" Red said. "I'm trying to think things through. Let's just wait and see."

A few minutes passed.

Billy Don said, "Colby's place is right around the next curve, so if the van stops, we'll know, because the Camry will hit his brakes."

Red didn't say anything.

The Camry kept going. No brakes. All the way around the curve.

Red touched the gas again, but Billy Don said, "Wait a second. Wait a second."

"Huh?"

"Think about it. Do we really need to keep following?"

"Why wouldn't we?"

"Syd's either gonna turn around, in which case he might bust us, because we'll pass right by him, or he's gonna go around to the back side of the ranch, like he did last night, is what Colby said. If he does that, we'll know, since he won't come back this way."

"So what're you saying?"

"That it makes more sense to wait here and see if he comes back."

Damn it, that *did* make sense. Except for one thing.

"What if the dudes in the Camry do something?"

"Like what?"

"Pull out an AR-15 and blow that van to smithereens."

"In which case we'll hear it, and Colby will hear it, and most all of the neighbors will hear it."

Red kept thinking.

Billy Don said, "Better decide pretty quick, because the van could be turning around right now, and when he gets back, we're gonna be sitting smack in the road like a couple of raccoon turds."

Damn it. There was no clear answer. The men in the Camry were screwing everything up. Who were they? Why were they here?

Red turned through Colby's open gate and immediately pulled off the driveway, heading across a grassy area toward a cluster of oaks and cedars that would shield the truck from view.

"Tell Colby," Red said, but Billy Don was already tapping away on his phone.

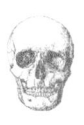

Colby was waiting quietly, knowing it could be a long night, when another text arrived from Craddock: *Van and camry passed your gate and now we're hiding just inside your entrance in case they come back because if we kept following they could of recconized the truck if they turned around*

Colby appreciated the updates, but good Lord, couldn't they use spell check and some occasional punctuation?

He sent back a thumbs-up emoji. O'Brien and Craddock had made the right choice.

What was Syd going to do? Enter the ranch from the county road on the back side, just as he'd done last night?

Colby quickly sent an update to Dixie.

Syd knew something wasn't right. When he'd turned onto Miller Creek Loop, the vehicle behind him on the highway had continued north, toward Johnson City. But within one minute, headlights had appeared in his rearview mirror again. Was he being paranoid? Where had that vehicle come from?

Now it was lingering behind him, staying at least fifty yards back. Was it those two idiot rednecks again? Who else would it be?

Maybe it was just some random person who lived on this road. Colby's gate was coming up, so Syd had to make a decision. He continued past it. So did the vehicle behind him.

Syd had to fight the urge to panic. Nothing good would happen if he panicked.

He kept his speed consistent. Tried to think. What were his options? If he simply pulled over and let the vehicle pass, that would be too conspicuous. It wasn't like they were following closely, so why would he pull over? Out here in the country, they might stop to see if he needed help.

He knew if he stayed on this road, it would take him on a winding path all the way to Johnson City. Screw that.

He was quickly approaching a left turn—the same turn he had taken last night. Blue Ridge Road. He couldn't remember where that road ended up. He hadn't needed to know that last night. He had only gone far enough to access the rear of Colby's ranch.

He eased off the gas and turned left. Crawled along at ten miles per hour.

The other vehicle was still on Miller Creek Loop—but it slowed and took the same turn.

Fuck.

It was nearly two o'clock in the morning in the middle of nowhere, and surely this wasn't a coincidence. Was he being stalked?

He followed the road, which was even narrower than Miller Creek Loop.

He came to a fork, but the road to the left was obviously a private entrance, complete with a closed gate. Syd stayed right and hoped the vehicle behind him would go left. But it followed him, now less than twenty yards back, not even pretending anymore.

The road dipped and then curved slightly left, and then it was blocked by a white wooden gate. A sign on a cross-brace read SELAH. There was nowhere to go. Syd was trapped.

Maybe...

Maybe the people in the vehicle behind him owned this ranch. Syd would tell them he was lost. He didn't know the road dead-ended. Could they back up and let him turn around?

He could see in his rearview mirror that somebody was getting out of the passenger side of the car behind him. It was a sedan of some kind.

Syd had been carrying one of his handguns between his legs, but now he quickly leaned down and slipped it under the seat. He lowered his window.

The person passed behind the van and was now approaching along the driver's side.

Syd waited and tried to smile. "Good evening," he would say. "I'm all turned around. Am I blocking your gate?"

Now there was a face in the open window, and for the tiniest sliver of time, Syd was confused.

This person was completely out of place. Unexpected. What was happening?

"Hey," Syd said. "I don't understand."

Armando raised a snub-nosed revolver and pressed the muzzle flat against Syd's forehead.

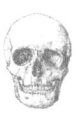

"Maybe they're not coming back," Billy Don said.

"Maybe not, but we already helped by letting Colby know they didn't enter through the gate."

"Maybe so, but it doesn't—"

"Shhh!" Red said.

Twenty-seven minutes after Red and Billy Don had parked the truck behind the trees, they saw headlights coming from the north, moving slowly along Miller Creek Loop.

"Is that it?" Billy Don asked.

"I can't tell," Red said.

The men were standing under a large oak, well in the shadows. If they'd stayed in the truck, they wouldn't have been able to see anything through the thick cluster of trees. Red had brought along his Colt Anaconda, just in case.

"It's slowing down," Billy Don said.

Red could hear the faint squeal of brakes, and the vehicle took a right through Colby's open gate. It was entering the ranch.

"Hot damn," Billy Don said. "Here it comes. Red, it's coming."

As the vehicle got closer, Red could see that it was in fact the black van. By itself. No Camry following.

Red had no idea what to make of that.

He opened his mouth, but Billy Don said, "Already on it," tapping out a text on his phone.

The van kept going, past the trees, and a moment later, the taillights disappeared into the night.

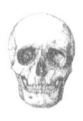

Van just pulled thru your gate coming up your driveway can't see it anymore not sure where the camry is right now will let you know if it shows up

Was this good news or bad news? Where was the Camry?

Colby sent Dixie another update.

Twenty minutes passed.

Syd was on foot by now, for sure.

If he was stupid, he would turn right off the main driveway and follow the road that led directly to the barn, which would allow Colby to see him coming. If Syd was a bit smarter, he would forego the road, sneak through the trees, and come in from a different angle. If he had done that, he could already be somewhere nearby, watching the barn's sliding door.

Colby would bet on the former—but he wouldn't bet much.

He saw movement by the barn door. Dixie had stepped outside.

She walked to Colby's old truck, opened the passenger door, got something from inside, then returned to the barn. Pure theater. She was bait. Her idea.

Her thinking—and she was probably right—was that Syd would not approach the barn if he didn't see some sign of activity. He would suspect it might be a trap, unless he actually saw Dixie.

"He might just shoot you without any warning," Colby had said earlier.

"He might not be here to shoot me," Dixie said. "If he is, you're the one who pointed out that he has a handgun, not a rifle. He'll want to be up close."

Which was true, but it didn't make him feel any more comfortable with the plan.

Ten more minutes passed.

Then Colby saw two dark figures moving slowly along the driveway. Two, not one. Syd must've brought his brother. O'Brien and Craddock had said only one man had gotten into the van at the motel, but at that distance, they easily could've been mistaken.

Well, hell, this sure complicated things.

Time to wing it.

First, he sent a text to warn Dixie.

37

"We could make ourselves useful," Billy Don whispered. "Instead of just sitting here."

"And do what?"

"Walk up the driveway and see if we spot the van. I mean, he couldn't have been dumb enough to drive all the way to the house, right?"

"And if we find it, then what?"

"We tell Colby."

"Who will already have figured the guy was gonna park it somewhere along the way, just like you said. How will that be useful?"

Billy Don didn't say anything.

"But now I'm thinking of something that *would* be useful," Red said.

"What?"

"We find the van and flatten all the tires."

"Let's do it," Billy Don said.

They slowly emerged from the trees and began to follow the curving driveway toward Phil Colby's house.

"Should we tell Colby what we're doing?" Billy Don asked.

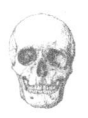

Two men coming, eighty yards out.

Dixie replied with a thumbs-up.

Was she really ready for this? Was she terrified right now? Colby could take the heat off her.

He braced the barrel of the .270 against the tree trunk and tried to find the men in his scope. Not easy, even with the moonlight. If he could get one of them in the crosshairs, maybe he would take him down. Then the other man would almost certainly cut and run.

Didn't matter, because a cloud had covered the moon and Colby couldn't see either man right now. He lowered the rifle and tried to find them with binoculars, which had a wider field of view.

Too dark.

Colby heard his phone vibrate with a text, but he ignored it. He couldn't look at his phone right now. The light from the screen, even muted, would make it harder for his eyes to readjust afterward and spot the men.

A sound came from inside the barn. A hammering or thumping. More theater from Dixie, making it obvious she was in there. Or maybe she was making noise as she proceeded with her part of the plan.

Just for reassurance, Colby reached down and found the steel cable on the ground. No, it hadn't moved. It was still there. Ready.

Finally, the cloud drifted on. More light. And movement again. Forty yards from the barn. Both men, but keeping some distance between themselves. On different sides of the caliche road. Stealthy. Slow. Picking each step carefully.

Was this really going to work? It all seemed so transparent to Colby right now—such an obvious trap. But Syd had been chasing Dixie for so long, maybe he was willing to take some risks to finally catch her.

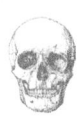

Red, in the lead, stopped walking and held up his left hand. His .45 was in his right.

They had just come around a curve in the driveway and there was the van, hunkered in the darkness no more than thirty yards ahead. All Red could see were the rear doors, and there was no way to tell if Syd was still in the front. Surely, he was long gone, though, right? Why would he park and then just sit there? Unless he was working up the nerve to approach the house. And how dumb was he not to have turned it around for a quick getaway?

Red moved forward as quietly as possible, but the soles of his boots crunched on the caliche driveway. Billy Don was even louder. Red moved off the road into the tall grass, but it wasn't much quieter.

When they were five yards away from the van, Red heard something. He stopped in his tracks. A grunt? A groan?

There it was again. From inside the van.

"MMmmmm!"

"Somebody's in there," Billy Don whispered.

Now they heard a thump—like somebody had banged the side of the van with an elbow. Again. And a third time.

"And they know we're out here," Billy Don said. "They heard us. What if it's Colby?"

"No way is it Colby," Red said. "How would it be Colby? That doesn't make any sense."

"Prob'ly not, but we gotta see who it is," Billy Don said.

"Well, yeah, obviously."

The person banged on the side of the van again.

"And it's your turn," Billy Don said.

"Huh?"

"I went first into the motel room," Billy Don said. "So now you check this out. If you have the balls."

"Oh, I have the balls," Red said.

"That's damn brave of you, considering you might get your face blown off."

"Just shut up, okay?" Red hissed.

Surprisingly, Billy Don shut up.

Red moved oh-so-slowly toward the van, and a moment later, he was within arm's reach of the handle that would open the double rear doors.

Then, instead of being sneaky, Red spoke loudly. "Whoever's in there: I'm about to open the rear door. You'd better be cool, because we're both armed like a son of a bitch."

"All four of us!" Billy Don said.

Jesus. So stupid.

Red grabbed the door handle. Held it for a second. Then yanked the door open. The rear cargo space was immediately bathed with light. As expected, there was Syd. He was prone on the carpeted floor of the van with his arms secured behind his back with duct tape. His legs were also bound, and he had several loops around his head, covering his mouth. His eye was still swollen shut and the bruising on his face had gotten even worse.

"Mmmm!" he said.

"That's the smartest thing I've ever heard you say," Red said.

He handed his revolver to Billy Don and hopped into the van. Then he unwrapped the tape around Syd's head, unavoidably taking quite a bit of hair in the process.

"Ow, damn it!"

"The price of freedom," Red said.

"Now my hands," Syd said. "My shoulders are killing me."

"Not so fast," Red said. "Who are the men in the Camry?"

"Long story, but they're killers. You gotta cut me loose or I'm a dead man."

"Killers for who?" Red said.

"I can't tell you all that, but right now they are on their way to kill a woman and maybe kill the man she's with."

"The lady with Phil Colby?" Red asked.

"Yeah. Now cut me loose."

"Billy Don," Red said, but Billy Don was already on it, sending another text to Colby.

"We gotta get out of here," Syd said. "All of us. They'll kill you, too."

"Why are they after that lady?" Red asked.

"I'll tell you everything, but we gotta go!" Syd said. "Before they get back."

"Where's the Camry?" Red asked.

"We don't have time for all this bullshit," Syd said. "Just take me somewhere else, even if you don't cut me loose. You gotta hurry. You don't know who you're messing with."

Red glanced to the front of the van and saw that the keys were in the ignition.

"Any answer from Colby?" he asked Billy Don.

"Nope."

Red looked at Syd. "The only way you're getting out of here is if you answer my questions."

"Okay, but hurry, man. Hurry."

Red knew he couldn't get the full story from Syd right now. There wasn't time for it. So what should he ask first? Think. He had to help Colby and the woman.

"Do these two killers know where Colby and the woman are?"

"They know where she is, for sure," Syd said. "Or where she was an hour ago."

"How do they know that?"

"Because I told them. They put a gun to my head and forced me."

"So where is she?"

"In a barn about five hundred yards east of Colby's house. He might be in there, too."

"And how did you know that?" Red asked. "Oh, wait. Shit. Is it one of those trackers?"

"AirTag, yeah," Syd said.

"You're a devious little fucker, aren't you?" Red said. "Is she still there?"

"I don't know. I turned my phone off before I left the motel."

"But you brought it?" Red said.

He could tell from Syd's hesitation that the answer was yes, but he didn't want to admit it. He had brought it along in case of some unforeseen emergency, but he still didn't want it turned on, so the cops couldn't connect his phone to the nearest cell tower.

"Where is it?" Red asked. His knees were starting to ache from hunching over in the back of the van.

"Fuck," Syd said, giving in. "The pocket in the side of the driver's door."

Billy Don went around the side of the van, opened the door, and found the phone.

"Turn it on?" he said.

"Yep," Red said.

"You gonna cut me loose or what?" Syd asked.

"Not yet. We can see if the woman's still in the barn, right?"

"Yeah, there's an app," Syd said. "If there's somebody nearby with an iPhone, like Colby."

They waited for the phone to finish booting up.

Billy Don had come back to the rear of the van, and now he said. "You got a text from some guy named Mark about ten minutes ago. A long one."

"We don't have time for that," Red said.

"No, no," Syd said. "Read it. What does it say?"

Five seconds passed.
"Holy shit," Billy Don said.
"Out loud!" Syd said.

Colby's phone vibrated yet again with an incoming text, and he still couldn't take the time to check it. Probably O'Brien and Craddock, wondering if they could do anything else to help.

Now one of the men had stopped behind the trunk of an oak tree, forty feet from the barn door, while the other slowly advanced, easy to see in the binoculars, thanks to the moonlight and the light from the barn.

By now, Dixie had scurried up a ladder to the loft and pulled it up after her. She had a radio playing in the barn that would've masked any small sounds she might've made or might make in the next few minutes.

The lead man was twenty feet from the barn door now.

Then fifteen.

He stopped.

Colby could see now that he was carrying a handgun. Looked like an automatic, but it was hard to tell, even through the binoculars.

Colby quickly checked on the other man, who was still hiding behind the trunk of the oak tree.

Colby swung the binoculars back to the first man, who was moving again, incredibly slowly. He was obviously wanting to reach the open door and have a good look inside before being detected.

One step.

Another step.

And so on.

Until he reached the door and peered inside. He stood unmoving for three solid minutes, just looking for any sign of Dixie.

The radio was in the back, in a corner that was blocked from view by a floor-to-ceiling shelf that held various tools and small equipment.

Colby grabbed the looped end of the galvanized steel cable. Five-sixteenths of an inch in diameter and two hundred feet long. Constructed from seven strands that gave it a working load limit just under two thousand pounds and a breaking strength of nearly five tons. Despite its suitability for the task at hand, the total weight of the cable was only thirty-seven pounds. Considerably less than a bag of cattle cubes. The steel felt slick in Colby's sweaty hand.

The man at the door of the barn looked backward, as if to confirm that his fellow thug hadn't bailed on him. Then he faced the door again and, after another pause, he took one cautious step inside. Then another, and he was no longer visible.

Colby waited five seconds, then he moved backward swiftly, pulling the cable with both hands, as if he were in a tug-of-war, and he slammed the door of the barn closed.

38

Hey Syd, enough of this bullshit. You shouldn't have dragged my wife into this. Right now I'm outside a sheriff's office and I'm about to go tell them I grew an illegal crop of weed and sold a lot of it. Way over felony level. And I'm going to tell them where to find the grow site. I'm confessing to it all. But I'm not going to tell them who I sold it to or who you work for as long as Dixie isn't harmed. So just leave her the fuck alone, you hear me? Maybe, once I know she's going to be okay, I'll give you the information you want. Tell that to your boss, too. Don't bother responding. I'm turning this phone off and going inside.

"I don't believe it," Syd said. "That crazy son of a bitch."

Red didn't understand every part of the text, except that it would protect the woman with Colby, who was named Dixie. Her husband was turning himself in to save her.

"Give us the background info," Red said. "The short version."

"If Mark follows through, there's no reason for us to go after Dixie."

"He's gotta be talking to the cops right now," Red said.

"I don't really follow, but what're we gonna do?" Billy Don asked.

Red looked at Syd. "So if the men up at Colby's right now know about this text, what will they do?"

"They'll give up and leave."

"Just like that?"

"I'm pretty sure. But they'll wanna take me with them and I—"

Red was already climbing out of the van, and he slammed the rear doors closed.

"Hey!" Syd yelled.

"Billy Don, get in the van," Red said, as he hurried around to the driver's side. "And call Colby!"

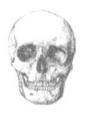

The slamming of the barn door was surprisingly loud, even from this distance.

Colby quickly looped the cable around the trunk of the cedar at ankle height, just as he'd practiced. When he was done, there was just enough cable left to hook the loop over the nail Colby had hammered into the tree earlier. Perfect. That cable wasn't going anywhere, and neither was the barn door.

Then Colby stood quietly behind the cedar for a moment. The calm was eerie. There had been no sound from inside the barn, but the man trapped inside was probably pretty freaked out.

All the windows on the ground floor of the barn were closed and locked from the inside, except for one that was open. Dixie had a clear view of that window from her hidden perch in the loft, and if the man began to climb through it, she would open fire with the shotgun. But their thinking was that the man would be hesitant to exit that window. He'd think Dixie was waiting outside, possibly with any number of armed allies. So he'd stay in the barn and text the guy behind the oak tree.

Colby's phone vibrated with a call, but he ignored it.

Colby lifted his binoculars and saw that the man was still behind the tree trunk. It was an enormous oak, with a trunk about three feet in diameter, so it provided plenty of cover. But from this angle, Colby could see the man's silhouette in the moonlight. That man most likely thought the barn door had been closed from the inside by his pal, who might have the woman caught, so he was waiting. He didn't know Colby was watching from his right.

Time to rock his world.

Colby knelt on one knee, raised the .270, and braced it against the trunk of the cedar tree. He had just enough ambient light to place the man in the crosshairs. Colby aimed for the man's chest, took a deep breath, and began to squeeze the trigger.

Was he really going to do this?

Was it murder, like Dixie had said? If so, did it matter?

Would she follow through and shoot the man inside the barn if he attempted to leave? They needed at least one of the men alive.

Now Colby was second-guessing himself. If they had two men alive, that made it twice as likely they could force one of them to talk.

Colby lowered the rifle and sighted on the man's knee. A smaller target and a tough shot under these circumstances, but he could make it. He felt better about this option. It wasn't irreversible.

Colby took another breath, held it, and once again began to squeeze the trigger. Gently. Slowly.

The rifle roared and spit a flame into the night.

The man behind the tree immediately fell to the ground.

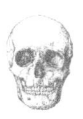

Red was proceeding along the caliche road at a moderate pace, with the headlights off. He couldn't do anything about the brake lights.

Billy Don was in the passenger seat with Syd's phone in his hand, checking on the AirTag.

Syd was still in the back, hollering to be turned loose, but Red was ignoring him.

"It shows her at the barn twenty-four minutes ago," Billy Don said. "No updates since then."

"That means Colby probably isn't with her, right?" Red said over his shoulder.

Syd didn't answer. He was pouting.

"Still nothing from Colby?" Red said.

"Nope," Billy Don said, checking his own phone now, although they would've heard a text alert if Colby had replied.

Red wanted to speed up, but he didn't want to stumble into the middle of…who knows what? They might ruin…something. Or they might somehow save the day. The problem was he had no idea what kind of trap Colby had laid. Surely he had planned some kind of trap, right?

Or maybe Colby was just waiting on a rooftop with a rifle, like the townsfolk in *High Plains Drifter*. Look how that had turned out. Red hoped Colby at least had a spotlight. Maybe the lady could hold the spotlight while Colby picked the two men off. That might work. Like road-hunting at night. Bing-bang and done.

"Tell us more about this Mark guy," Red called back to Syd, just to ease the tension they were all feeling.

"Y'all are fuckin' crazy. We should be leaving. They won't know why we're coming, so they might try to kill us all. Even when they know, they might want to kill me."

"I might cut you loose if you talk," Red said.

"Or you might not."

"True," Red said. "Depends on what you tell me."

Five seconds passed.

"Okay, this guy Mark knew how to grow some really good pot, so I told my boss about it, and he wanted Mark to tell us how he did it. For money. Like a consultant. It was going to work out for everybody until Mark's wife figured out what was happening and said she was going to report it all to the cops."

"So your boss wanted her dead for that?" Red asked.

"Yeah, but the wife was giving Mark a couple of days to talk to a lawyer first, which was stupid. My boss wanted me to find her before she talked to the cops."

"Wait a second," Billy Don said. "How did y'all figure out what the wife was saying?"

"Mark told us," Syd said.

"Holy shit," Billy Don said. "He gave her up. What kind of lowlife husband is that?"

"Yeah, but he changed his mind and warned her, and then they both hauled ass, and he ghosted me."

"So why go after her and not him?" Billy Don asked.

"I thought they were together at first," Syd said. "But it was just her, which was fine, because at the time, I figured Mark wouldn't go to the cops. I guess I was wrong about that."

"How come she never followed through and went to the cops?"

"She was too scared of what we might do to her family."

"That sounds really shitty," Billy Don said. "You need to find a better line of work."

Syd didn't reply.

They rounded a curve and Billy Don, looking at a map on his phone, said, "We need to turn here, I think. That's faster than going to the house and then going to the barn from there."

It was another caliche road—not as well traveled as the main road, but smooth and generally free of weeds and ruts.

Red took the turn.

"You were supposed to kill her?" Red said to Syd.

"Yeah, and Mark, too. I know, it sucks, but it was them or me."

"Why's that? What did you do?" Red asked.

"Made a deal directly with Mark and cut my boss out," Syd said.

"Damn, son," Billy Don said. "That was stupid."

"This was my chance to make up for it."

"So they wouldn't kill you," Red said.

"That was the idea."

"And you dragged your brother into it? That wasn't cool," Billy Don said.

Syd didn't say anything.

"And I bet the real money in the bag was in case you decided to make a run for it," Red said.

"If you knew these guys, you might run, too."

Red was really hoping Colby had killed them both by now.

"You see me running?" Red asked.

"Are you gonna cut me loose now or what?" Syd asked.

"Not yet," Red said.

The van was now just a few hundred yards from the barn, but trees prevented them from seeing it.

Red said, "So last night you tried to—"

Boom!

Red was used to rifle shots, but that one, at this particular moment, made him jump.

"Whoa," Billy Don said. "That was at the barn, I think. Hard to tell."

"So you're gonna stop now, right?" Syd asked. "Your friend is probably dead already. And maybe the woman. You wanna be next?"

39

The hay against Dixie's skin had become unbearably itchy. She was drenched with sweat, and her entire body was beginning to ache from the lack of movement. But she didn't dare move. She might make a sound and give herself away.

How did it come to this? She was a forestry technician, for crying out loud.

What would have happened if she hadn't randomly wandered onto this particular ranch?

She didn't want to kill the man below, but she would if she had to. She was prone on the floor of the loft, deep in shadows, bales of hay stacked in such a way as to create a perfect sniper's nest. At this distance, the shotgun would inflict fatal damage if she hit him in the torso, neck or head.

She didn't recognize him. Not one of the men from the van. But a danger nonetheless. Had to be. He had been pacing. Looking around the barn, expecting to see somebody with a gun. He had a gun of his own—an automatic. He carried it as if he'd been born with it in his hand.

A moment ago, he had taken out his phone and sent a text. He hadn't looked at it since, so it probably had not vibrated with a reply.

He stepped toward the open window, as he had several times before, but he stopped five feet short of it. Wary of getting shot.

He stood there a moment. Then he stepped closer—just a foot away from the window. If somebody were pressed against an outside wall, gun in hand, leveled, waiting for him to stick his head out, he wouldn't be able to see them.

He suddenly stuck one hand out and waved it up and down. Testing the waters. Risking his hand. Smart. There was, of course, no shot.

But Dixie was ready to shoot. If he started climbing out that window, she would aim for whichever part of him was exposed. His back, his butt, his head, or anything else. Take him out. She could do this. She *had* to do this.

She flinched hard as a shot thundered from not far away.

Deer rifle. Had to be. Not a handgun. That meant Phil had fired it.

The man below moved away from the window—an instinct, although the shot plainly had not been intended for him. He was becoming impatient. He went to the sliding door again and tried to push it open, but it gave no more than a few inches.

Then he checked his phone and apparently saw nothing.

Was the other man dead? If so, they needed to keep this man alive. That meant she would need to be more careful with her shot. She didn't dare risk checking her phone for a message from Phil.

Should she yell at the man to put his gun down and get on the ground? If she did, would he do it?

Maybe winging it wasn't the best idea.

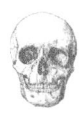

Colby kept his eye on the scope, waiting. The man was on the ground behind the tree, but he wasn't writhing or shouting in pain. Had Colby missed?

Then the man raised his pistol and fired a round blindly in Colby's direction, but he still didn't know Colby's exact location. Based on the sound of the shot, Colby guessed it was something larger, like a .357 or a .45.

Colby worked the bolt and jacked another shell into the chamber. Steadied the rifle and waited for another shot. He had hoped to incapacitate the man completely by destroying his knee, but that hadn't happened.

A full minute passed. The man stayed put.

Then another cloud covered the moon, and there was just enough light for Colby to see the man spring to his feet and run in the opposite direction of the barn.

Colby looked through the scope, but it was no use. With the movement and the lesser light, he couldn't focus on anything recognizable.

Now the man had reached the tree line and was lost into the night.

Colby dropped the rifle, grabbed the shotgun, and took off after him.

This was going to end tonight, one way or another.

Red didn't know what to think when they heard a second shot, this one sounding like a handgun.

"You're still not gonna turn around?" Syd asked. He had managed to struggle to his knees, so he could see through the windshield.

"Shut up," Billy Don said.

"Cut me loose," Syd said. "They're gonna kill me either way."

"You sure acted tough in front of the motel, and now look at you," Billy Don said.

Red kept going, around a curve, and now the barn came into view, less than one hundred yards away. There was one exterior light shining above the sliding door, and all the windows he could see were glowing with light from inside.

Red eased off the gas, but Billy Don said, "Keep going."

"I wasn't stopping," Red said.

"You were slowing down," Billy Don said.

"Not the same thing," Red said.

"It nearly was," Billy Don said. "You were creeping along."

"But still moving forward," Red said.

"This is so stupid," Syd said.

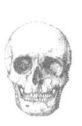

Dixie heard a second shot—not quite as loud, and north of the barn. Not from Colby.

The man below the loft heard it too, and he checked his phone again. Obviously he'd been texting his partner outside and was hoping for an update, but his glance was too quick. There was no text. He went to one of the closed windows beside the door and looked out. He wouldn't be able to see much. He certainly wouldn't be able to see Phil, who was well off to the left.

Was he dead at this point? Maybe he thought his shot earlier had hit the man, and he'd approached, and that second shot, just now, had gotten him.

The idea gave Dixie a feeling of heartache she had never experienced. If it were true, she would never forgive herself.

The waiting was terrible. The not knowing.

Dixie had the barrel pointed just inside the open window. The man wouldn't attempt to exit any other way. But he wasn't going to leave. In fact, he was letting out little moans of anguish. He had no good options—not without more information.

Try to leave the barn and get shot, knowing his partner might be perfectly fine?

Or remain inside, fearful, while his partner was outside dying?

A man like this probably wasn't used to being the hunted one. Surely it felt humiliating. Or humbling. He had never before been on the—

The man suddenly bolted for the window and dove through headfirst.

Dixie got off one roaring shot, but she was pretty sure it was too late.

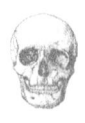

Colby could hear the man crashing through the brush, panicked, much like a wounded deer. Distance? Maybe one hundred feet.

The moon was behind a cloud again, so the light was faint, at best. Colby kept to a deer trail that meandered neatly through the trees, only requiring Colby to duck under low limbs on occasion. He knew exactly where he was and where the trail led.

They were moving westward—away from the house, the barn, and the nearest county roads. It was the worst direction for the man to flee, for several reasons. He was only going deeper into the ranch.

The sounds kept coming. Dry sticks snapping underfoot. Small rocks tumbling. Grunts of surprise as the man caught another unexpected cedar bough brushing across his face.

Colby had slowly closed the gap, and now he could hear the man's labored breathing—and then a sudden *Oopph!* as the man apparently took a spill.

Colby stopped and waited. A moment later, he heard the man rise to his feet and continue his trek, albeit a bit slower than before. If Colby's shot had hit him, it hadn't done much damage.

Colby heard a shotgun blast from the direction of the barn. Dixie.

The man ahead picked up speed, now moving at a light trot.

Colby kept moving forward, choosing each step as carefully as possible, but even knowing the land as well as he did, it was possible he could be the one to have a misstep that would end the chase.

The man came to an abrupt stop, so Colby did, too, now less than fifty feet behind. He was caught in the open, possibly somewhat visible, depending on the quality of the man's eyesight. The man was hoping to catch the sound of Colby behind him, to confirm that he was being followed.

Then the worst thing happened. The cloud moved on and both men were suddenly bathed in moonlight. The man was looking right at Colby.

Colby immediately raised his shotgun just as the man turned and dashed into another cedar break, now more frantic than ever. He had no idea he was heading for a cliff with a forty-foot drop. It couldn't be far ahead now. Maybe forty yards.

Colby had no choice but to follow as quickly as he could, deep in the cedars now, knowing he might step into a gully or an armadillo hole at any moment and break an ankle. Impossible to get a clean shot. Colby couldn't even see the man now, even though he couldn't have been far ahead.

But he could certainly hear him—especially when the man suddenly let out a shriek that chilled Colby to his core.

40

As they rolled closer to the barn in the van, everything was quiet. Where was everybody? Who had fired those shots?

Now Red came to a stop fifty feet from the northwest corner of the barn. From here they could see the front door and the windows on the west side.

"Where's Colby?" Billy Don asked.

"I don't know," Red said.

"And the woman?"

"They're both fuckin' dead," Syd said.

"Shut up," Billy Don said.

Red said, "Billy Don, it's your turn, so why don't you get out and check the—"

Red heard a shotgun blast just as a man dove headfirst out the west-side window, hit the ground, scrambled to his feet, and looked right at them.

"That's Armando!" Syd said.

Armando raised a handgun and Red reacted instinctively by mashing the gas pedal to the floor.

Red heard a shot, but by then he had slunk low in his seat and Billy Don had done the same, as best he could.

Red heard a second shot and then a heavy thump.

Red stomped the brakes and risked a quick glance over the dashboard.

Armando was scrambling to his feet again, somehow still holding the handgun, and he began to limp as quickly as he could along the length of the barn.

"What happened?" Syd yelled from the back, where he had been thrown to the floor.

"Get him, Red!" Billy Don said. "Hurry!"

Red gunned it again, hoping to reach Armando before he could round the southwest corner. It was going to be close.

Armando glanced over his shoulder and his expression of panic was almost comical. He fired backwards blindly, but his bullet flew harmlessly into the night.

The van was going roughly thirty miles per hour when the front bumper made contact and Armando went down, out of sight, under the vehicle.

"Wow," Billy Don said.

"Did you get him?" Syd asked.

Red hit the brakes hard and came to a stop. He and Billy Don scrambled out of the van and looked behind it, where Armando was writhing on the ground, muttering and groaning. Red couldn't see any obvious injuries or broken bones, but that didn't mean anything. Maybe his insides were all messed up.

"Fucked around and found out," Billy Don said. He saw Armando's gun ten feet away on the ground, so he walked over and picked it up.

"What's happening?" Syd yelled from inside the van.

"Don't move!"

It was a woman's voice from somewhere above.

Red looked up to a window on the loft level of the barn. A woman was pointing a shotgun at them. *The* woman. Apparently, she couldn't see them well and didn't recognize them from their meeting with Colby on the side of the highway. Even after Red and Billy Don had agreed to help, Colby hadn't let them meet the woman, perhaps so they couldn't identify her later.

"We're on your side," Red said, raising his hands. "We were the guys watching the motel."

She slowly pulled the shotgun back into the window. "Any idea where Phil is?"

"Not a clue. We just rolled up as this guy jumped out the window."

"Keep an eye on him. I'm coming down."

Boy, she was as bossy as Mandy.

"Ask him where Fernando is!" Syd yelled.

"Where's Fernando?" Red asked Armando.

"And where's Colby?" Billy Don added.

Armando shook his head, still grimacing.

"Tell him about Mark!" Syd yelled.

"What about Mark?" Dixie said, suddenly at Red's side. She was covered with hay and drenched with sweat, cradling the shotgun in the crook of her left elbow. "Tell me! What about Mark?"

"Billy Don, read her the text," Red said.

Billy Don pulled Syd's phone from his pocket and did as Red asked.

After he finished, Dixie appeared frozen for a moment, as if she weren't quite willing to believe it.

Then she said, "I need to call Phil." She felt the pocket of her shorts and must've realized her phone wasn't in there. She turned to go back into the barn, but she stopped and looked at Red. "Honk that van horn and don't stop."

Then she dashed back into the barn.

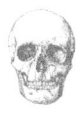

Colby stood silently for ten seconds, just waiting, in case it was a bluff.

The man had plainly not fallen off the cliff, because Colby could hear him just ahead, cursing in Spanish and shouting with rising and falling levels of intensity—as if his pain would begin to subside, only to worsen again. Odd.

Colby took a few tentative steps forward, and now he could see the man's dark figure facedown on the ground, squirming. It appeared he was trying to stand, but each time, he fell again and let out a cry of pain.

What was happening?

Had he had a stroke? A heart attack? A seizure?

Colby stepped forward slowly, the shotgun aimed and ready. He was now ten yards away from the man, and he could finally see what had happened.

The man had stumbled directly into a large cluster of prickly pear cactus. This particular bed was perhaps six feet in circumference, and the man was lying in it. Every time he tried to push himself up, he was stabbing some new part of his hands or elbows or knees with needles. Colby had stepped on his share of prickly pear, but he had never wound up in this particular predicament.

The man's gun was on the ground, a few feet away from the cactus.

The man couldn't see Colby, but he was speaking to him, and Colby's Spanish was just good enough to know the man was asking for help.

"Take it easy," Colby said, slowing moving closer. "Quit moving. That's not helping any."

Was it possible the man had two guns? Colby could see both of his hands, but the man might have a second gun tucked into his waistband.

Now the man was asking Colby to help him up. He promised not to run.

Colby took two more steps forward, and now he was ten feet away.

"You speak English?" Colby asked.

Colby heard a shot near the barn. Then another one. He tried not to imagine what that might mean.

"*Sí*, some," the man said. "A little."

"Who's your boss?" Colby asked.

"*Que?*"

Colby heard a third shot from the barn. He couldn't waste any more time.

"Who is your boss? *Su jefe*."

It would be good if this man gave him a name, but Colby knew he could probably get it from Syd. He *would* get it from Syd.

The man remained silent.

"No answer?" Colby said.

He raised the shotgun and aimed it at the back of the man's head. He would never see it coming, which was the only blessing Colby was willing to bestow.

"You help me up?" the man asked. He tried to turn his head to see Colby.

"Afraid not," Colby said.

"If I tell you name of my boss, you will kill me anyway."

Now Colby heard a car horn near the barn. Honking over and over, without stopping. He didn't know what to make of that, but it wouldn't be Dixie. They had agreed she would call if she absolutely needed to reach him.

Perhaps it was the other man from the Camry. Maybe that was his way of telling this man he had captured Dixie. Or he had killed her. Colby knew that was a strong possibility and that he needed to return to the barn right now. He couldn't afford to drag this man along with him. There was only one option.

"Last chance," Colby said. "*Su jefe.*"

"I can't help you, my friend," the man said.

Colby's finger began to tighten on the trigger. This was going to be the hardest thing he had ever done, but it was the only way out for Dixie.

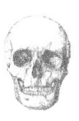

Dixie put the shotgun on the ground and scrambled up the ladder to her sniper's nest in the loft. Where the hell was her phone? She didn't see it.

She'd had it right beside her, in view, so she could read any incoming texts from Phil. Where had it gone? Think.

The man dove through the window.

Dixie fired a shot.

Then she heard a vehicle outside, a revving engine, and a thump.

She scrambled to her feet as she heard more commotion outside, and some groans of pain. Then she hurried to the window to see what was happening, leaving her phone where it was. Then she'd put the ladder back in place...

It had to be right here. She dropped to her knees and began to dig through the loose hay.

The honking outside was grating on her nerves.

It was no use. The phone had disappeared. How could that be?

She shifted and her knee hit something hard.

Finally. She had it.

She heard a shot in the distance.

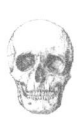

Colby dropped to one knee and let the shotgun point toward the ground.

He released a long, slow breath. Tried to calm himself.

There would have to be some other solution.

He hadn't been able to do it.

He'd squeezed the trigger, but at the last second, he'd jerked the barrel upward. The buckshot had flown harmlessly over the man's head.

If Dixie was dead, well, Colby had done his best, and killing this man now wouldn't bring her back. Colby would march him back at gunpoint and—

His phone rang.

Sweet Lord, his phone rang. It was ringing, not vibrating. It could only be Dixie.

Colby quickly pulled his phone out and answered the call.

41

The next afternoon, Colby looked over at Dixie and saw an expression of contentment on her face. He liked seeing her that way. The stress was obviously gone. The anxiety. The fear.

If any neighbors had heard the gunshots last night, they hadn't been concerned enough to call it in. After all, it wasn't unusual to hear shots in rural areas after dark, often because it was easier to hunt feral pigs, varmints, and predators at night. Besides, how many shots had there been in total? Eight or ten, maybe? Colby had lost track. Not that many, really.

He could only marvel at how quickly the situation had changed. He had been so close to pulling the trigger. That would have been a disaster, but how could he have known? Then everything had turned on a dime, like a sudden cease fire in the middle of a war. Amazing.

Syd had left in the van before Colby made it back to the barn with Fernando. O'Brien had cut him loose, and before anybody knew it, he fired up the van and drove away without a word. Colby had seen the taillights just as he and Fernando were returning from the chase through the woods. Did it matter? Maybe it was better that way. Let him go.

Fernando and Armando both had some injuries, obviously, but nothing urgent. Scrapes, abrasions, puncture wounds. When they'd heard about Mark's text to Syd, they hadn't said much, but they almost appeared relieved. The one called Fernando agreed that it was time to go home, and they asked for a ride to their car, which was parked on the road leading to Selah Ranch, one of Colby's neighbors. O'Brien and Craddock agreed to take them. That was the last Colby had seen of them—the four men walking away on the caliche road, heading toward the ranch entrance, where O'Brien's truck was parked. Fernando was still pulling cactus thorns as they went, and Armando was walking with a pronounced limp. Craddock sent a text two hours later saying they had followed the Camry all the way to Pearsall, halfway to Laredo, just to make sure the men were really returning home.

Less than twenty minutes after Colby had answered the call from Dixie last night, the two of them had ended up alone again outside the barn. They'd gone back to the house and stayed up until sunrise, adrenaline still pumping, sharing information and examining the events of the night from every angle, trying to determine if there was any lingering cause for Dixie to worry about the cartel. They found none. She was in the clear.

What did the future hold? Colby wasn't sure, but he knew Dixie would be okay. That's what mattered.

"You getting hungry?" Colby asked.

It was nearly one o'clock now. They had slept together in Colby's bed until eleven. Now they were seated on the back deck, drinking coffee, with their feet propped on the railing.

"Ravenous," Dixie said.

"We should go into town," Colby said.

"That sounds good. In a minute, okay? It's nice to just sit here and not worry about anything."

He knew that would change soon enough.

Deputies would find the grow site—possibly late today or maybe tomorrow morning—and life would be hectic for her again. She would be besieged by cops and the media and her bosses and family members and friends. She would get tired of explaining the situation. She would get tired of people speculating that she was part of it.

But, over time, that would pass, too.

Now she pulled her phone—her original phone—from her pocket. She hadn't checked it since yesterday evening, right before they'd spotted Syd's van at the motel. That's when she'd found the voicemail from Lionel.

"I'm tempted to crush this with a hammer instead of turning it on," she said, holding the phone up.

"Can't blame you."

"But I can't."

"I know."

"Want me to wait? Maybe do it tomorrow? Give us a full day to decompress?"

"Whatever you want to do."

"Well, if I turn it on and there's nothing urgent, I'll be thrilled. But if I find an ocean of voicemails and texts waiting, then I'll wish I'd put it off until tomorrow."

"I completely understand."

"You're no help."

"Never said I was."

"That's not true, by the way. What I just said. Without your help..." She shook her head. "You got me through it."

He reached for her hand and held it.

A minute later, she said, "Okay, I'm going to turn it on."

"Go for it," Colby said.

She pushed the button on her phone and it slowly booted up.

There was a text from Mark that he had sent last night, just minutes before he had left the voicemail for Syd.

I'm sorry. I truly mean that. I don't know what else to say, except that I wish you all the best in your new life.

Dixie read it out loud, not sounding particularly moved by it one way or the other.

Then she played a voicemail left two hours earlier from an unknown number.

"Mrs. Morrow, my name is CJ Francisco and I'm an investigator with the Tyler County Sheriff's Office. Can you give me a call at your earliest convenience?"

That was it. Nothing more. No other details.

Colby had been wondering if perhaps Mark's text to Syd last night was just his latest enormous lie, but apparently not.

"You don't have to call him back," Colby said.

"You know what? I know I don't, but I think I will. I'm just too damn curious."

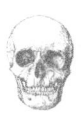

"Now *that* was one wild-ass night," Red said.

"You can say that again," Billy Don said.

"He already did," Mandy said. "Multiple times. You both did."

They were in Red's truck, going to have lunch somewhere, although they hadn't decided where yet. Maybe they'd go back to CJ's in Blanco and get another pizza. Or go back to the Chess Club. Then there was the Red Bud Café, which was damn tasty. Barbecue at the Old 300, where Melissa wore her T-shirt tight. So many choices.

"It's hard not to keep thinking about it, because it was so wild," Red said.

"Thinking and saying are two different things," Mandy said.

"We helped save that woman," Billy Don said.

"Well, you sure as hell could've avoided a lot of drama if you hadn't tried to steal that bag of fake money, but at least you accidentally ended up doing the right thing," Mandy said.

"Admit it, you had fun," Red said. "That's what you said earlier."

"Okay, I did, but I'm glad I missed the last part."

They were passing the Blanco County Inn and Red couldn't help but glance over for the black van. It wasn't there, of course. Red was relieved, to be honest.

"I ran over a guy," he said. "A cartel killer. I ran smooth over him."

"Sure as hell did," Billy Don said.

"I kinda liked it, too," Red said.

"I thought for sure he was dead, or at least you broke his legs or something," Billy Don said.

But that wasn't the most rewarding part of the night. That came later, after Phil Colby arrived at the barn with the killer named Fernando, who looked a lot like the guy named Armando. Hell, they could've been brothers. It was weird to give a couple of cartel killers a ride to their car, but before the four of them left the barn, Colby took Red aside and said, "You and Billy Don were a big help. I won't forget it."

Simple and to the point.

And it *was* true. They *had* been a big help. He and Billy Don could've bailed out at any time and let Colby and the woman fend for themselves, but no, they hung in there and did the right thing.

Maybe this would finally settle the bad blood between them and Colby.

Maybe Colby wouldn't glare at them the next time he passed Red's truck at dusk on Miller Creek Loop, obviously suspecting that they might be looking for a deer to shoot on the side of the road, although there were times when that wasn't even true.

Maybe Colby wouldn't make disapproving remarks anytime Red

and Billy Don leered at some of the younger ladies at the wild game dinner, even though those ladies were of perfectly legal age.

Maybe Colby and his pal John Marlin would invite Red and Billy Don over to have a few cold beers and shoot the breeze and they would all forge a new, long-lasting friendship.

Maybe.

But probably not.

Red could live with that.

42

"This is CJ."

"This is Dixie Morrow returning your call."

"Oh, Mrs. Morrow. Thanks for getting back to me. Would it be possible for you to come down to the sheriff's office this afternoon for a chat?"

"I'm several hours away, so I'm afraid that won't work. What is this regarding?"

"Your husband Mark—y'all are married, right?"

"At the moment."

"Well, uh, okay. He walked into our offices late last night and confessed to growing a large crop of marijuana on the property where y'all are living. He also said he sold fifty pounds of his pot to a member of a drug cartel, but he won't identify that person. Can you confirm that any of this is true?"

Dixie looked at Colby and shook her head. *The craziness never stops.*

"I'm sorry, do you not believe him?" Dixie said.

"That's the thing—I've interviewed him for about six hours now, and I gotta be honest, it's hard to know what's true and what's not. Does he have any kind of mental issues that I should be aware of?"

Colby couldn't help but grin.

"You could put it that way. Mark has a problem telling the truth. Actually, I'm being too generous—out of habit, I guess. Mark is a pathological liar. If you talk to anyone else who knows him well, they will confirm it."

"I sort of figured as much. He's all over the place. Still, we've got a couple of deputies taking Mark out to the property right now to see if the crop really exists. You think we'll find something?"

Dixie hesitated for a moment, then said, "You will."

"Have you seen this crop yourself?"

"I have no comment on that."

"I understand. Guess I don't blame you. He said he had a partner, but he won't tell us who it was. You know who it might be?"

"I have no comment on that, either."

"He had ten thousand dollars in counterfeit currency in his possession, but he didn't even know the money was fake. Or that's what he told us."

Dixie's eyes widened. "That's all news to me."

"Okay, well, when are you gonna be back in town?"

"Mr. Francisco?"

"Yes, ma'am."

"With all due respect, I don't want to get involved any more than I already am."

"I getcha. You don't need to be dragged into his mess. One last question, though, if you don't mind. Any idea why he would suddenly turn himself in like that? Just out of the blue?"

Dixie thought about it for a moment.

"I guess he finally decided to do the right thing."

The following morning, Colby and Dixie drove his truck south to San Antonio. They took the exit for Dee Howard Way and went east to the economy parking lot for the airport.

Colby got lucky and found an empty space near Dixie's light-blue Honda Passport. He pulled in and killed the engine, so she wouldn't feel rushed.

They hadn't discussed what would come next, and Colby had an empty feeling in his stomach.

Was this the end of it? How could it not be? What did she need with a rapidly aging rancher?

"I need to go back home," Dixie said.

Colby nodded.

"I'm sure they've got a team of deputies at the grow site today, cutting down the plants and dismantling everything. I feel like I need to be seen, so people won't think I'm hiding."

"Don't let anybody give you any bullshit."

"They'll probably want to search the house."

"Get yourself a nice hotel room. The best in all of Tyler County."

"Which isn't saying much," Dixie said.

"Then sleep on a creek bank somewhere. You'll be fine."

Dixie laughed. "I can't believe they didn't fire me. They still might. Guess we'll see."

Right after her call with CJ Francisco, she'd called her supervisor with the timber company. Told him deputies were on the way to the property to look for an illegal marijuana crop, and they would probably find one, and it was her husband who had grown it. Told him she'd had nothing to do with it and was embarrassed to have brought the company bad publicity. He had handled it remarkably well and said that he would contact the company attorneys for advice on how to proceed.

"How much time is left on your contract?" Colby asked.

"Four weeks."

"Surely they'll just wait it out," Colby said. "Otherwise, it'll look like they're punishing an innocent person."

"Weird, but I don't feel so innocent," Dixie said. "I don't know why that is."

"The only thing you were guilty of was having a big heart. You tried to give Mark a small break—enough time to consult a lawyer—and he used it against you. You didn't do anything wrong."

"I appreciate that. Speaking of which, I also need to start the divorce proceedings."

"The sooner, the better," Colby said.

Her eyes were welling up. For Mark, or because she was leaving?

A jet flew overhead and prevented any conversation for at least thirty seconds.

When the cab of his truck got quiet again, Dixie said, "Exactly one month from today, at, say, three o'clock, if you were to hike to your creek and find a woman swimming by the waterfall, what would you do?"

"That depends. Would that woman look exactly like you?"

"Yeah. She would."

"I'd probably stay in the shadows for a minute or two and just appreciate the view," Colby said. "Then I'd walk down to the creek and join her."

"That sounds really nice," Dixie said.

"It sure does."

"Can I ask you a favor?"

"Yeah, sure."

"Bring a towel and a couple of beers."

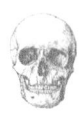

Nine days later, Syd was having breakfast at the Boomarang Diner in Perry, Oklahoma, when he learned he could finally go home.

He was halfway through Elvin's Ultimate Breakfast—three eggs over easy, bacon, sausage, hash browns, and a biscuit swimming in gravy—when he pulled his phone out and saw a text from Nicky.

After they'd left Blanco, Syd had taken Nicky home and immediately left in his own vehicle, a gray Ford Freestyle.

Nicky had no idea where Syd was now, because if Syd told him, that meant Nicky could tell someone else later, probably against his will. But he *could* tell. And he *would* tell, just as Lionel had talked readily when Syd and Nicky had put some pressure on him. Syd hadn't even actually harmed him. Not physically, anyway. Mentally? Well, maybe. They'd tied Lionel up and Syd had put a .380 to his head and pulled the trigger. It was empty, of course. Scared the crap out of him, though. After Syd did that a few more times, Lionel gave up Mark's address, along with detailed instructions on how to get there. Syd was all amped up and he couldn't resist firing a couple of shots into the floor of the trailer, although in hindsight, that was kind of stupid, because those bullets could theoretically be matched to his gun if they remained intact.

Also, well, it just wasn't cool. He knew it right after he did it. This poor guy Lionel was just a pothead trying to make a few bucks and Syd had basically terrorized him.

Syd felt like an asshole, but he tried to ignore it, focus on the task at hand, and stay alive. Then that big, dumb redneck, Billy Don, said something that really stung.

Syd had mentioned that the woman, Dixie, hadn't gone to the cops because she was scared of what might happen to her family, and Billy Don said, "That sounds really shitty. You need to find a better line of work."

Syd had been thinking about that ever since. Nine days. Not every minute, of course, but it would pop into his head a couple of times a day.

"You need to find a better line of work."

It was true, wasn't it? Even if Draco had a mood swing and welcomed Syd back, which wasn't likely, wasn't it time to move on to something else? Something where he didn't have to be a shitty person?

That was too much to think about right now.

He checked the text from Nicky.

Did you hear the news?

What fucking news? That was pretty vague. How would Syd know if he'd heard the news if he didn't even know what news Nicky was talking about?

Nicky had included a link, so Syd clicked it.

Then he put his fork on the table and simply stared at the article he was seeing.

Drug Kingpin Slain

The bullet-riddled body of Felipe "Draco" Vargas, a lieutenant in one of North America's largest drug cartels, was found on an isolated stretch of highway ten miles outside of Laredo late last night.

Authorities believe the killing is the result of power struggles within the cartel. Vargas had a reputation for mercurial behavior and impulsive decision-making that opened the cartel to vulnerability from the police and other drug gangs. He was the prime suspect in the murder of his ex-wife four years ago, although police were never able to collect enough evidence to bring charges.

This is a developing story. Check back later for more details.

Email Alerts

Want to know when Ben Rehder's
next novel will be released?

Subscribe to his email list at www.benrehder.com.

Have you discovered Ben Rehder's
Roy Ballard Mysteries?

Turn the page for an excerpt from *Gone The Next*,
the first novel in that series.

GONE THE NEXT

1

The woman he was watching this time was in her early thirties. Thirty-five at the oldest. White. Well dressed. Upper middle class. Reasonably attractive. Probably drove a nice car, like a Lexus or a BMW. She was shopping at Nordstrom in Barton Creek Square mall. Her daughter — Alexis, if he'd overheard the name correctly — appeared to be about seven years old. Brown hair, like her mother's. The same cute nose. They were in the women's clothing department, looking at swimsuits. Alexis was bored. Fidgety. Ready to go to McDonald's, like Mom had promised. Amazing what you can hear if you keep your ears open.

He was across the aisle, in the men's department, looking at Hawaiian shirts. They were all ugly, and he had no intention of buying one. He stood on the far side of the rack and held up a green shirt with palm trees on it. But he was really looking past it, at the woman, who had several one-piece swimsuits draped over her arm. Not bikinis, though she still had the figure for it. Maybe she had stretch marks, or the beginnings of a belly.

He replaced the green shirt and grabbed a blue one covered with coconuts. Just browsing, like a regular shopper might do.

Mom was walking over to a changing room now. Alexis followed, walking stiff-legged, maybe pretending she was a monster. A zombie. Amusing herself.

He moved closer, to a table piled high with neatly folded cargo shorts. He pretended to look for a pair in his size. But he was watching in his peripheral vision.

"Wait right here," Mom said. She didn't look around. She was

oblivious to his presence. He might as well have been a mannequin.
Alexis said something in reply, but he couldn't make it out.
"There isn't room, Lexy. I'll just be a minute."
And she shut the door, leaving Alexis all by herself.

~ ~ ~

When he first began his research, he'd been surprised by what he'd found. He had expected the average parent to be watchful. Wary. Downright suspicious. That's how he would be if he had a child. A little girl. He'd guard her like a priceless treasure. Every minute of the day. But his assumptions were wrong. Parents were sloppy. Careless. Just plain stupid.

He knew that now, because he'd watched hundreds of them. And their children. In restaurants. In shopping centers. Supermarkets. Playgrounds and parks. For three months he'd watched. Reconnaissance missions, like this one right now, with Alexis and her mom. Preparing. What he'd observed was encouraging. It wouldn't be as difficult as he'd assumed. When the time came.

But he had to use his head. Plan it out. Use what he'd learned. Doing it in a public place, especially a retail establishment, would be risky, because there were video surveillance systems everywhere nowadays. Some places, like this mall, even had security guards. Daycare centers were often fenced, and the front doors were locked. Schools were always on the lookout for strangers who —

"You need help with anything?"

He jumped, ever so slightly.

A salesgirl had come up behind him. Wanting to be helpful. Calling attention to him. Ruining the moment.

That was a good lesson to remember. Just because he was watching, that didn't mean he wasn't being watched, too.

2

The first time I ever heard the name Tracy Turner — on a hot, cloudless Tuesday in June — I was tailing an obese, pyorrheic degenerate named Wally Crouch. I was fairly certain about the "degenerate" part, because Crouch had visited two adult bookstores and three strip clubs since noon. Not that there's anything wrong with a little mature entertainment, but there's a point when it goes from bawdy boys-will-be-boys recreation to creepy pathological fixation. The pyorrhea was pure conjecture on my part, based solely on the number of Twinkie wrappers Crouch had tossed out the window during his travels.

Crouch was a driver for UPS and, according to my biggest client, he was also a fraud who was riding the workers' comp gravy train. In the course of a routine delivery seven weeks prior, Crouch had allegedly injured his lower back. A ruptured disk, the doctor said. Limited mobility and a twelve- to sixteen-week recovery period. In the meantime, Crouch couldn't lift more than ten pounds without searing pain shooting up his spinal cord. But this particular quack had a checkered past filled with questionable diagnoses and reprimands from the medical board. My job was fairly simple, at least on paper: Follow Crouch discreetly until he proved himself a liar. Catch it on video. Testify, if necessary. Earn a nice paycheck. Continue to finance my sumptuous, razor's-edge lifestyle.

~ ~ ~

You'd think Crouch, having a choice in the matter, would've avoided rush-hour traffic and had a few more beers instead, but he left Sugar's Uptown Cabaret at ten after five and squeezed his way onto the interstate heading south. I followed in my seven-year-old Dodge Caravan. Beige. Try to find a vehicle less likely to catch someone's eye. The windows are deeply tinted and a scanner antenna is mounted on the roof, which are the only clues that the driver isn't a soccer mom toting her brats to practice.

Anyone whose vehicle doubles as a second home recognizes the value of a decent sound system. I'd installed a Blaupunkt, with Bose speakers front and rear. Total system set me back about two grand. Seems like overkill for talk radio, but that's what I was listening to when I heard the familiar alarm signal of the Emergency Alert System. I'd never known the system to be used for anything other than weather warnings, but not this time. It was an Amber Alert. A local girl had gone missing from her affluent West Austin neighborhood. Tracy Turner: six years old, blond hair, green eyes, three feet tall, forty-five pounds, wearing denim shorts and a pink shirt. My palms went sweaty just thinking about it. Then I heard she might be in the company of Howard Turner — her non-custodial father, a resident of Los Angeles — and I breathed a small sigh of relief. Listeners, they said, should keep an eye out for a green Honda with California plates.

Easy to read between the lines. Tracy's parents were divorced, and dad had decided he wanted to spend more time with his daughter, despite how the courts had ruled. Sad, but much better than a random abduction.

The announcer was repeating the message when my cell phone rang. I turned the radio volume down, answered, and my client — a senior claims adjuster at a big insurance company — said, "You nail him yet?"

"Christ, Heidi, it's only the third day."

"I thought you were good."

"That's a vicious rumor."

"Yeah, and I think you started it yourself. I'm starting to think you get by on your looks alone."

"That remark borders on sexual harassment, and you know how I feel about that."

"You're all for it."

"Exactly. Anyway, relax, okay? I'm on him twenty-four seven." Crouch had taken the Manor Road exit, and now he turned into his apartment complex, so I drove past, calling it a day. I didn't like lying to Heidi, but I had a meeting with a man named Harvey Blaylock in thirty minutes.

"Well, you'd better get something soon, because I've got another one waiting," Heidi said.

I didn't say anything, because a jerk in an F-150 was edging over into my lane.

"Roy?" she said.

"Yeah."

"I have another one for you."

"Have scientists come up with that device yet?"

"What device?"

"The one that allows you to be in two places at the same time."

"You really crack you up."

"Let me get this one squared away, then we'll talk, okay?"

"The quicker the better. Where are you? Has Crouch even left the house?"

"Oh, yeah. Been wandering all afternoon."

"Where to?"

"Uh, let's just say he seems to have an inordinate appreciation for the female form."

"Which means?"

"He's been visiting gentlemen's clubs."

A pause. "You mean tittie bars?"

"That's such a crass term. Oh, by the way, the Yellow Rose is looking for dancers. In case you decide to — "

She hung up on me.

~ ~ ~

I had the phone in my hands, so I went ahead and called my best friend Mia Madison, who works at an establishment I used to do business with on occasion. She tends bar at a tavern on North Lamar.

Boiling it down to one sentence, Mia is smart, funny, optimistic, and easy on the eyes. Expanding on the last part, because it's relevant, Mia stands about five ten and has long red hair that she likes to wear in a ponytail. Prominent cheekbones, with dimples beneath. The toned legs of a runner, though she doesn't run, but must walk ten miles a day during an eight-hour shift. When Mia gets dolled up — what she calls "bringing it" — she goes from being an attractive woman you'd certainly notice to a world-class head turner.

On one occasion, she revealed that she has a tattoo. Wouldn't show it to me, but she said — joking, I'm sure — that if I could guess what it was, and where it was, she'd let me have a look. Nearly a year later, I still hadn't given up.

"Is it Muttley?" I asked when she answered.

"Muttley? Who the hell is Muttley?"

"You know, that cartoon dog with the sarcastic laugh."

"You mean Scooby Doo?"

"No, the other one. Hangs with Dick Dastardly."

"I have no idea what you're talking about."

"Before your time, I guess. Are you at work?"

"Not till six. Just got out of the shower. I'm drying off."

"Need any help?"

"I think I can handle it," she said.

"Okay, next question. Want to earn a hundred bucks the easy way?" I said.

"Love to," she said. "When and where?"

3

Harvey Blaylock was maybe sixty, medium height, with neatly trimmed gray hair, black-framed glasses, a white short-sleeved shirt, and tan gabardine slacks. He looked like the kind of man who, if things had taken a slightly different turn, might've wound up as a forklift salesman, or, best case, a high-school principal in a small agrarian town.

In reality, however, Harvey Blaylock was a man who held tremendous sway over my future, near- and long-term. I intended to remain respectful and deferential.

Blaylock's necktie — green, with bucking horses printed on it — rested on his paunch as he leaned back in his chair, scanning the contents of a manila folder. I knew it was my file, because it said ROY W. BALLARD on the outside, typed neatly on a rectangular label. I'm quick to notice things like that.

Five minutes went by. His office smelled like cigarettes and Old Spice. Rays of sun slanted in through horizontal blinds on the windows facing west. As far as I could tell, we were the only people left in the building.

"I really appreciate you staying late for this," I said. "Would've been tough for me to make it earlier."

He grunted and continued reading, one hand drumming slowly on his metal desk. The digital clock on the wall above him read 6:03. On the bookshelf, tucked among a row of wire-bound notebooks, was a framed photo of a young boy holding up a small fish on a line.

"Boy, was I surprised to hear that Joyce retired," I said. "She seemed too young for that. So spry and youthful." Joyce being

Blaylock's predecessor. My previous probation officer. A true bitch on wheels. Condescending. Domineering. No sense of humor. "I'll have to send her a card," I said, hoping it didn't sound sarcastic.

Blaylock didn't answer.

I was starting to wonder if he had a reading disability. I'm no angel — I wouldn't have been in this predicament if I were — but my file couldn't have been more than half a dozen pages long. I was surprised that a man in his position, with several hundred probationers in his charge, would spend more than thirty seconds on each.

Finally, Blaylock, still looking at the file, said, "Roy Wilson Ballard. Thirty-six years old. Divorced. Says you used to work as a news cameraman." He had a thick piney-woods accent. Pure east Texas. He peered up at me, without moving his head. Apparently, it was my turn to talk.

"Yes, sir. Until about three years ago."

"When you got fired."

"My boss and I had a personality conflict," I said, wondering how detailed my file was.

"Ernie Crenshaw."

"That's him."

"You broke his nose with a microphone stand."

Fairly detailed, apparently.

"Well, yeah, he, uh — "

"You got an attitude problem, Ballard?"

"No, sir."

"Temper?"

I started to lie, but decided against it. "Occasionally."

"That what happened in this instance? Temper got the best of you?"

"He was rude to one of the reporters. He called her a name."

"What name was that?"

"I'd rather not repeat it."

"I'm asking you to."

"Okay, then. He called her Doris. Her real name is Anne."

His expression remained frozen. Tough crowd.

I said, "Okay. He called her a cunt."

Blaylock's expression still didn't change. "To her face?"

"Behind her back. He was a coward. And she didn't deserve it.

This guy was a world-class jerk. Little weasel."

"You heard him say it?"

"I was the one he was talking to. It set me off."

"So you busted his nose."

"I did, sir, yes."

Perhaps it was my imagination, but I thought Harvey Blaylock gave a nearly imperceptible nod of approval. He looked back at the file. "Now you're self-employed. A legal videographer. What is that exactly?"

"Well, uh, that means I record depositions, wills, scenes of accidents. Things like that. But proof of insurance fraud is my specialty. The majority of my business. Turns out I'm really good at it."

"Describe it for me."

"Sir?"

"Give me a typical day."

I recited my standard courtroom answer. "Basically, I keep a subject under surveillance and hope to videotape him engaging in an activity that's beyond his alleged physical limitations." Then I added, "Maybe lifting weights, or dancing. Playing golf. Doing the hokey-pokey."

No smile.

"Not a nine-to-five routine, then."

"No, sir. More like five to nine."

Blaylock mulled that over for a few seconds. "So you're out there, working long hours, sometimes through the night, and you start taking pills to keep up with the pace. That how it went?"

Until you've been there, you have no idea how powerless and naked you feel when someone like Harvey Blaylock is authorized to dig through your personal failings with a salad fork.

"That sums it up pretty well," I said.

"Did it work?"

"What, the pills?"

He nodded.

"Well, yeah. But coffee works pretty well, too."

"You were also drinking. That's why you got pulled over in the first place, and how they ended up finding the pills on you. You got a drinking problem?"

I thought of an old joke. *Yeah, I got a drinking problem. Can't pay my bar tab.* "I hope not," I said, which is about as honest as it gets. "At one point maybe I did, but I don't know for sure. Probably not. But that's what you'd expect someone with a drinking problem to say, right?"

"Had a drink since your court date?"

"No, sir. I'm not allowed to. Even though the Breathalyzer said I was legal."

"Not even one drink?"

"Not a drop. Joyce, gave me a piss te — I mean a urine test, last month, and three in the past year. I passed them all. That should be in the file."

"You miss it?" Blaylock asked. "The booze?"

I honestly thought about it for a moment.

"Sometimes, yeah," I said. "More than I would've guessed, but not enough to freak me out or anything. Sometimes, you know, I just crave a cold beer. Or three. But if I had to quit eating Mexican food, I'd miss that, too. Maybe more than beer."

Blaylock slowly sat forward in his chair and dropped my file, closed, on his desk. "Here's the deal, son. Ninety-five percent of the people I deal with are shitbags who think the world is their personal litter box. I can't do them any good, and they don't want me to. Most of 'em are locked up again within a year, and all I can say is good riddance. Then I see guys like you who make a stupid mistake and get caught up in the system. You probably have a decent life ahead of you, but you don't need me to tell you that, and it really doesn't matter what I think anyway. So I'll just say this: Follow the rules and you can put all this behind you. If you need any help, I'll do what I can. I really will. But if you fuck up just one time, it's like tipping over a row of dominoes. Then it's out of your control, and mine, too. You follow me?"

~ ~ ~

After the meeting, I swung by a Jack-In-The-Box, then sat outside Wally Crouch's place for a few hours, just in case. He stayed put.

I got home just as the ten o'clock news was coming on. Howard Turner had been located in a motel in Yuma City, Arizona, there on business. Police had verified his alibi. He had been nowhere near

Texas, and the cops had no reason to believe he was involved.

So Tracy Turner was still missing, and that fact created a void in my chest that I hadn't felt in years.

ABOUT THE AUTHOR

Ben Rehder lives with his wife near Austin, Texas, where he was born and raised. His novels have made best-of-the-year lists in *Publishers Weekly, Library Journal, Kirkus Reviews*, and *Field & Stream*. *Buck Fever* was a finalist for the Edgar Award, and *Get Busy Dying* was a finalist for the Shamus Award. For more information, visit www.benrehder.com.

OTHER NOVELS BY BEN REHDER

Buck Fever
Bone Dry
Flat Crazy
Guilt Trip
Gun Shy
Holy Moly
The Chicken Hanger
The Driving Lesson
Gone The Next
Hog Heaven
Get Busy Dying
Stag Party
Bum Steer
If I Had A Nickel
Point Taken
Now You See Him
Last Laugh
A Tooth For A Tooth
Lefty Loosey
Shake And Bake
Free Ride
Better To Be Lucky
Boom Town
Another Man's Treasure

For more information, visit www.benrehder.com.